Adam found himself
at a loss for words

Even if she did have amnesia, and even if she did look like Christie, it didn't mean she was Megan's mother. Mentally, he noted the differences in the two women. The voice. The clothing. The jewelry. The figure.

"Because you can't remember who you are does not make you Christie Anderson," he stated firmly, as much for her sake as for his.

"But I could be," she said with a spark of hope in her eyes.

"No, you're not Christie. She died, Faith." He kept his voice deliberate. "Six months ago, while sailing her small boat. The St. Louis County coroner signed her death certificate."

"You said they never found her body," she reminded him.

He didn't want to believe any of what she suggested could be true, nor did he want to remember that only a few hours ago he'd wondered about the very same possibility.

Dear Reader,

Intrigued by a news story about an amnesia victim, I found myself thinking about the consequences of memory loss. I know how frustrating it can be to forget the smallest of details. I could only imagine what it would be like to wake up and discover that I'd forgotten my entire past. As I thought about how different my life would be if I couldn't remember the people I love, a story began to take shape in my mind and a heroine was born—Faith Miller.

As you begin this story, you know as much about Faith as I did when I first met her. She is a woman with amnesia, remembering nothing prior to the night she was found on the side of a road with a head injury. The only clue she has to her identity is a bracelet with the letters F-A-I-T-H imprinted on it.

In order to write this book I had to uncover the mystery of her past. Did she have a family? Where was her home? What was her occupation? Did she have a happy childhood? How did she end up on the side of a road?

I'm happy to say I found the answers to all of those questions and many others. And with the help of a bachelor father and his six-year-old daughter, Faith finds them, too. She also discovers the answer to another question that's very important to her. It's one even those of us who don't have amnesia ask. "Where do I belong?"

Because that's what every romance story is really about— finding that special someone who makes you feel as if you've come home.

If you would like to write to me, I love hearing from readers. Send your letters to Pamela Bauer, c/o MFW, P.O. Box 24107, Minneapolis, MN 55424, or you can visit me via the Internet at www.pamelabauer.com.

All the best,

Pamela Bauer

Bachelor Father
Pamela Bauer

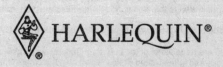

HARLEQUIN®

TORONTO • NEW YORK • LONDON
AMSTERDAM • PARIS • SYDNEY • HAMBURG
STOCKHOLM • ATHENS • TOKYO • MILAN • MADRID
PRAGUE • WARSAW • BUDAPEST • AUCKLAND

ISBN 0-373-71252-9

BACHELOR FATHER

Copyright © 2005 by Pamela Bauer.

For someone who shares my love of books,
my aunt, Opal Ronning, and her real life hero, my uncle Jim.

Books by Pamela Bauer

CHAPTER ONE

"ISN'T IT ABOUT TIME for a changing of the guard?"

Faith glanced up to see Dr. Avery Carson walking toward her, his dark wool parka peppered with melting snowflakes. Wearing a plaid woolen cap with earflaps and a pair of clunky rubber boots, he looked more like the guy who plowed the snow from the driveway than a retired doctor.

Faith smiled. "This is a surprise. I didn't expect to see you here today."

"I was in the neighborhood and thought I might as well stop in and offer you a ride home. It's not much fun waiting for a bus in this weather and I find having a pretty girl next to me makes the traffic tolerable," he said with an endearing grin.

"Is the driving difficult?"

"Only if you're not used to a Minnesota winter. I've been here sixty-eight years. I can navigate through a bit of snow." He glanced at the baby in her arms. "Who's that little bundle of joy?"

"Her name is Emma," Faith said, loving the scent of baby powder that emanated from the infant. "Isn't she precious? She fell asleep the minute I started rocking her."

"She certainly looks content in your arms. Will she

wake if you put her down?" he asked with a nod toward the row of cribs along one wall.

"I don't think so, but I'd rather hold her until her parents return."

"That might not be for a while," he warned.

"I know. I don't mind staying. Actually, I was thinking I should stay since one of the other volunteers called in sick."

"No one will ever accuse you of not putting in a full day," he remarked.

"Hard work is healthy for the body and soul. Besides, rocking babies isn't exactly what I would call work." She glanced again at the angelic face peeking out of the pink blanket.

"I think the hospital is fortunate to have someone so devoted to other people's children. Anyone who comes through that door can see you're good with kids."

His compliment warmed her insides. For two weeks she'd been volunteering in the hospital's child-care center where there had been a steady stream of infants and toddlers who had sat on her lap in the wooden rocking chair. Most of the hospital staff knew that Faith had a talent for quieting even the unhappiest of visitors. What they didn't know was that she found comfort in tending to them. It made her feel useful and wanted, but more importantly it gave her an identity—something she needed desperately. As long as she was at the hospital she knew who she was. She was the baby rocker.

"I like kids," she stated simply.

"And it's obvious they like you, but you're still entitled to have some time for yourself at the end of the day," Dr. Carson said.

Faith could have told him that the one thing she didn't need was free time. Just the opposite was true. The busier she was, the better she liked it. When her hands were occupied, her mind didn't have time to dwell on what was missing in her life. It was much easier to rock a fussy baby to sleep or calm a toddler having a temper tantrum than it was to be alone with her thoughts.

"I want to stay," she insisted. "And Mrs. Carmichael will appreciate having the help. She's always saying we don't have enough hands even when we are fully staffed."

To Faith's surprise, however, when her supervisor heard her offer she said, "That's very sweet of you to want to stay, Faith, but I think Dr. Carson's right. You've put in enough hours already today."

"But you're short one worker," she reminded her. "What if it gets busy?"

"I don't think that's going to happen—not with the way it's snowing. You go home and relax," Mrs. Carmichael ordered her.

Most people would have been happy to hear such words, but not Faith. She didn't have a place to call home, just a room at the Carsons'. And work was relaxing for her. No matter how welcome the Carsons made her feel, at the end of the day she was still alone in a strange house with only her troubled mind and its unanswered questions.

Carefully Faith got up from the rocker, holding

Emma steady so as not to wake her. As she placed the
baby in one of the cribs, she felt a shiver of loneliness.
She brought her fingertips to her lips, then blew a kiss
in the infant's direction.

Watching her, Dr. Carson said gently, "There will be
more babies for you to rock tomorrow."

Faith nodded, knowing that what he said was true.
The child-care center would be open to parents who
wanted a place to leave their children while they visited
patients in the hospital. Chances are she would be the
one taking care of them—if tomorrow began the same
way every day of the past three weeks had begun, with
her waking up and not knowing who she was.

Although doctors had been successful in treating her
physical injuries from her accident, she still hadn't recovered from the amnesia that was as puzzling to doctors as it was to her. Memory loss due to trauma was not
uncommon, but rarely did it include a loss of identity.
She'd been told it was a temporary condition and that
her memory would either return suddenly or gradually,
like pieces of a puzzle falling into place. So far, neither
had happened. Her past was a blank canvas and the only
life she knew was the one that had started the day Avery
and Marie Carson had stopped to help her as she lay unconscious at a roadside rest stop.

From the moment she'd met the doctor and his wife,
they had showed her nothing but kindness, taking her
into their home, providing her with clothes from a local
charity and treating her like the daughter they'd never
had. They were good, honest people who hadn't hesitated to come to her aid when she was desperately in

need of help. Faith hoped that if she did have a family somewhere, they would be as generous and as compassionate as the Carsons.

She had to belong somewhere, yet where that someplace was and with whom she shared it remained trapped in a past she couldn't remember. Even though she hadn't been wearing a wedding ring when she'd been rescued, she knew she couldn't rule out the possibility that she had a husband. Or children. That thought always brought an ache to her heart. She didn't want to think that she could ever forget her own child. Yet until her memory returned, just how much family she did have would remain a mystery.

As she tugged on her winter coat, Mrs. Carmichael mentioned that she had a cart full of children's books to be taken to the second floor. Faith looked at Dr. Carson and asked, "Would you mind if we dropped them off on our way out?"

"Not at all," he said with a smile, and held the door for her as she pushed the book cart into the hallway.

Although pediatrics was her favorite unit in the hospital, every time she visited the young patients her throat filled with emotion. This time was no different. As Faith and Dr. Carson made their way through the unit, she noticed a little girl who was being pushed down the long corridor in a hospital bed. When the orderly stopped for a moment to confer with a nurse, Faith found herself staring into an ashen face framed by blond hair. At first she thought she was asleep, but then she saw her eyelids flutter.

Faith automatically smiled, wondering if the girl was

even aware of her presence. Slowly the girl's sleepy eyes opened and stared directly at Faith. They were the color of the blue jays that fed outside the Carsons' kitchen window every morning, and were trying to focus on Faith's face. As they did, a hint of a smile parted the parched lips.

"Hello," Faith said softly.

Small fingers slipped out from beneath the white blanket and reached for Faith who didn't hesitate to take the delicate hand in hers and gently squeeze it.

"Am I in heaven?" The girl's voice was barely above a whisper.

Faith exchanged glances with Dr. Carson before looking back at her. "No, you're in the hospital."

"And you're here, too?" The voice remained weak.

"Yes, I work here."

"Does that mean you can stay with me?" she asked, a ray of hope flickering in her eyes.

"No, I'm sorry I can't. I'm not a nurse. I work downstairs in the child-care center," Faith explained. "I rock babies."

Confusion clouded the blue eyes. "But I want you to stay with me."

The plea in the tiny voice tugged on Faith's emotions.

Before she could say another word, the orderly had returned. "Sorry, but we need to get this young lady into her room." He gave Faith an apologetic look as he returned to the foot of the bed.

"The people here are nice. They'll take good care of you," Faith said, but the girl's lower lip quivered in dismay as Faith released her small hand.

"But I want you to take care of me," she said in such a pathetic little voice that Faith felt a lump in her throat.

"I'm sorry, but I can't. You'll be fine," she said with a smile of encouragement. Then she put her fingers to her lips and blew her a kiss and was touched when the girl returned the gesture.

As the bed rolled away Dr. Carson said, "You were tempted to go with her, weren't you?"

"Yes," Faith admitted. "She looked so frightened."

"You were able to chase away that fear—at least for a moment or two. You truly have a gift to make children feel better," Dr. Carson said with a pat on her arm.

His words were of little comfort. She felt as if she'd let this one particular child down. "She wanted me to stay with her."

This time Dr. Carson put an arm around her and gave her a gentle hug. "Of course she did. She took one look into your eyes and saw compassion and kindness. It's true what they say, Faith, that the eyes are the window to a person's soul. The day I met you yours told me there's not a mean bone in your body. And watching you interact with children, I'm convinced that I read yours correctly."

She wanted to believe that what he said was true, that when she did finally remember who she was and what was in her past that she would discover that his trust was not misplaced. Yet there were so many unanswered questions running through her mind.

"I don't know what I would have done if I hadn't met you and Marie." She told him the one thing of which she was certain. "Thank you for believing in me."

"You make it easy, Faith."

She forced a weak smile. "I think you're the kind of person who looks for the good in people. I just hope that someday you don't discover that…" She trailed off, not wanting to express her fears.

"What? That you're someone I shouldn't have trusted?"

"It's a possibility," she admitted.

He shook his head. "No, I don't think it is."

"But what if…"

Dr. Carson stopped her with a lift of his hand. "We're not going to talk about the what-ifs. Now let's get these books to where they're supposed to be so we can get home. Marie's got dinner in the oven and we don't want to be late."

"I'M LOOKING FOR Megan Novak. She was admitted early this morning," Adam told the woman at the hospital reception desk. "I'm her father."

He wondered why it should still feel awkward to identify himself as a parent. Maybe because his relationship with Megan still felt uncomfortable. He hadn't expected her to rush into his arms and call him Daddy the first time they'd met. After all, she'd been told she didn't have a father, a fact that still caused the hair on his neck to rise. He'd missed out on six years of Megan's life because of Christie's decision not to tell him she'd had his child.

And he knew that if it hadn't been for a tragedy, chances were he still wouldn't know he had a daughter. Adam didn't understand why, after going through so much trouble to keep Megan's existence a secret, Christie had named him as her legal guardian in the will. He probably would never know, but the reason was of no consequence at this point. What mattered was that Christie had ensured that, in the event of her death, Megan would have someone who was able to take care of her. He was that someone.

While the lawyers had worked out the legal details of guardianship, Megan had stayed in the small town of Silver Bay in the house she'd shared with her mother and her uncle. She'd said very little to Adam when they finally met for the first time, regarding him suspiciously as she clung to Tom Anderson's side. It shouldn't have come as a surprise to him that she would want to live with the uncle she'd known all of her life rather than with a father who was a stranger to her.

There was a lot to like about Tom Anderson. He had that same "live for today" attitude that Adam remembered of Christie, enjoying every minute of life and believing that tomorrow would take care of itself. It was obvious to Adam that he adored Megan and provided a much-needed male authority in her life. What he lacked in reliability he made up for in generosity. He wasn't, however, her father. No matter how much she wanted to stay in Silver Bay, Megan belonged with him in St. Paul.

"She's in room 217, Mr. Novak," the receptionist told him, bringing his thoughts back to the present. "If you go down the hall and take a left, you'll see the elevators."

Adam didn't wait for an elevator but took the stairs. When he reached the second floor he followed the arrows that directed him to the pediatric unit. Standing outside room 217, leaning against the wall was his sister-in-law, Lori. As soon as she noticed him, she straightened and started toward him, her arms outstretched.

"You made it!" she said, hugging him as close as her pregnant belly would allow. "I was worried the snow would close the airport before your plane could land."

"I got lucky."

She glanced past his shoulder. "Naomi's not with you?"

"No. She stayed in Miami." Which was how he'd wanted it. Not that Naomi Windell would have cut short her vacation for someone else's sick child. He glanced at the closed door. "Why are you out here?"

"There's a nurse and a lab technician in with Megan. It should only be a few minutes and we can go back in."

"How is she?"

"She's been sleeping ever since she came back from recovery. Have you talked to Dr. Lindgren?"

"Yes. He said the surgery went well."

She nodded. "That's what he told me, too. They're giving her antibiotics, which should take care of the infection, but she's going to have to stay in the hospital longer than if it had been a simple appendectomy…probably another five to seven days."

"I don't suppose she's going to like that," he surmised with a lift of one eyebrow.

Lori rolled her eyes. "Not if the way she behaved before surgery is any indication. She cried and begged me to take her home. Not that I blame her. Having an operation is scary enough when you're an adult—but when you're only six…" She shrugged helplessly.

"The worst should be over."

"Yes, and now her daddy's here." Lori sighed in relief. "She's going to be happy to see you."

Adam hoped she was right. As hard as his sister-in-law had tried to smooth over the rough edges in their relationship, he knew that Megan regarded him as the man she'd been forced to go live with when her mother had died. In the short time she'd been with him, they hadn't managed to get beyond that. Any affection she had for a father figure still went to her uncle. She treated Adam with a suspicion that at times bordered on indifference.

"Have you called Tom Anderson?" he asked, suddenly remembering the other man.

Lori nodded. "I told him I would keep him posted on what's happening. He asked if he could talk to her this evening once she was back in her room, but until now she's been too sedated to do much of anything but sleep."

"I'm sure she's going to want to call him as soon as she's able to use the phone," Adam noted.

"That probably won't be before morning. I don't expect she'll be awake much tonight." Lori glanced at her watch and said, "I can't believe it's only seven-thirty. It feels much later than that to me."

"How are you holding up?"

"I'm okay," she answered, although the circles under her eyes contradicted her. "It's just the usual complaints of a pregnant lady." She stretched, rubbing the area near the base of her spine.

"Backache?"

"Everything aches," she quipped.

He saw the lines on her face and realized how stressful the day had been for her. "When I asked if Megan could stay with you while I was gone I never expected something like this would happen. I'm sorry, Lori. I probably should have just taken her out of school and brought her with me."

"We both know why that wouldn't have worked."

"I wouldn't have brought Naomi if Megan had come with me." He didn't want to sound defensive, but ever since Megan had come to live with him he'd felt as if his personal life were suddenly under a magnifying glass.

Lori raised both hands as if to ward off an argument. "I was happy to have Megan stay with me."

He knew that was true, but it didn't make him feel any less guilty about the situation. "I know, but you shouldn't have had to be the one going through all of this, especially not in your condition."

She brushed away his concern with a wave of her hand. "Now you're sounding like Greg. Just because I'm pregnant doesn't mean I have to sit at home with my feet up. I managed just fine today."

"I knew you would. Just knowing you were with her was a great comfort to me, although I have to admit, that probably was the longest flight I've ever taken."

"I hope I didn't sound too frantic when I called you, but honestly, Adam, until that doctor came out of surgery and told me she was going to be all right, I was scared. Really scared." Her voice broke with emotion and she bit down on her lip.

"Waiting in a situation like this is never easy, is it?" he asked rhetorically. "I'm just glad you brought her to the emergency room when you did. You saved her life, Lori."

She leaned back against the wall, her shoulders sagging. "I know, but I can't help but wonder if the infection couldn't have been prevented if I had only taken her to the doctor last week."

"She wasn't having an appendicitis attack last week."

"No, but last night wasn't the first time she's complained of stomachaches, Adam," she said soberly.

"No, it wasn't," he agreed. "She's had a lot of them— like when she didn't want to eat her dinner or she didn't want to go to school. You remember the story about the boy who cried wolf?"

"Yes, but…"

"Lori, she had a physical exam before she started school here and the doctor said she was in good health," he reminded her, not wanting to admit that the same thought had crossed his mind when he'd learned that Megan's appendix had ruptured. Images of her rubbing her tummy and telling him it hurt had flashed relentlessly in his head.

"She had none of the other symptoms of appendicitis until this morning," Lori added, as if trying to convince herself she wasn't to blame. "It's not easy to diagnose, even with all of the symptoms."

"No, it isn't, as Dr. Lindgren told us. Nor does it do any good to second-guess the situation at this point. Yes, Megan did complain of stomachaches, but she's complained about a lot of things since she's been here." He rubbed a hand around the back of his neck. "Sometimes I feel as if that's all she does."

"She's had a lot to deal with these past few months," Lori said sympathetically.

"I realize that. I'm also aware of what a huge change it was for her to come live with me. Sometimes I wonder if I shouldn't have simply accepted the financial responsibility of her care and allowed her to stay with Tom."

Lori placed her hand on his arm. "No, you are her father. She belongs here with you. I know that it's been a little difficult for the two of you—"

"A little difficult?" He interrupted with an incredulous chuckle. "She's been with me for eight weeks and she still calls me Adam." A clear sign to him that she didn't want to be with him.

"She's not used to having a father and you're not used to having a daughter. It's going to take time for the two of you to adjust to your relationship." It was the same argument Lori had used repeatedly for the past few weeks.

Time was the one thing he hadn't been given. Most men had nine months to prepare for a fatherhood that began with an infant. He'd had to take a crash course that had ended with him being delivered a kindergartner. He'd expected there to be a period of adjustment while the two of them got to know one another. What he hadn't expected was that after so many weeks he would feel as if he'd failed the first test of fatherhood.

"I'm not sure what else I can do," he said, feeling frustrated by his efforts. "I've given her everything I can think of to make her feel at home with me."

"Things will get better," she predicted. "You just have to patient." She arched her back, again placing a hand at the base of her spine. "I wonder how much longer it'll be before we can go in? I could use a chair about now."

"Are you sure you're okay?"

She smiled weakly and nodded. "I'm just tired." She put a hand on her stomach. "And it doesn't help that your nephew has decided today is the day to practice his soccer kicks."

"Why don't you go home?"

She shook her head. "Can't. I promised Megan I'd be here when she woke up."

"She's probably not going to know who is and who isn't here tonight," he noted.

Lori glanced apprehensively at the closed door. "I am tired," she admitted.

"Then do me a favor and leave. On top of all of this I don't need the wrath of my brother on me. He's not happy that I made him go to the boat show in the first place, and if he comes home and finds you've run your-self ragged while he's been gone, he's going to be all over me."

"It's a good thing he is there," she remarked. "Your grandfather can't really handle a show on his own anymore."

"I called Bill Grainger and he's going to fly out first thing in the morning to help in any way he can," Adam told her.

"That'll be good." She placed a hand on his arm. "I'm sorry you had to leave in the middle of the show. I know how excited you were about the *Seababy*."

He shrugged. "Things happen."

Although Adam often oversaw construction at Novak Boats, his first love was design. It was why he was the company's best spokesperson. He knew every inch on each custom-designed yacht that came out of the factory. Boat shows were the perfect place for him to showcase the cutting-edge technology that had earned him numerous industry awards. This year it was the *Seababy*, a midsize motor yacht, that was his pride and joy and already the buzz in the boating world.

But then Novak Boats often was at the center of attention in the industry. What his grandfather had founded as a small family business to build pontoons for local lakes had evolved into an internationally known yacht manufacturer creating pleasure cruise boats easily handled at sea. From a single employee to nearly one hundred and fifty, the company had earned its place in the boating world with a reputation envied by many.

Building boats was a passion Adam had discovered at an early age. While some kids went to nursery school, Adam had tagged along with his father to the factory where his grandfather had put him to work fetching tools. He'd learned the art of boat building at the knee of a master, and by the time he went off to college to earn his engineering degree, he knew every aspect of the business, including how to represent Novak Boats at the various shows across the country.

When the door to Megan's room opened and a lab technician came out carrying a tray of medical supplies, Adam asked, "Is everything okay?"

The woman nodded. "You'll be able to go in in a few minutes. Her nurse is just finishing up in there."

"Is she asking for me?" Lori wanted to know.

"Oh, yes. I think she must have said 'I want my mommy' at least five times."

Lori's startled glance caught Adam's before she said to the tech, "I'm her aunt. Her mother died last fall."

The tech grimaced. "Oooh. I'm sorry. I thought…"

Lori shook her head. "It's okay."

"It's probably the medication confusing her," the tech said with an apologetic shrug, then disappeared down the hall.

The door opened again and this time a nurse stepped out. "You can come in now."

Adam introduced himself and asked, "How is she?"

"She's resting comfortably. She was having quite a bit of pain so I gave her something to help her sleep," the nurse explained. "Mr. Novak, if you'd like to spend the night, we can put a cot for you in her room."

Lori looked at Adam. "One of us should probably stay in case she wakes up."

He nodded. "I'll stay. You go home and get a good night's sleep."

"What if she asks for Christie again?"

"I doubt she will." He dismissed her concern with a shake of his head. "But if she does, I'll clear things up." As he watched his sister-in-law walk away, he realized it was a heck of a time for him to hope to improve communications with his daughter. But he would. Somehow. Someway.

CHAPTER TWO

WHAT THE NURSE CALLED a bed was actually a padded vinyl chair that collapsed in the middle so that it resembled a cot. There were times when being six foot three had its advantages. This was not one of them. As Adam tried to stretch out on the makeshift bed, his feet dangled over one end. After a period of tossing and turning in search of a comfortable position, he put the chair back into its original position. It wouldn't be the first time he would have to sleep sitting upright.

Not that he expected to sleep. He needed darkness and silence. Megan's hospital room had neither. If there wasn't some piece of equipment blinking, there was an electronic machine beeping. Then there were the frequent visits by various medical staff.

And, of course, there was Megan herself. She was not a quiet sleeper. Although she wasn't tossing and turning, she made little sounds that were a cross between a groan and a hiccup. The first time he heard one he thought that she was in distress. He'd jumped up from the chair and called for the nurse who had assured him Megan was not in any danger.

To his surprise he finally was able to get a couple of hours of sleep. When he awoke he discovered someone had pulled the drape around Megan's bed, separating him from his daughter. Although he couldn't see the two people on the other side, he could hear them.

"It hurts," Megan cried.

"I know it does, dear. I'm going to give you some medicine to help make you feel better."

When the only sound to be heard was Megan's whimpering, Adam called out, "Is everything all right?"

"Everything's fine, Mr. Novak," a woman's voice answered from the other side of the curtain. "We're just taking care of some business."

Then he heard Megan say in a voice that was slightly hoarse, "Is Adam here?"

Adam. Being in the hospital hadn't suddenly made his daughter want to call him Dad. He wondered if she would ever regard him as her father.

"If you're referring to your dad, yes, he is here," Adam heard the nurse say. "He's been here all night actually, and as soon as I'm finished we'll open the curtain and you can see him."

"I'd rather see my mommy. Can you get her for me?"

Adam frowned. It had been almost six months since Christie had drowned. Megan knew her mother had died and gone to heaven, so why was she asking for her now?

The nurse didn't answer her question about her mother but went on to advise Megan to be very careful and lie still because it was important that she not disturb the bandages on her tummy.

Adam could see nothing but darkness through the sliver of an opening in the window blind. He glanced at his watch. It was five-fifteen. He had a crick in his neck, his clothes were wrinkled and he was in desperate need of a cup of coffee. Thinking he might take a break and find a coffee machine, he was about to ask the nurse how long she'd be with Megan when the drape swung open.

"How is she?" he asked in a low voice.

"She's still pretty sleepy, but she's doing much better, aren't you, Megan?" the nurse said, walking over to write some numbers on a white board hanging on the wall.

Adam moved closer to the bed. Although Megan still looked tiny and frail, her face wasn't as pasty as it had been when he'd first seen her. The medical equipment surrounding her reminded him, however, that she was one very sick little girl.

"How do you feel?" he asked her, wishing he could do something to make her more comfortable. She reminded him of how she'd looked the first time he'd seen her. It had been in the attorney's office and she'd stood perfectly still next to the lawyer, as if she were afraid to move a muscle for fear of something horrible happening to her.

"It still hurts," she replied in a voice that begged for his sympathy. "Lori told me the operation would make me feel better."

The nurse came back to her bedside. "It doesn't hurt as badly today as it did yesterday, does it?"

"No." The response was barely audible.

"Each day it will hurt a little less," the nurse told her. "Once your tummy heals you're going to feel as good as new. Now I'm going to leave you so you can get some more sleep." She checked the IV unit next to the bed, then said, "If you need anything, you know what to do, right?"

"I push the button," Megan said weakly.

"That's right." On her way out, the nurse said to Adam, "I'll just be down the hall if you need me."

He nodded. "Is there someplace where I can get a cup of coffee?"

"There's a lounge near the elevators with vending machines, but at this time of night, the coffee's pretty strong. You might want to go across the street. There's a small diner that's open twenty-four hours."

Adam thanked her then took the place she'd vacated next to the bed.

Megan glanced at him through half-closed eyes. "Where's Lori?"

"She's at home."

"She said she was going to stay," Megan said in a voice that was on the verge of tears.

"She wanted to, but she was tired so she went home to get some sleep. She'll be back in the morning. I'm here if you need anything." He noticed a cup with a straw in it on the tray table next to her bed. "Would you like a sip of water?"

She shook her head. "Did you come home on an airplane?"

"Yes."

"Didn't you like the boat show?"

"Yes, I did, but I wanted to be here with you." It was the truth. The moment Lori had called with the news that she'd taken Megan to the hospital his first thought was to get home as quickly as possible so he could be with her.

She scrunched up her face. "I feel funny."

"Funny how?" he wanted to know.

"Like my head's fuzzy," she murmured.

"That's from the medicine. The more you sleep, the less fuzzy you'll feel."

"But I don't want to go to sleep," she whined. "I want to find her."

He leaned closer to her. "Who do you want to find?"

"Mommy. She's here in the hospital, you know. I saw her. When the man was pushing me in my bed." Megan yawned, her eyelids fluttering as she fought to stay awake.

So that was the reason for her confusion. While she'd been sedated she had seen someone who resembled Christie and mistaken her for her mother. Adam knew he needed to correct her. He couldn't let her go on believing that she'd really seen her mother, yet he wondered if she would even remember such a conversation tomorrow morning? What she needed was sleep. There would be plenty of time to talk about what she did or didn't see tomorrow.

"Shhh. Don't talk now," he told her. "You need to rest."

Megan's voice trembled as she said, "I wish she'd take me home with her."

Adam felt as if two hands reached right into his chest and squeezed his heart. "You'll get to go home when you're feeling better," he said gently. He took her small hand in his and brought it to his lips, kissing the knuckles ever so gently.

"Will Mommy be there?" The question came out on a pathetic little whimper, then before Adam could answer, she had closed her eyes and succumbed to sleep.

It was obvious Megan was still not over the death of her mother. He supposed it shouldn't have surprised

him. She was so young and innocent—too young to
have to cope with the loss of a parent. Now the trauma
of surgery had been added to her already-confused emotional state. He could only hope that once she recovered
from the effects of the anesthetics, she wouldn't be asking about her mother.

As he watched her sleep, he stared at her face, trying to see why his relatives thought she looked like him.
All he saw was a younger version of Christie. With her
blond hair, blue eyes and small rounded nose, Megan
definitely looked more like an Anderson than a Novak.
Lori insisted that she had his smile, but he was reserv-
ing an opinion on that one until the space where her
tooth was missing had been filled.

His brother, Greg, had pointed out that Megan had
several of Adam's mannerisms, like biting down on her
lower lip when she concentrated and wiggling her feet
while she slept. He glanced to the end of the bed, knowing that if he watched it long enough, he'd see the blanket twitch. After only a few seconds it did wiggle and
he smiled.

Adam thought it was strange that she should have any
of his traits considering they'd spent so many years
apart. Again he looked at her face, so peaceful in slumber. She had so much potential, so many possibilities
ahead of her. From the day he'd first seen her he'd promised himself that he would make up for the years he'd
missed in her young life.

And he would. He was going to do his best to protect her from getting hurt again. And he would spend
more time with her. Ever since she'd come to live with

him he'd been working like a fiend getting ready for
the debut of the newest Novak yacht. He'd had little
free time to do the fun things that fathers and daughters were supposed to do. But that was going to
change. As the sun's first morning rays slowly appeared through the slits in the window blinds, he
pulled out his Palm Pilot to see where he could schedule her in.

AFTER SPENDING THE NIGHT in a chair, Adam needed a
shower and a change of clothes. While his sister-in-law
kept his daughter company, he took his laptop and went
home where he was tempted to grab a few hours of
sleep, but chose instead to call his brother in Miami to
get a report on the boat show and to take care of several
other business matters.

It was after noon when he returned to the hospital.
Before going up to see Megan, he stopped at the gift
shop in the lobby and bought a bouquet of balloons and
a small white bear that had Get Well Soon embroidered
inside a pink heart on its chest.

When he walked into Megan's room, he saw Lori
was sitting next to the bed reading her a story. The
blinds were open, allowing a stream of sunshine in and
Megan's bed had been raised so that she was no longer
lying flat on her back.

"Oooh, what pretty balloons," Lori cooed when she saw
what was in Adam's hands. "What do you think, Megan?"

"Are they for me?" she asked, a gleam of interest in
her eyes.

"They certainly are." Adam set the bear down next

to her on the bed. "Along with this guy, they're supposed to help you feel better," he told her, giving her a smile.

As he glanced around for a place to put the balloons, Lori said, "You can probably tie them to the foot rail. That way Megan can see them even if the curtain is drawn around her bed." She reached for the bear and moved it closer to her niece, tucking it under the covers so that it was beside her. "Isn't he soft?"

Megan nodded, her small hand closing around the bear and bringing it to her face. "He's very soft. Thank you," she said politely.

"You're welcome. How are you feeling?" he asked, taking the chair on the opposite side of the bed from Lori.

"Okay," she answered without much enthusiasm.

"Dr. Lindgren was here earlier and said that she should start feeling much better once she's able to eat," Lori told him. "She's going to try some Jell-O for lunch."

"Yes, I heard. That's good news," Adam said.

"And the other good news is that while you were gone, she got up and went to the bathroom," Lori told him.

"That has to be a good sign," Adam acknowledged.

"I didn't like doing my business in that pan," Megan said with the frankness of a child. She told him several other things she didn't like about being in the hospital before asking him the one question he didn't want to hear. "Have you seen Mommy today?"

Lori's eyes met his and she shrugged helplessly. He sat down in the chair next to the bed and said, "Megan, you know we can't see her. She's in heaven."

"Not anymore she isn't. She came back," Megan said in a small voice. "Will you find her for me?"

He leaned closer to her. "I can't do that because she's not here."

She licked her lips with her tongue before saying, "But I saw her yesterday when I was getting a ride in my bed."

"You mean you saw someone who looked like her," he corrected her.

"Uh-uh. I saw *her*," she told him.

Adam reached for her hand and clasped it within his. "We've talked about this before, Megan. From time to time you're going to see women with blond hair and blue eyes who remind you of your mother. That's only natural. You loved her very much and you miss her."

"But this lady was my mommy," she insisted.

"No, she wasn't," he said gently, but firmly.

She pulled her hand away. "I knew you wouldn't believe me." It was an accusation accompanied by a look that reminded Adam of all that was wrong in their relationship.

"It's not that I don't believe you. I think you're confused because you saw someone who *looks* like your mother," he said.

"It was her," she stated as emphatically as she could considering she had very little strength. "She smiled at me and she blew me a kiss. Mommy always did this when she said goodbye." She raised two fingers to her lips, then held them up in the air as if sending a kiss his way.

"Lots of people blow kisses, Megan."

"It was my mommy," she stated. Her gaze shot to Lori. "You believe me, right?"

Lori sighed. "Oh, sweetie, it's not a question of believing you. I'm sure the woman you saw looked a lot like your mom…."

Realizing neither of them thought she'd seen her mother, Megan couldn't stop her lip from quivering and the tears from falling. Pain tightened Adam's chest.

"It's only natural that you'd be thinking about her while you're here in the hospital," he said. "She used to comfort you when you were sick, remember?"

Megan nodded. "Sometimes she'd climb into bed with me to keep me warm." She hiccuped as she struggled not to sob. "She could make my tummyaches go away without having to have an operation."

"I know." He brushed a stray blond hair away from her cheek. "Unfortunately your mommy's not here. She's in heaven."

"Maybe she came back."

The hope in her eyes had the same effect on him as a punch in the stomach. "People don't come back from heaven, Megan. Once you go there, you stay there forever."

"But you came back," she told him.

Adam exchanged glances with Lori before saying, "No, I didn't. I was never in heaven."

"Mommy said you were."

Again he caught Lori's glance and it was filled with empathy.

"Well, your mommy made a mistake. She only thought I'd gone to heaven," he explained, trying not to feel frustrated with something over which he'd had no control.

"Maybe you made a mistake and Mommy didn't really go to heaven, either," she argued.

His anger with Christie for keeping Megan's existence from him surfaced. He could only imagine how different things would be this very moment if instead

of disappearing from his life, Christie had told him she
was pregnant with his child.

"Other people believe your mommy's in heaven,
too," Lori said. "Even your uncle Tom knows she's
there."

"Maybe he made a mistake, too," Megan countered
innocently.

Adam could see that he was accomplishing nothing
by trying to convince her she hadn't seen her mother.
If there was one thing he'd learned in the short time he'd
known his daughter it was that once she had her mind
made up about something, she wasn't about to change
it. He could see this was one of those times.

"Tell me why you think she's here in the hospital,
Megan," he said patiently.

"When I saw her she told me she works here. She
rocks the babies," she answered.

"She told you that?" he asked, wondering if there actually was an employee who rocked babies.

"Yes. In the child-care center."

He looked at Lori who said, "It's on the first floor."

He thought for a long moment before getting to his
feet. "I'll tell you what. I'll go downstairs and look for
this woman so we can find out what her name is."

"I know what her name is. She's my mommy." Megan's voice sounded weary, reminding Adam that she
had a long recovery ahead of her.

Lori raised a finger to her lips. "Shh. Don't talk, just
rest. Let your dad go and see if he can find her."

Adam glanced down at his daughter. "I'll be back as
soon as I've talked to her, okay?"

Megan's response was a satisfied grin. On any other occasion it would have made him happy. Today it only made him anxious.

Lori looked at Adam. "I'll walk with you to the elevators." As soon as they were in the hallway she said, "I'm worried about her, Adam. She really does believe that she saw Christie."

"I know. Last night I thought it was simply the medication, but she's lucid today and she's still asking for her," he said as they walked toward the bank of elevators at the end of the corridor.

"She thinks people can come back from heaven," Lori said on a sigh.

"Yes, and we know why." He found it difficult to hold back his frustration with Megan's mother. "All of this could have been avoided if Christie had simply allowed me to be Megan's father from day one." Impatiently he raked a hand through his hair. "I still don't know why she never told me she was pregnant."

"You said it was a one-night stand, Adam," she reminded him, as if that explained Christie's behavior.

"That didn't give her the right to keep Megan's existence from me," he argued. "I may not have been the most mature guy seven years ago, but I wouldn't have turned my back on my own daughter."

"Of course you wouldn't," his sister-in-law said in a tone definitely meant to appease him.

Lori had been married to his brother long enough to know that he had strong family values. She'd also seen enough women come and go in his life to know that making a commitment to one wasn't a priority in his life. Although she rarely commented on his personal relationships, he knew that she hoped that marriage and a family would be in his future. One of the reasons they got along as well as they did was because they had an unspoken agreement between them. He didn't interfere in his brother's marriage and she respected his privacy when it came to his love life. Now that he had Megan, he could see she was finding it difficult to honor her end of the agreement.

They'd reached the elevators and stood facing each other. "It does no good to wonder what might have been," Lori told him. "We need to get this resolved and soon. Megan can't go on thinking her mother's come back from the dead."

Adam pressed the call button. "It will be resolved. If this woman she's mistaken for Christie works in the child-care center, I'll find her. Will you stay with Megan until I get back?"

"Of course. I do have a doctor appointment later this afternoon, though."

He nodded. "This shouldn't take long."

An elevator car arrived and he stepped inside. As the doors slid shut, he tried not to think about how fragile and vulnerable Megan had looked as she'd asked about her mother. He'd wanted to take her in his arms and tell her that nothing would ever harm her as long as he was around.

He hadn't. And not just because of the hospital equipment connected to her. She had given him no reason to believe that she wanted him to be her father. If anything, she'd shown him in a hundred different ways that she didn't regard him as her parent.

She wanted a mother, not a father. It's why she preferred to be with Lori rather than with him. He wondered if it also wasn't the reason why she wanted so badly to believe that she'd seen Christie in the hospital.

He tried not to feel as if he'd flunked another fatherhood test, but after six weeks of being a parent, he'd made very little progress in earning her trust and love. That had to change. How it would happen, he wasn't sure, but he knew it had to start with finding the baby rocker.

"THERE WAS A MAN looking for you while you were at lunch," Mrs. Carmichael told Faith when she came back to work after her break.

She frowned. "What did he want?"

"He said he wanted to thank you for being kind to his daughter."

"Did you tell him I was just doing my job?" she asked, pulling on the blue and green smock all hospital volunteers wore.

"Oh, he didn't leave his daughter here at the center. She's a patient on the second floor." Her supervisor pulled a slip of paper from her pocket. "A little girl named Megan Novak."

The name didn't ring a bell. "Are you sure he wanted me? I don't remember meeting anyone by that name."

"He asked specifically for the woman who rocks the babies, and even described you as having blond hair and blue eyes," Mrs. Carmichael answered. "I told him I'd pass on his thanks but if he wanted to do it himself in person he could come back this afternoon."

Puzzled, Faith shook her head. "He must have me confused with someone else."

"I know you like to visit the kids in pediatrics. Maybe it's someone you met while you were there?"

"It could be, but I don't remember anyone named Megan."

The older woman shrugged. "I wouldn't worry about it. If he comes in, it will all get straightened out."

Faith didn't give it another thought but went back to work. She had just finished buttoning her smock when a little boy arrived at the center. He was a two-year-old named Isaac who didn't want to be separated from his mother. Unfortunately, his father was a patient on the fourth floor and his mother wanted to visit him.

It wasn't the first time Faith had to calm a kicking and screaming child who thought a temper tantrum would bring his mother back to the nursery. With a patience that had earned her the nickname "the peacemaker" from another of her co-workers, Faith waited until he had vented his frustration before attempting to take him on her lap. Eventually he saw that no amount of ranting was going to bring his mother back. Faith spoke to him in a gentle tone, urging him to sit with her in the rocker. Within minutes she had rocked him to sleep.

"Do I dare talk or will he wake up?" The voice was almost a whisper.

She glanced up and saw a tall man with dark hair and even darker eyes looking at her. He wore a pair of corduroy slacks and a tweed sweater. Although he was at least a foot away from her, she felt as if he had invaded her space. So intimidating was his presence. Her heartbeat increased. For the first time since her accident, someone was looking at her with a familiar glint in his eye.

The fact that it was such an attractive man caused her stomach to do a flip-flop, as well. She glanced at the boy on her lap. "I think this one can sleep through just about anything. Can I help you with something?"

He glanced at her name tag. "You're Faith, the baby rocker, right?"

"Yes, I am." When he continued to stare at her without saying a word she asked, "Do I know you?" Her mouth went dry at the possibility and every nerve in her body tensed as she waited for his answer. He hesitated, staring at her the way the toddlers in her care often examined the wooden puzzles on the table—with both fascination and uncertainty.

When he said, "You don't recognize me?" her heartbeat quickened.

She shook her head. "Should I?" It was obvious from the way he was staring at her that he thought she should. Hope mushroomed inside her that she might finally learn her identity. Ever since her accident she'd been anticipating the day when someone would recognize her. She wondered if this man was that someone.

Then he said, "No, we haven't met. I'm Adam Novak. Megan's father."

The man who'd come looking for her to thank her for being kind to his daughter. Just as quickly as it had surfaced, the hope disappeared. Faith did her best to hide her disappointment, but her voice was subdued when she said, "I'm sorry, but I don't know who Megan is."

"She's six years old. Blond hair. Blue eyes. A couple of days ago she had surgery," he explained. "While they were moving her to her room on the second floor, she must have seen you. She said you talked to her and told her you rock babies here in the nursery."

The memory of the frightened little girl came to her and made Faith's voice soften with concern. "That was your daughter?"

He nodded. "I don't know what you said to her, but she's been talking about you ever since."

Something in his tone gave her the impression he wasn't exactly pleased about that, despite his cordial smile. "Sometimes with children all that's necessary is a smile," she told him, wishing he'd leave, but he lingered, his hands in his pockets as he stood next to the rocking chair, his gaze intense. "How is she feeling? Is she going to be all right?" Faith asked.

"She's slowly improving," he answered. Even though he'd told her he didn't know her, he continued to stare at her as if she were of particular interest to him.

Faith could feel her face warming under his scrutiny and was grateful when out of the corner of her eye she noticed Isaac's mother had come back to the day-care center. "I'm glad to hear she's getting better. You'll have to excuse me. It looks as if this little guy's mother has come to pick him up." She looked past his shoulder and smiled at the woman walking toward them, hoping he would take the hint and leave.

"I understand," he said with a glance over his shoulder at the approaching woman. "I just wanted to say thank you for what you did for Megan."

"No thanks are necessary," she told him.

He smiled then, an incredibly sexy grin that made Faith feel funny in places she didn't know existed inside her. "Goodbye, Faith, the baby rocker."

"Bye," she mumbled, then turned her attention to Isaac's mother, hoping he would leave without saying another word to her. He did and she felt a pent-up stream of tension ease from her muscles. She hoped it was the last she'd see of him. Being in his presence was like something she'd never experienced before. For a brief moment she'd felt a longing inside her that made her wonder what it would be like if Adam Novak were to take her in his arms and kiss her. She didn't want to have such feelings. They didn't seem right. Not now, when she didn't even know her own name.

Goodbye, Faith, the baby rocker. Long after he was gone she heard his deep voice echoing those words in her head, and each time they sent a tiny shiver of pleasure through her.

CHAPTER THREE

ADAM KNEW WHY Megan wanted to believe Faith was her mother. If he didn't know better he might have mistaken the child-care worker for Christie, too.

But he did know better. Unlike his daughter, Adam was certain that when people died and went to heaven, they didn't come back.

Christie had drowned in Lake Superior last September. An eyewitness had seen her small sailboat capsize in a storm, sending its lone occupant into the lake. The Coast Guard had been summoned to the scene but rescue attempts had failed.

Anyone who lived near Lake Superior knew that because of the temperature of the water, there was little hope of surviving such an accident. That hadn't stopped Christie's brother, a professional diver, from looking for her. It hadn't taken him long to realize that he wasn't going to find her. Tom Anderson, like the other residents of the small town of Silver Bay, knew that very few bodies were ever recovered from the huge body of water. It was too deep and too cold and the great lake had a history of not giving up its dead. Megan's mother was one of them. Although her body had never surfaced from the icy waters of the lake, the authorities had declared her legally dead.

As Adam stood outside the child-care center looking in at Faith, the baby rocker, he had to remind himself of that fact. Although she wore a hospital smock and plain black slacks, with the right clothes and makeup he thought she could easily pass for Christie. He doubted, however, that a woman who rocked babies during the day in a hospital nursery would strip off her clothes at a nightclub after dark.

He watched as she said goodbye to one child and welcomed another. She led her newest responsibility to a child-size table where she set him on a chair, then knelt beside him, encouraging him to build a tower of wood blocks. For every one square she added to the pile, he tossed another onto the floor and every time she'd bend over to pick up a block, her blond hair would fall like a curtain of silk across her cheek.

Adam felt something stir inside him. Like Christie, she had a look about her few men wouldn't notice. It was uncanny just how much of a resemblance she had to Megan's mother. So much of one that when he'd first seen her, his breath had caught in his throat. He knew he'd made her uncomfortable staring at her the way he had, but he hadn't been able to help himself. He debated whether he should go back inside and explain the reason for his interest in her.

He decided against it. He needed to talk to his daughter, and there was no point in putting off the inevitable. He needed to go back upstairs and tell Megan that the woman she'd seen yesterday was not her mother.

For once in his life he found himself wishing that miracles could happen and the impossible would come true. He could think of nothing more satisfying than being able to tell her that he'd been wrong—that her mother hadn't drowned. She was alive and well and right here in this hospital. The past six months had been just one big, nasty nightmare. It was the one thing he could tell his daughter that would for certain put a smile on her face.

He knew he was being fanciful to even allow such thoughts. Megan needed him to be a parent even if it meant he had to tell her what she didn't want to hear.

Adam sighed. It seemed as if every day brought a new challenge to him as a father. Just when he thought he'd crossed the last of the major hurdles, another one always managed to pop up in the middle of the road. Never would he have expected he would be having a conversation with his daughter about her mother's reincarnation. But then he'd been unprepared for so many of the things that had happened between the two of them, it really shouldn't have come as that big of a surprise.

Reluctantly he turned away from the window and headed back to Megan's room.

"HAS IT BEEN BUSY?" Zoe, a college student who worked the evening shift, asked Faith when she arrived at the child-care center.

"It hasn't been too bad," Faith told her replacement as she wiped down the wood slats of a crib.

"Who's the guy in with Mrs. Carmichael?" the young girl wanted to know.

Faith turned around to glance at the office and saw

Adam Novak leaning over Mrs. Carmichael's desk. She wondered why he had come back.

"I think his daughter's a patient here." Faith returned her attention to scrubbing the crib, not wanting the other woman to suspect she had any interest in the conversation taking place in the office.

"He's hot, isn't he?" Zoe asked.

Faith mumbled, "I wouldn't know," which wasn't exactly the truth. She knew very well that he was attractive. It's why she'd had a funny feeling in her stomach when he'd stared at her earlier that afternoon.

"He's probably married," the other girl surmised. "Most good-looking guys are."

Faith didn't comment, not wanting to admit that she had wondered about his marital status, too. Since he'd left the child-care center earlier that day, she'd wondered about quite a few things about him, none of them she wanted to share with her co-worker.

To her relief, Zoe changed the subject. "How come you're doing Gina's job? I thought it was her week to wash the cribs."

"It is, but I had some extra time so I thought I'd do it."

When a mother arrived with a little girl, Zoe was forced to give them her attention. Faith emptied her bucket and was about to take off her smock and go home for the day when she heard Mrs. Carmichael call her into her office.

"Mr. Novak would like to speak to you for a few minutes," she said when Faith paused in the doorway. Mrs. Carmichael gestured for her to enter the small room. "You can talk here," she said before pulling the door shut on her way out.

Adam Novak stood next to the desk, looking every bit as attractive as he had earlier that day. Faith knew that Zoe was dead-on with her description of him when she'd called him hot. Just the way he looked at her could make her skin warm. Her heart began to beat faster and she clasped her hands together so they wouldn't reveal her nervousness.

"You're probably wondering why I'm here," he began, his gaze not as intense as it had been the first time they'd spoken, yet it had the power to send a shiver through her.

"Why *are* you here?" Once again, the way he looked at her created all sorts of funny sensations inside her. She nervously moistened her lips with her tongue.

"You like children, don't you." It was more of a statement than a question.

"Of course. I wouldn't be much help around here if I didn't," she answered with a weak smile.

He returned her smile with a grin that sent a tingling through her. "That's why I came back. Because you like children and I have a pretty good idea that if you knew there was something you could do to help one, you'd do it. Am I right?"

"Yes." She eyed him warily. "Mr. Novak, if you want me to visit Megan, all you have to do is ask."

"There are circumstances that might make it a little awkward," he said, his eyes still holding hers.

"I often visit the pediatrics unit to read to the patients. This is a hospital, Mr. Novak. I see children with all kinds of illnesses. It won't be uncomfortable for me. If I can cheer Megan by visiting her, I'd be happy to do so."

"Her physical condition is not the reason I think it could be awkward for you," he told her.

"Then what is the reason?"

He took a deep breath, ran a hand over his dark head, then propped a hip on the corner of the desk. "I need to tell you a little about Megan. Maybe you want to sit down."

She shook her head. "No, I'm fine, thank you."

He shrugged. "Megan lost her mother last fall. She drowned in a boating accident."

Faith's chest tightened. "I'm so sorry. It must have been horrible for both of you."

"Yes, it was. Losing a parent at such a young age is traumatic. It's very difficult for a six-year-old to comprehend the concept of death. She had so many questions. I thought I'd answered all of them, but..." He trailed off with a shake of his head.

"I'm sure you did the best you could," Faith said.

Grimacing, he admitted, "I'm afraid my best wasn't good enough."

"Why do you say that?"

"Because no matter how many times I explain that once a person dies and goes to heaven that person cannot come home again, Megan doesn't believe me."

"She thinks her mother's going to come back?" Faith asked in dismay.

"It's worse. She believes she's seen her."

Emotion rose in her throat. "That is very sad."

"Sad, but true. After surgery when they were moving her from recovery to her room, she saw a woman she believes is her mother." He looked her straight in the eye and said, "You."

"Me?" Faith was so startled that she was surprised she could say anything at all.

"Yes, and I can understand her mistake. You do look like Christie."

Faith gasped. "That's why you were staring at me? Because I reminded you of your dead wife?" She hated the frantic tone that had come into her voice, but at the moment she was feeling far from calm.

"Yes, you look very much like Megan's mother," he said quietly.

"You said she drowned."

He nodded soberly. "In Lake Superior." A shadow passed over his face. "That's what makes this difficult for Megan to understand. They never recovered her mother's body and for months after her death she believed it was all a mistake." He continued to talk about the period of adjustment Megan was going through, but Faith had a hard time concentrating on what he was saying. There was only one thought going through her head. *They never found her body.*

Faith swallowed with difficulty. It couldn't be. It was too bizarre to even contemplate. She couldn't be this Christie person whom everyone thought was dead. Lake Superior was over three hours away. What would she have been doing on the side of the road in southern Minnesota if she lived on the North Shore?

"So that's why I need you to visit Megan," he said, unaware of the turmoil going on inside her.

With her skin becoming clammy and her heart pounding in her chest she said, "You want me to tell her I'm not her mother?"

"Yes. It's the only way she's going to accept that her mother is gone. She won't listen to me."

"But you're her father." Her legs grew weak beneath her and she reached for the desk to steady herself. "Surely she trusts you to tell her the truth?"

"It's been a while since I saw her mother."

She frowned. "But you do remember what she looked like?"

"Yes. She looked very much like you."

The room began to spin and Adam's voice grew fainter in her ears.

"That's why I stared at you the way I did earlier this morning. For a moment, I thought you were Christie. I..."

Faith didn't hear the rest of what he said because she was falling into darkness.

As she gradually regained consciousness, she heard a man's voice calling her name. When she opened her eyes, Adam Novak and Mrs. Carmichael were at her side looking very anxious.

"Do you think we should take her to the E.R.?" the older woman asked Adam.

"No, I think she's coming around," he answered.

Faith's first attempt at speaking resulted in silence. She wanted to tell them she was okay, but no matter how hard she tried, she couldn't get the words out.

"I'll get a glass of water," Mrs. Carmichael said before disappearing from the room.

As Faith tried to raise herself up, Adam lent her his arm. He felt solid and steady as she used it as a lever.

"Take it slow," he warned, sliding his other arm around her.

She was tempted to sink back against him. He smelled good—like the forest after a rain—and he was looking at her as if she were a delicate piece of china that might break. A pleasant sensation rippled through her as she caught the look in his eyes.

"I'm okay," she said, scrambling to her feet and away from his touch.

"You'd better sit for a few minutes," he said, pushing a chair toward her.

Her legs still wobbly, she did as he suggested. When he hovered over her she said, "You don't need to worry. I'm not going to do that again."

"Maybe you should go to the E.R. and have a doctor look at you," he suggested.

"I live with a doctor. I'll tell him about it when I get home," she told him, straightening her smock.

"How are you getting home? I don't think you should travel alone."

"I'll be fine." She wished he'd quit looking at her with those dark eyes of his.

Mrs. Carmichael returned with a glass of water, which Faith downed in one gulp.

"I don't think you should go home unescorted." Mrs. Carmichael echoed what Adam had said. "I'm going to call Dr. Carson to come pick you up."

Faith didn't protest, thinking it might be a good idea to talk to the doctor about what she'd just learned. While Mrs. Carmichael was on the phone, she turned to Adam.

"I'm sorry, but I don't think I should visit Megan just yet," she told him.

"No, of course not. You need to go home and take

care of yourself. I would like to get this all taken care of before much longer, however. We need to put a stop to this fantasy she has that you're her mother."

She shook her head. "That might not be possible."

His eyes narrowed. "Why not?"

Faith took a deep breath and said, "Because there's a possibility I am her mother."

ADAM STARED AT FAITH in disbelief. Either she hadn't heard a word he had said or she truly was ill. He looked at her pale cheeks and her troubled eyes. "I think maybe you should get checked out in the E.R."

"I told you I'm okay," she insisted.

"Do you realize what you just said?"

She nodded. "I think I might be this Christie person."

"No, you most definitely are not," he stated emphatically. She didn't look confused and he found his patience dwindling. "Are you playing some kind of game with me?"

"No. I'm just trying to tell you the truth." There was a vulnerability about her that made it difficult for him to be suspicious of her, yet he didn't understand what she was hoping to accomplish by saying that she might be Megan's mother.

He reached for the other chair in the office and sat down in front of her. "Tell me why you would make such a statement."

"A little over three weeks ago a doctor and his wife were traveling along Highway 52 just south of the cities when they saw me lying on the side of the road. I was unconscious and looked as if I'd been beaten," she began. "Thanks to the kindness of Dr. Carson and his wife and the excellent medical attention I received, I regained consciousness and most of my injuries are healed. My hair covers the scar on my scalp." She removed her smock and pushed back the sleeves of her shirt to show him her arms. "These are almost gone now, but you can still see where I was bruised."

A shudder echoed through him at the sight of the areas of discoloration. It angered him to think that someone had assaulted her and left her to die on a roadside.

"I'm sorry. I hope they caught who did this to you."

She shook her head and he felt a rush of emotion at the injustice. As she lowered her sleeves, he realized that there was another significant difference between her and Christie. Faith had larger breasts.

When she noticed where his eyes were focused she blushed. That was something Christie wouldn't have done. As an exotic dancer she'd enjoyed the looks men cast her way.

Not wanting to make Faith uncomfortable, he asked, "Do you have any permanent damage?"

"One part of me didn't recover," she said. "For some reason—they think either a blow to my head or some other trauma—I've forgotten everything that happened prior to that night."

He narrowed his eyes. "Are you saying you have amnesia?"

"The doctors say it's retrograde, meaning I can't remember anything of my past that took place before the accident, but I do remember everything that has happened since then," she explained. "So what I was doing or where I was living…" She shrugged. "I just don't know what that was…or where I was…or with whom."

Adam found himself at a loss for words. He stared at her, thinking that she was putting two and two together and coming up with five. Even if she did have amnesia and even if she did look like Christie, it didn't mean she was Megan's mother. Mentally he noted the differences in the two women. The voice. The clothing. The jewelry. The figure.

"Because you can't remember who you are does not make you Christie Anderson," he stated firmly, as much for her sake as for his.

"But I could be," she said with a spark of hope in her eyes.

"No, you're not Christie. She died, Faith." He kept his voice firm and deliberate. "Six months ago while sailing her small boat. The St. Louis County coroner signed her death certificate."

"You said they never found her body," she reminded him.

"Because they don't find any bodies in Lake Superior." His voice rose as his frustration increased. He didn't want to believe any of what she suggested could be true, nor did he want to remember that only a few hours ago he'd wondered about the very same possibility.

"But you have to admit that theoretically speaking, she could be alive," Faith persisted.

"I don't want to speak theoretically." He was a man who worked with facts and figures. His world was concrete. "It isn't good enough for my daughter. Theories could break her heart so badly that I'm not sure the damage could ever be repaired. Until we sort this out, I'd appreciate it if you wouldn't see Megan."

"I don't want to hurt Megan, but you can't expect me not to be curious about my identity. Until today, not a single person has recognized me. You're the first one who has said I remind him of somebody else."

"You do look like someone I once knew, but there's a difference between resembling someone and actually being that person," he argued.

She cocked her head to one side. "You said you hadn't seen Christie in a while. Can you honestly look at me and be one-hundred-percent positive I'm not her?"

He wanted to say yes, but the truth was, he did have a nagging sliver of doubt. He didn't want it to be there, but it was. It was why he said, "I'll tell you what I'm going to do. I'll contact the attorneys who handled Christie's estate and get their advice on this matter. Does that sound fair to you?"

She nodded. "It won't take long?"

"No. I'll do it today."

"All right," she said, getting to her feet. "I'd better get my coat. Dr. Carson should be here any minute."

He nodded. "Before you go, can I ask you a couple of quick questions?"

She shrugged. "Sure."

"How do you know your name is Faith if you can't remember who you are?"

"The night I was found I had no identification on me, only a braided leather bracelet with the name Faith on it." She pulled back the cuff of her sleeve and showed him her wrist. Hand painted in pink were the letters *F-A-I-T-H*. "Everyone assumed it's my name."

"It could have religious significance," he suggested.

She ran a finger over the narrow band of leather. "It could, but it's a lovely name, don't you think?"

She looked up shyly at him with those blue eyes and he was charmed by her innocence. "Yes, it's lovely," he answered, thinking more of her face than her name.

"You have another question?"

"How is it that you ended up working here at the hospital?"

"The doctor who found me on the side of the road used to be on staff here. He suggested I do volunteer work until my memory returns. I earn my room and board by helping his wife out around the house."

"I see. Then you don't know what your occupation is?"

She shook her head. "What did Christie do for a living?"

"She was a dancer." He didn't think she needed to know about the exotic part. At least not yet.

She thought for a moment, her eyes narrowing and her lips pursing. Then she said, "I don't think I know how to dance."

He looked her up and down one more time and thought he'd like to see her try.

AS HE HAD the previous night, Adam decided to sleep at the hospital in Megan's room. Not that he expected to get much rest. They'd wheeled in the same uncomfortable convertible chair he'd used the night before and Megan still had a monitor next to her bed beeping intermittently.

However, it wasn't his physical discomfort or the hospital distractions that kept him awake. It was the relentless stream of thoughts racing through his mind. He couldn't stop thinking about Faith and the startling information she'd told him.

As soon as he'd arrived at home he'd pulled out Megan's photo albums to see how closely Faith resembled Christie. As much as he wanted to say they weren't the same person, the snapshots of Megan's mother could have been pictures of Faith.

It was too preposterous to even contemplate that the two women were one and the same, yet it was exactly what he did think about as he tried to get to sleep. All the logic in the world couldn't keep him from concocting the most absurd reasons for Christie to have faked her own death and disappeared from the lives of those she loved.

It didn't matter that as soon as he'd left the day-care center he had phoned the attorney who had handled Christie's estate and had been told the chances of her surviving the drowning were slim to none. Everything the lawyer said should have convinced Adam that Faith wasn't Megan's mother. It should have, but it didn't because Adam had seen and spoken to Faith. The attorney hadn't.

"If this woman has only had amnesia for the past few weeks, how could she be Christie?" the lawyer had asked. "The accident happened last September. Where would she have been for over five months and why wouldn't she have contacted Megan?"

Adam could have given him one of the farfetched

scenarios he had come up with, but he knew he would only sound like someone who'd watched one too many B movies. Besides, they were rhetorical questions that the lawyer didn't expect Adam to answer.

"Everyone in town knew Christie loved Megan," the attorney had reasoned. "It would take a lot for you to convince me she would ever abandon her own daughter. She wasn't that kind of person."

Adam wished he could state with the same confidence as the attorney that he knew what Christie would or wouldn't have done, but the truth was he hadn't spent enough time with her to get to know her at all. They'd spent one night together. Less than twelve hours. It had been enough time to make a baby, but not enough time to discover who she was. Most of what he knew he'd learned after her death from a lawyer and a six-year-old.

His thoughts returned to the night they'd met. He'd followed her out of the bachelor party calling after her, "Hey, it's a great night for a cruise down the St. Croix. I've got a yacht if you want to go."

That had raised an eyebrow on her pretty face. "A yacht?"

She hadn't believed him, but then why would she? Not many college students had a boat moored at Marine on St. Croix. "I designed it myself," he'd boasted, then had proceeded to use the same words he'd heard his grandfather use to lure customers at boat shows.

It had worked. She'd said she would go with him to see his boat on one condition—that they take her car. He hadn't argued and within minutes they'd been on their way to the marina.

Once there, he discovered she knew more about boats
than any other woman he'd dated. That was because
she'd grown up in the small town of Silver Bay on Lake
Superior where her father had been the captain of an iron-
ore freighter and her brother had been in the merchant
marine. She'd told him that she planned to return to the
North Shore once she got her life back on track. Adam
had wanted to know why it had gone off track, but she'd
said it wasn't important how it happened. All that mattered was that she was now going in the right direction.

When he'd questioned whether stripping was the
right direction, she'd told him that it was the best way
to make a lot of money in a short amount of time. "Not
all of us are born with a silver spoon in our mouths,"
she'd said in a derisive tone.

Then he'd been the one on the defensive, making sure
that she knew he wasn't some rich kid who'd taken her
to his father's yacht. He'd given her a brief history of
Novak Boats, emphasizing that it was only because of
hard work and long hours that it was a success.

He'd never had a problem charming women and this
time was no different. She'd spent the night with him
and the following morning he'd awakened with a hang-
over and the realization that he was alone on the yacht.
She'd gone, leaving nothing behind except a small scrap
of paper with her phone number on it.

He hadn't called her. After his friend's wedding, he'd
left for a summer internship in California and gotten
busy with life. He hadn't thought of Christie again, until
the lawyer had called with the news that she'd named
him as Megan's guardian in her will.

They were memories Adam thought he had buried in the back of his mind. He'd brought them out briefly when he'd learned of Christie's death, but he'd had no trouble returning them to their rightful place. Now that he'd met Faith, they'd resurfaced again and were refusing to be put away.

And he doubted he would be able to put them back in their place until he had proof that Christie and Faith were not the same person. For his peace of mind as well as his daughter's, he needed to know the truth. The attorney said there were two alternatives he could pursue. One was to contact Christie's brother, Tom, and have him come to St. Paul and meet Faith. Unfortunately Megan's uncle had been called out of town and would be gone for at least six weeks, so Adam knew he would have to use the second method. A DNA test.

Adam was familiar with DNA testing. When he'd been notified that he was Megan's father, his own attorney had recommended he be tested to make sure what Christie had stated in her will was true, that he was Megan's father. His DNA had been a match.

Now a lab test could be used to see if Faith was Christie—and Megan's mother. With a simple swab of the inside of a cheek the relationship between a child and her parents could either be established or denied. All Adam had to do was convince Faith to take the test and wait three to five days to get the results.

To a man who hated waiting for anything, three to five days seemed like an eternity. He wanted the matter resolved. He wanted his daughter to stop fantasizing about having a mother again. Most of all, he wanted peace of mind. Proving Faith the baby rocker was not Christie was going to bring that to him.

CHAPTER FOUR

FAITH LAY AWAKE in her bed, wishing she could stop replaying the conversation she'd had with Adam Novak. She fluffed her pillow and turned over for what had to be the hundredth time, refusing to look at the clock. She didn't want to know how late it was. Sleep would eventually come. It always did, no matter how troubled her thoughts were. The past few weeks had proven that.

Only, tonight was different from any of the other nights she'd spent at the Carsons'. Her insomnia wasn't due to the fact that she couldn't remember her past, but rather the possibility that she could be about to find it. She'd been given a ray of hope that a force existed strong enough to crack the darkness that held her memory in its grasp. And all because of a little girl who'd needed surgery at the hospital.

Megan Novak. The thought of the six-year-old crying for her mommy made her heart ache. She remembered how the girl had begged Faith not to leave her after surgery. At the time Faith had thought she was simply frightened, but now she realized it was more than fear that had Megan reaching out to her.

If Megan were her daughter—and Faith knew that possibility was a slim one—she would find one giant piece of her memory puzzle. Unfortunately she would need a lot more pieces to understand what had happened to cause her to be found far away from the North Shore where Christie had disappeared.

Although Faith hadn't admitted it to Adam, she knew it was unlikely that she was Megan's mother. Adam believed that the authorities were right, that there was no way Christie would have survived the boating accident last autumn. It was that very aspect of the situation—the fact that they hadn't found a body—that gave Faith a spark of hope that she could be the missing woman. Her heart, however, refused to believe that she could ever abandon her own child. As much as she wanted to solve the mystery of her identity, she didn't want to be the reason why an innocent child like Megan had been forced to suffer such grief.

After much tossing and turning, Faith's weary body finally succumbed to sleep. She awoke several times, her slumber interrupted by disturbing dreams. At Dr. Carson's suggestion, she'd placed a pencil and paper next to the bed in the event that she might find clues to her past from the images passing through her mind while she slept, but so far her notepad was empty with the exception of one word. *Outcast.*

She'd written it down not because of anything she remembered dreaming, but because of the feeling she always had when she awoke—as if she were being excluded from something. Faith questioned whether that feeling was associated with the content of her dreams or if it was simply the result of having no memory of her past. Because her amnesia made her a stranger to her own life, denying her access to people and places, she often felt like an outsider to her own thoughts.

That morning, she was wakened by a dream. This time she could recall the content and quickly reached for her notepad and pencil. She jotted down the words and images flashing through her head. *Megan. Baby. Doll.* She wrote as fast as she could, but the pictures faded quickly and before she knew it the dream was nothing but a blur.

Eager to talk with Dr. Carson to see if he thought there was any significance to what she had remembered, she scrambled out of bed and hurried downstairs only to find Marie was alone in the kitchen. "Is Avery still asleep?"

"No, he's gone. He had an appointment early this morning," Marie answered. "Aren't you feeling well?"

The question made Faith aware that in her haste to talk to the doctor she hadn't pulled on her robe and slippers. She stood barefoot in her nightgown, her hair tousled from sleep.

"I had a dream," Faith said with a sense of urgency. "One that I could remember." She held up the piece of paper on which she'd jotted her notes. "I thought I should tell him about it...you know, to see if it has any significance."

"You mean any clues to your past." Faith nodded and Marie said, "I'm afraid I don't know as much on the subject of dreams as Avery does, but I'm willing to listen if you want to talk about it."

Faith did want to talk about it, and since Marie had

become her friend, she didn't hesitate to say, "I'd like that." Feeling the cold floor beneath her feet, she shifted from one foot to the other.

Marie noticed and said, "Why don't we go into the living room and I'll turn on the fireplace? We'll be much more comfortable there."

Faith agreed, then followed her into the adjoining room where with the flick of a switch, Marie made gas flames dance in the brick fireplace. Then she reached for a lap robe that had been draped over the back of the love seat and gave it to Faith, motioning for her to take a chair near the hearth. "This should keep you warm."

Faith tucked her feet beneath her as she sat down, thanking her hostess as she covered herself with the soft woolen robe. "I can't believe I actually remembered something from a dream."

Marie took the wingback chair next to her. "It sounds as if you think it may be important."

"I'm not sure. It really wasn't much, but I did write down what I could remember when I woke up—just like Avery told me to do. Unfortunately the images faded quickly."

"Dreams have a way of doing that," Marie commented, leaning closer to her. "Now tell me about yours."

She glanced down at the notes on her paper. "I was holding a baby. Actually, I was rocking it."

"Were you at the child-care center?" Marie asked.

"I'm not sure, but I think I may have been because it's the only time I rock babies, and Megan Novak was there, too." She paused, rubbing her fingers across her brow as she struggled to remember more details.

"Go on, dear," Marie encouraged.

"Megan asked me if she could see the baby, but when I pulled back the blanket, it wasn't a baby in my arms at all. It was a doll. A faceless doll. And when Megan saw it she began to cry." She shrugged. "That's it. That's all I can remember."

The look Marie gave her was intent. "No other details? Clothing, furniture, time of day?"

Faith shook her head. "I think Megan wore a hospital gown, but I'm not sure."

When Marie didn't say anything for several moments, Faith asked, "Do you think the doll could be a real baby? My baby?"

"And she didn't have a face because you can't remember her?" Marie accurately followed the direction of her thoughts.

"It would explain why Megan cries when she sees the doll."

Marie's brow wrinkled. "Why do you say that?"

"If Megan is my daughter and the doll represents her as an infant, then it's only natural that she'd be upset that I don't remember her," Faith reasoned.

Marie was quiet for a moment, her eyes thoughtful while she contemplated the possibility. "You might be right," she finally admitted. "Or it could be that your subconscious is simply trying to sort through everything Adam Novak told you yesterday. After all, you only had this dream after he told you about Megan's mother."

Faith nodded pensively, aware that Marie made a valid point. "You're saying if Adam hadn't told me about Megan mistaking me for her mother, I might not have had the dream at all."

Marie's voice softened as she said, "That's not what you wanted to hear, is it?"

She shook her head again. "I keep looking for signs…." Faith struggled to keep her disappointment from showing.

Marie reached across to place her hand on Faith's arm. "I know how difficult it's been for you these past few weeks. You want answers, but I'm not sure you're going to find them in your dreams."

"Then where do I find them?"

"Avery said a simple DNA test would prove whether or not you're Megan's mother."

Faith remembered Avery mentioning a medical test that could be done to determine whether a biological relationship existed between two people. Because she was exhausted both physically and emotionally, she'd had difficulty following his explanation of genetic coding and he'd told her not to worry because they would talk about it again if it was necessary.

"By finding out who you're not, you'll at least have one answer," Marie continued.

Faith nodded, biting on her lower lip as she mulled over what Marie said. "It'll take a while to get the results."

"And you're in a hurry," Marie stated with an understanding smile. "You want the answer now, don't you?" When Faith nodded she added, "Maybe you don't need a DNA test."

Faith frowned. "What do you mean?"

"You could go straight to Megan Novak. You said last

night that her father hadn't seen her mother recently. Megan, on the other hand, saw her daily. Even if she is only six, she should be able to identify her own mother," Marie reasoned. She tapped a finger against her forehead. "Amnesia has affected what's inside here, not your physical appearance. I doubt Megan's forgotten the sound of her mother's voice or the feel of her hands."

"You think she'll be able to tell right away?"

"Don't you?"

It was something Faith had contemplated last night as she'd tossed and turned before falling asleep. Right or wrong, Megan believed Faith was her mother based on an encounter they'd had while she'd been sedated. She no longer suffered the effects of anesthesia. The next meeting between them could very well force Megan to accept that she'd been mistaken, that Faith wasn't her mother.

As Faith showered, thoughts of the six-year-old continued to occupy her mind. *Be responsible.* A man's voice echoed in her memory, startling her. She had no idea from what part of her past the voice had come, but there was no denying its presence. She shut off the water, hoping to hear other voices, but there were none. Briefly she closed her eyes, willing her mind to remember the time when she'd heard that voice, but all she saw was darkness.

Answers. She wanted answers, which was why when she arrived at the hospital she didn't go to the day-care center but took the elevator to the second floor and went straight to the nursing station. When she asked which room Megan Novak occupied and if she was allowed to have visitors, she learned that Adam Novak had spent the night in his daughter's room. Butterflies began to flutter in her stomach.

Just the thought of seeing him again sent a delicious shiver of anticipation through her. She remembered how those dark eyes had pierced her with an intensity that had made her go weak at the knees.

When she reached room 217, the door was open but a curtain had been pulled around the bed. Faith could hear voices—a child's and an adult's. The adult's voice belonged to a woman. Faith paused outside the room, not wanting to intrude.

Within a few minutes, a nurse came out. When she saw Faith she said, "Are you here to see Megan?"

"If you think it's all right if I visit her. I work downstairs in the child-care center," she answered. "I don't want to intrude if she's with her family."

"There's no one in there but Megan."

"I thought her father was here?"

"He was but he must have stepped out. Go on in," she urged Faith. Before scurrying off down the hallway, the nurse poked her head back into the room and called out, "You have a visitor, Megan."

Faith stepped tentatively into the room, wondering if she shouldn't have waited for Adam Novak to be with his daughter when she approached her. Then she heard a tiny voice call out, "Is anybody there?" and she pushed her doubts aside.

The nurse had raised the back of Megan's bed so that she was almost in a sitting position. Her eyes widened when she saw Faith and a smile spread across her face.

"It's you!" she said on a delightful note.

"Yes, it's me." Faith wasn't quite sure what else to say. "How are you feeling?"

Megan didn't answer the question but said, "I knew Adam was wrong. He said people can't come back from heaven, but I told him I saw you and now you're here."

"I've never been to heaven, Megan," she said gently, noting that she'd referred to her father by his given name instead of calling him Dad or Daddy.

"Then where have you been?" Blue eyes looked at her with an innocence that tugged at Faith's heartstrings. They grew cloudy as Faith moved closer to her. "You are my mommy, aren't you? You look like her." Uncertainty crept into her voice, replacing the joy that had greeted her arrival.

Faith gazed into blue eyes that begged her to answer the question with a yes. Faith wished she could. The last thing she wanted to do was destroy the hope this beautiful child harbored, yet until the answers to her own questions were found, she had no choice but to be candid.

She pulled a chair close to the bed and sat down. "I don't know if I'm your mommy."

Megan frowned, her eyes losing some of their sparkle as she looked in bewilderment at Faith.

"You're probably wondering how a mommy can not know that she's a mommy, but if you'll listen, I'll try to explain it to you, all right?" Faith said calmly.

"All right," the small voice answered.

"Megan, you came to the hospital to have an operation, didn't you?"

She nodded. "My appendix was broken."

"Yes, and it was making you feel badly, wasn't it?" Again she nodded and Faith continued. "I have something inside me that's broken, too."

"Are you going to have an operation like I did?"

"No. What's broken inside me can't be fixed by being in the hospital."

"Then how can it get fixed?"

"That's the problem. The doctors aren't sure how to make it work again." She tapped her forehead with her finger. "My broken part is up here in my memory. Because it's not working, I forget things I should know. Like my name."

Megan's blue eyes widened. "You don't know your name?"

Faith shook her head. "Or where I live or who my family is." She lifted her wrist with the leather bracelet on it. "Everyone calls me Faith because of this, but I can't remember if it really is my name. I could be someone named Faith or I could be another person with a different name."

Megan fingered the leather band and Faith asked, "Do you remember seeing your mother wear a bracelet like this?"

She shook her head. "Uh-uh. Who gave it to you?"

"I don't have the answer to that question," she answered honestly.

"Can't you remember?"

"No, I can't. It's another one of those things—like my name—that's been put in a place inside of my head where I can't find it." She leaned forward. "I want to find all those things I can't remember. That's why I came to see you. I think you might be able to help me."

"How?"

"I want you to tell me why you think I could be your mother. Would that be okay with you?"

Megan nodded vigorously, her innocent eyes showing her eagerness to please.

"Great." She gave her a big smile, then shoved her hands out in front of her, palms down. "You said my face looks like your mother's. What about my hands?"

Megan reached for them, her tiny fingers turning them over. Her touch was soft and warm as she studied them as if they were of utmost importance. "They kinda look like my mommy's hands, but you're not wearing the mommy ring and your nails are a mess."

Faith passed on the criticism of her short, stubby fingernails, focusing on the missing jewelry. "What's a mommy ring?"

"It's a ring that mommies wear. Uncle Tom helped me pick it out for my mommy's birthday. It has a heart on it and a blue diamond cuz that's my birthstone."

"And your mother wore it all the time?"

"Uh-huh. She said she was never going to take it off because every time she looked at it she would know I love her."

Faith had to swallow back the emotion that wanted to lodge itself in her throat. She glanced at her bare fingers, wishing she'd been found wearing such a ring. Of course the fact that she wasn't wearing one didn't rule out the possibility that she was Megan's mother. She could have lost the ring or it could have been stolen.

"You said my fingernails are a mess," Faith reminded her.

Again Megan nodded her blond head. "Doreen would have a hissy fit if she saw them."

"Doreen? Who's that?"

"Mommy's best friend. She works at the Cut and Curl except she always comes to our house to do our nails because it cost too much to go to the beauty parlor. She made little flowers on mine one time. Lori doesn't know how to do flowers. See?" She held up her hands and Faith saw each tiny nail had a coating of dark purple.

"They're very pretty," she commented, wondering who Lori was. "Does Lori live here in the Twin Cities?"

"Uh-huh. Her house is just around the corner from Adam's, which is good because that means I can go to her house after school. She's going to have a baby. She's this fat." She extended her hand out in front of her stomach as far as it could reach.

"Is she your day-care provider?"

"I don't go to day care. I go to Lori's."

"And Lori is?"

"Her aunt," a male voice answered, startling Faith.

She turned to see Adam Novak looming behind her, looking even more attractive than he had the last time she'd seen him. He was not happy to see her with his daughter. That much was evident by the narrowness of his dark eyes.

"Hello," she said weakly. "I was just talking to Megan."

"I can see that," he observed dryly.

"I'm helping her fix what's broken," Megan declared in her small voice. "She can't remember she's my mommy."

"She's not your mother, Megan," Adam stated firmly, his eyes daring Faith to contradict him.

She wouldn't have even if she disagreed with him, but Megan did. "She looks like Mommy."

"We'll talk about this later," he told his daughter, then turned to Faith. "I'd like to speak to you out in the hall."

"You're not leaving, are you?" Megan's face fell at the possibility.

She wanted to say no, but from the look on Adam's face she knew he really didn't want her to stay. "I'm sorry, but I have to go to work in the child-care center downstairs," she told Megan.

"But you're coming back, aren't you?" she asked, looking at Faith with an appeal in her eyes.

Faith didn't dare glance at Adam as she said, "If you want me to."

"I do," the small voice pleaded. "I don't want you to go!"

"I'm sorry, but I have to." Faith gave her a smile, said goodbye and hurried out of the room.

Adam Novak followed. He nodded toward the lounge at the end of the hallway.

Wanting to get the conversation over, she walked briskly down the corridor. In her haste, she didn't notice the hospital worker pushing a laundry cart. It was only because Adam reached out and caught her by the arm that she avoided a collision with the cart.

It was in that split second that her world changed. No longer was she in the hospital but standing with a suitcase in hand, watching cars whiz by on a highway. So startled was she by the flash of memory, that she gasped and took a step backward, trying to pull her arm away from him. "No!"

Adam reacted immediately to her protest. He released her, raising his arms in the air, palms outward, his entire body language acting as an apology.

From the look on his face she knew he thought she'd been offended by his touch. "It wasn't you…." She started to explain but then stopped. What could she say? That she'd recoiled from his touch because she'd had a sudden memory that had caught her off balance? How could she explain something she herself didn't understand?

"I was only trying to keep you from colliding with the cart," he told her.

"I didn't think you were trying to do anything else," she said. "It's just that—"

He waved a hand in the air. "No explanations necessary. Look, would you be more comfortable if we communicated through our attorneys?"

"I don't have an attorney."

He ran a hand across the back of his neck and sighed. "Then I guess we'd better sit down."

"DID YOU FIND OUT anything about…?" Faith didn't finish the sentence. They both knew to what she referred.

"I've spoken to the attorney who handled Christie's estate," he answered.

"And?" She stared at him with a look in her eyes that reminded him not of Christie's impudence but rather Megan's innocence. For Adam, who'd spent the past eighteen hours trying to convince himself that Faith couldn't possibly be Megan's mother, it was unsettling.

He didn't want to feel anything toward her and especially not protectiveness.

"He doesn't believe you're Christie, either." The tiny glimmer of hope that had been in her eyes disappeared.

"Oh." The word was barely audible.

An unwanted wave of sympathy for her unfurled inside him. "Why did you go see Megan?"

"Because I had to. Do you have any idea what it's like to get out of bed each morning and feel as if you're living someone else's life? I don't know who I am, where I live, if I have a family, or even how old I am. Until yesterday, everyone I met looked at me as if I were a stranger. Then you came along and told me about your daughter and for the first time I had the hope that someone might be able to help me answer all the questions I have about my past."

"Megan doesn't have the answers," he stated.

"You don't want to believe she does."

"Are you saying she said something to make you believe you could be?"

"You heard her."

"She's confused."

Faith rubbed her temples, her face weary. "So am I."

Again he felt the stirrings of sympathy, but he pushed them aside. He didn't want to be drawn to her on an emotional level. It was enough that he had to fight the physical attraction that existed between them. And that in itself was strong.

"If the doctors haven't been able to help you overcome the amnesia, what made you think a conversation with a six-year-old girl would?"

Faith shook her head and looked down at her hands. "I guess I hoped that maternal instinct would be stronger than whatever it is that has robbed me of my memory. I thought maybe something she said would trigger a memory. When your entire life history consists of twenty-seven days, you don't have a lot of options."

She was making this about her situation and it wasn't. It was about Megan. "I told you yesterday I would take care of resolving this matter."

"Yes, and I appreciate that, but I'm the one without an identity here. I feel as if I've been running through this long dark tunnel without even a hint that there could be a light at the end."

"Megan isn't that light."

"You don't know that for sure," she said, refusing to agree with him.

He could see that beneath the shy, vulnerable exterior there was a bit of a stubborn streak. He wanted to be annoyed but unfortunately it only made her all the more attractive to him. "Megan doesn't need a reason to continue to believe in this fantasy she has that her mother is alive."

"I didn't give her one."

"Did you tell her you're not Christie?"

"No."

"Then you didn't discourage her, either, did you?"

She sighed. "I think it's best to always be honest with children so I told her the truth. That I don't know who I am."

At least that was a positive, he thought. "I'm glad to hear that."

"I also suggested she try to notice things about me that are different from her mother."

"And did she find anything?"

"Yes. I'm not wearing a mother's ring—apparently Christie always wore one. And Megan also said my nails are a mess." She held up her hands, her fingers splayed.

Adam looked at the long fingers with their short unpolished nails. Despite the fact her hands were a bit rough, they were beautiful.

"There may have been other differences Megan could have pointed out had we had more time," she said pointedly.

"It really doesn't matter. The reason I wanted to talk to you is that there's a fast and easy way to prove you're not Megan's mother. A DNA test."

Her delicate eyebrows drew together. "Dr. Carson mentioned something about some kind of a lab test last night."

"Then you already know it's fairly simple to do. You don't have to have any blood drawn. The sample can be taken from your mouth with a cotton swab. It's so simple they even sell home kits so people can do it themselves."

"You're saying that by putting a stick in my mouth you'll be able to determine if I'm Megan's mother?" She eyed him with suspicion.

"Yes. I thought you said Dr. Carson explained it to you."

"He just briefly referred to it."

She looked bemused by his explanation, which he thought was unusual. He thought it rather odd that she would be unfamiliar with the procedure. One could hardly turn on a television crime show or watch a murder mystery in the theater without there being some reference to DNA testing.

"There are several labs in the Twin Cities that do this kind of testing," he told her. "If you can take time off from work I can see that it gets done today. If not, I'll get one of the home-test kits and you can do the swab sample yourself. Either way, we'll have the results in three to five days. You need to tell me which you prefer."

She thought about it briefly before saying, "First I would like to talk to Dr. Carson about this."

He didn't understand why, but he didn't object. "All right, but the sooner this matter is resolved, the better it will be for everyone." He reached into his pocket and pulled out his business card. "Here's the number where I can be reached. If you get my voice mail, leave a message and I'll get back to you as soon as possible."

She took the card and slipped it into her pocket. "I'll talk to Dr. Carson today."

"I'd appreciate that. It would be better for Megan if you didn't visit her. She's still a very sick little girl and it wouldn't be good to upset her."

"What if I am her mother?" she asked.

"You're not. I'm certain of it."

"Then Megan will realize that, too. Haven't you considered that the more time she spends with me, the more differences she'll notice?"

He knew she could be right. It was, after all, what had happened to him. The more he saw Faith, the less she reminded him of Christie. For one thing there was a shyness about her that was in direct contrast to the confidence Christie had exuded. Faith carefully chose her words when she spoke, often using silence for emphasis. Christie, on the other hand, had been a fast talker, blurting out whatever was on her mind. And then there was their physical appearances. At first glance one would say they bore an incredible likeness to one another, but Adam could see that Christie's appeal had a lot to do with the expert way she applied her makeup and wore her clothes. Faith, on the other hand, had a natural beauty, her skin free of cosmetics, her wardrobe simple.

He had no doubt that as soon as the DNA test was complete, he would have proof that they were not the same person. He worried, however, that Megan might only see what she wanted to see.

He shook his head. "You could be right, but I'm not sure I want to take the chance."

He thought she would protest but she simply said, "I understand." She glanced at the clock on the wall. "I guess there's nothing more to say then, is there? If you'll excuse me, I need to get to work." And without another word, she walked toward the bank of elevators.

CHAPTER FIVE

WHILE FAITH WAITED for the elevator she refused to glance in Adam Novak's direction. She needed to put the man out of her thoughts and wished she could banish him to the part of her memory that was malfunctioning.

He'd treated her as if she were some kind of threat to his daughter, which was ridiculous. She loved children and would never do anything to harm Megan. She was a beautiful, sweet little girl. Possibly *her* beautiful, sweet little girl.

Faith wished she could either confirm or deny that possibility. So far, the closest thing she'd had was the flash of an image that had placed her on the side of a highway with cars whizzing by. She would need a lot more pieces of the puzzle before she would have any sort of picture.

Unfortunately, today she only had one piece and it didn't answer questions, but raised them. Why had she been standing on the side of a busy highway? Had she been waiting for a bus? Where was she going? Was it a memory from the night Avery and Marie had rescued her?

Whatever it was, it had stunned her momentarily. She could have told Adam the reason she'd jerked away from him, but he'd made it clear that her lost memory was not his concern. To him, all that mattered was getting the proof that she wasn't Christie Anderson.

As hard as she tried, she couldn't resist one last look in his direction. He'd stopped at the nursing station, but he chose that moment to glance back to the elevators. It was almost as if he knew she was looking for him. Their eyes met briefly. The look she saw there made her insides feel as if someone were running a feather up and down her body. She wondered what it would be like to kiss those lips. Then it dawned on her. The possibility existed that they had been lovers at one time.

She looked away, not wanting to think about it, but it seemed to echo through every nerve inside her, sending a blush from her head all the way down to her toes. It was an eerie feeling, knowing that a man could have seen her naked and touched her in her most intimate places without her having any recollection of it. Was it any wonder that every time she saw him her heartbeat increased and she found it difficult not to be attracted to him?

She jabbed a finger at the elevator call button for a second time, wanting to be far away from his gaze. She needed to get him out of her thoughts, and was relieved when a car arrived.

As she took the brief ride to the hospital's main floor she realized that for the first time since she'd been volunteering at the child-care center, she wasn't eager to go to work. What she wanted to do was talk to Dr. Carson.

But after only a few minutes in the nursery, she was glad she hadn't given in to the temptation to ask for time off. As usual, the children left in her care gave her a sense of purpose, and she put all thoughts of Adam and Megan out of her mind until her lunch break. Then she phoned the Carson home and left a message for Avery to call her.

He did better than that. He stopped by to see her on her afternoon break. Over a cup of hot chocolate in the hospital cafeteria, she told him everything that had been weighing on her mind all morning. The dream she'd had the night before, the talk she'd had with Megan, the flash of memory and Adam's request for the DNA test.

"I think the DNA test is a good idea," the retired doctor told her in his baritone voice that always made her feel as if she had a warm blanket draped around her. On a white paper napkin he drew a diagram as he explained the genetics of parents and their children. "If you are Megan's mother, this side of her DNA will match yours."

Faith picked up her mug of hot chocolate. "So in three days time I could know who I am."

"Or who you're not."

She took a sip. "Adam Novak doesn't think I'm Christie Anderson."

"He could be right."

"He could be," she agreed. "He's hoping the DNA doesn't match. He doesn't want me to be Megan's mother."

"I think you may be wrong about that," Avery Carson said, slipping his pen back into his sport jacket. "Any father who loves his daughter would want to spare her the grief of losing her mother if it were at all possible."

She didn't disagree, but took another sip of her hot chocolate. "They have an unusual relationship."

"Why do you say that?"

"She calls him Adam, not Dad."

Avery frowned. "Maybe she's trying to sound grown-up."

"I don't think that's it."

"You think it means they have a troubled relationship?"

She shrugged. "Something's not right."

"From the little time I spent talking with the man yesterday he struck me as a very concerned, loving father," the older man commented.

"When did you speak to him?"

"He called last night to make sure you were all right. He was concerned about you."

That sent an unwanted shiver of pleasure through her. "There was no reason to be." She set down her mug.

"This can't be an easy situation for him," Dr. Carson pointed out.

"No, I'm sure it isn't, but Megan wants to talk to me. She thinks I'm her mother."

"And that's tugging on your heartstrings, isn't it?" She nodded and he continued. "Her father could be right…she could be confused. At any rate, you'll know in a few days."

Faith toyed with the spoon sitting next to her mug. "It's a very strange feeling…being totally dependent on someone else to identify who you are."

"That could soon change. If today is any indication, it may be that those pieces of the puzzle you're missing are going to start falling into place."

"You think my memory might be returning?"

"It could be. That one piece this morning could be the first of many that will pop into your head. You're going to have to be patient, however. It could take time for all of them to come together," he cautioned her.

Faith knew it was useless to ask him how much time. For weeks she'd been asking that question of the doctors and each time she received the same answer. She needed to focus on the fact that for the first time she had seen a glimpse into her past. It was what she'd been waiting for, yet she couldn't help but feel apprehensive at the same time.

"You look worried." Avery read her face accurately.

"I am," she admitted. "You know how much I want to find out who I am, but today, when I finally saw a part of my past…" She trailed off, not sure how to put into words what she was feeling.

He reached across the table and covered her hand with his. "Are you frightened of what you're going to discover?" When she nodded he added, "That's to be expected. It's the fear of the unknown. It can make all of us apprehensive at times. There was nothing about this particular glimpse of your past that would cause you to think you need to be fearful, was there?"

"I'm not sure. It happened so quickly and was gone in an instant. It's almost as if I imagined it. You don't think I did imagine it, do you?"

"No, I don't. And I think if you try hard enough, you can recall the image again." He leaned forward and took her hands in his. "I want you to close your eyes and try to bring the memory back. I'll help you."

She did as he told her, listening closely as he spoke to her in his soothing voice, urging her to relax and let the memory return. "You said you were standing on the shoulder of a highway. Can you see yourself watching the cars go by?"

She did see them. "Yes. It's dark and there's snow on the ground. And I have a suitcase."

"Just play the image over and over in your mind." He let a brief silence stretch between them before saying, "Do you remember what you were thinking as you stood on the side of the road?"

Faith shook her head. "I was unhappy."

"Why were you unhappy?"

She shrugged. "I don't know. I just know I wanted to get away."

"Away from what?"

She paused, trying to recall the emotions the image refused to tell her, but was unsuccessful. "Just away."

"What was your destination?"

"I don't know."

"How were you planning to get there?"

"I don't know." Faith sighed in frustration and opened her eyes. "It's not much, is it?"

Again Avery Carson patted her hand. "It's a start. In time you'll learn more."

"Like what I was running away from."

"Or whom," he suggested gently.

"And where I was going. And why I never got there. That's the scary part," she admitted, suppressing a shudder.

"We know you had some kind of trauma. Your injuries indicate that," he stated evenly. "And if you had a suitcase there's the possibility you were simply visiting someone who lived in this area."

"Wouldn't they have reported me as missing when I didn't arrive?"

His thick gray eyebrows drew closer together. "I wish I had the answer for you, Faith."

"You don't think I'm from this area, do you?"

"Your description didn't match any of the local missing-person reports and I have to think that someone in your family or a friend would have notified the authorities that you're missing."

"Unless they don't know I'm gone. Maybe I was going away and not expected to be in communication," she speculated.

"It's a possibility," he noted, although she could tell by the tone of his voice that he didn't think it was likely. "Eventually we'll have all the answers."

"You sound confident about that."

"I am. If this DNA test doesn't tell us who you are, in time your memory will. The answers are out there, Faith. You just have to be patient."

Faith only hoped that when she did find them she wouldn't regret wishing she had a past.

ALL AFTERNOON Faith watched the door of the child-care center, expecting Adam to return with information regarding the DNA test. When five o'clock came and there'd been no word from him, she was both relieved and disappointed. She didn't want to see him again, yet she was anxious to have the DNA issue resolved.

As she pulled on her coat she noticed a pregnant woman in the corridor. When the woman realized that she'd been caught staring at Faith, she quickly averted her eyes. She didn't, however, move away from the window.

Any doubt Faith may have had that she hadn't been the object of her scrutiny was erased when she stepped out into the corridor and the woman approached her.

"You're Faith, aren't you." It wasn't a question, but a statement.

"Yes. Can I help you?"

"I'm Lori Novak. Megan's aunt." She smiled as she held out her hand.

Faith didn't hesitate to shake it. "Of course. Hello." She now understood why the woman had been staring at her.

"Adam asked me to give you this." It was then that Faith noticed she had a small package in her left hand. "It's the DNA kit. He said everything you need is inside, along with instructions. If you have any questions, there's a number you can call, but I don't think you'll have any problems. It's pretty straightforward and easy to understand."

"Thank you. I appreciate you bringing this." Faith held on to the box as if it contained something fragile, relieved that the purpose of Lori's visit was to deliver the package. It was nice to know Lori hadn't come simply to gawk at her and compare her resemblance to Megan's mother.

"Adam would have delivered it himself but he was eating dinner with Megan and I was on my way home, so I offered to bring it," she said with a cheerfulness that sounded forced to Faith's ears.

"Please relay my thanks to him and tell him that I'll take care of this as soon as I get home."

"He'll be glad to hear that. He wants this resolved quickly…for everyone's sake, but especially for Megan's."

"Of course. She's a lovely child."

Lori smiled. "Yes, she is. The poor thing's had a rough go of it the past couple of days with the surgery and all."

Faith knew that the "and all" referred to her. "I'm sorry that my appearance has upset her."

Lori shrugged. "It's not your fault that you look like her mother. It's easy to see how any child could be confused under the circumstances. It would be a shame for her to be hurt after what she's already suffered."

Faith didn't appreciate the implied warning. She already had Adam Novak treating her as if she were an adversary. She didn't need another one of Megan's relatives regarding her in the same light.

At that moment a mother and a small child came out of the child-care center. The little boy ran up to Faith.

"I made a picture for you," he boasted, shoving in her direction a paper scribbled with crayon.

"Why, thank you!" she gushed, bending down to his level to speak to him. "Are you sure you don't want to take it home for your mommy?"

Suddenly shy, he had his finger in his mouth as he said, "Uh-uh. It's for you."

Faith held the picture at arm's length. "This is perfect. I'll hang it up so I can see it every day." She exchanged a few comments with the boy's mother before she whisked her son away.

As Faith watched them leave, Lori said, "You like kids, don't you?"

Faith wondered what Adam had said about her to his sister-in-law. "I may not know what's in my past, but I do know that children are to be treated as the gifts from God they are, Ms. Novak. So if the reason you really came today was to warn me not to hurt your niece, it was unnecessary." She didn't want to be on the defensive, but she felt as if Adam Novak had put her there.

Lori Novak's face softened in apology. "I'm sorry. I haven't handled this very well." She arched her back and grimaced. "Do you think we could sit down?"

Faith led her to the lounge where she fell back against the cushions of a sofa with a sigh. Faith took the chair next to her.

"I'll admit I came to see you because I was curious," Lori began. "And yes, I'm worried about my niece. Wouldn't you be?"

Faith simply said, "Yes." She thought about telling her why she'd gone to Megan this morning, but decided against it. She was certain Adam had already given his sister-in-law his version of what had happened.

To her surprise, however, Lori said, "Megan told me you came to see her this morning."

"What did she say?"

"Oh, lots of things. All of them good." This time her cheerfulness wasn't forced. "You managed to do something that her father and I haven't accomplished since she's been in the hospital."

"And what would that be?"

"Make her smile. She's hoping you'll come see her again."

"I plan to."

"Even though my brother-in-law asked you not to?"

"You said Megan wants to see me."

"Yes. She thinks you're her mother and honestly, I can see why. When she said you looked just like her I expected there to be a similarity but…" Lori paused, scrutinizing her face closely. "It's amazing how much you look like Christie."

"Do I sound like her, too?"

"I don't know," she admitted. "We never had a chance to meet. My knowledge of Christie comes from what Megan's told me and from the pictures I've seen. And I must say, you look very much like the woman in those photographs."

"Your brother-in-law doesn't think I do and he should know. They did have a child together."

"Yes, but…" Lori paused, chewing on her lip for several moments before saying, "There are circumstances you don't know about."

Faith didn't feel as if she had any business asking what they were. "Tell me something. Do you think I'm her mother?"

"Considering everything that happened, it doesn't seem likely," she admitted.

"No it doesn't, but the fact is it's not impossible, either."

"You're hoping you are Christie, aren't you?" Lori observed accurately.

"At least if someone claimed me, I would have a name and a family. It might not help me remember my past, but I would know who I am. It's terrible not having an identity."

"You do realize that finding out you are Megan's

mother would mean more unanswered questions," she cautioned her.

"You mean because she's been missing since September?"

Lori nodded.

Faith sighed. "Until my memory returns, there will be unanswered questions. Lots of them. There's nothing I can do about it. I have to believe though, that finding out who my family is will help."

"It must be terribly lonely for you," Lori said.

"Yes, it is." Faith lowered her eyes. "No woman wants to believe she could ever forget her own child. Even if Megan isn't my daughter, there could be another little girl or boy out there who's feeling the same kind of loss as she's experienced."

"Do you feel like you're a mother?"

"I'm so unsure about everything that I honestly don't know. I love kids—that much I am sure of—and the first time I looked at Megan I felt some kind of connection. She's a beautiful little girl any mother would love to claim as her own. Now whether that's wishful thinking or if it's some maternal instinct that's working even if my memory isn't, I can't say."

Lori's brown eyes were filled with compassion. "My brother-in-law wouldn't appreciate me saying this, but I think you *should* visit Megan."

"But you said you don't think I'm her mother."

She shrugged. "I know, but I still think you should go see her again. It's just a feeling I have. I know my niece…probably better than her father does."

Faith nodded. "Megan said you take care of her."

Lori smiled with genuine affection. "Yes, when Adam's gone…which is a lot. He's hired several different sitters but none has worked out and she always ends up back at my house. Which is fine. I love having her. She's quite precocious for a six-year-old. The first day she stayed with me she was giving me cooking tips. Do you like to cook?"

"Yes, although I haven't had much opportunity to do any. I don't have my own kitchen where I'm staying."

"Christie must have spent a lot of time baking because Megan is very comfortable in the kitchen. She told me she would help me when I make my bread because she likes to punch it down." Lori chuckled. "I had to tell her the only bread that ever shows up on my table is the kind that comes out of a plastic wrapper."

"Kneading dough can be very therapeutic," Faith told her.

"Then you've made your own bread, too?" Lori looked at her curiously.

"I don't know," she answered, rubbing her fingers across her forehead. "I mean I don't remember making it, but I must have because I know I like the sensation of dough in my fingers." Seeing the other woman's puzzled expression she added, "That's what's so odd about this amnesia. I have knowledge yet I can't remember specific events." Not wanting to focus on herself she said, "Tell me more about Megan…if you don't mind, that is."

"No, I don't mind at all. She's very excited about the baby coming." Lori glanced down as she placed a hand on her stomach. "She says she can't wait to meet her cousin. She likes to sit next to me and read aloud to the baby and she's begging us to allow her to be present at the birth."

"It looks as if that will be soon," Faith observed.

"Not for another month according to the doctor. I don't know how I'm going to survive that long. I can barely bend over to tie my shoes, I'm waddling when I walk and some days it feels as if this little guy is going to kick his way out." She grimaced as she shifted on the sofa. "He's at it right now. I think he's telling me it's time to go home."

Faith smiled in understanding.

Lori pushed herself up from the sofa and extended her hand. "It was nice meeting you, Faith."

Faith echoed the sentiment, adding, "Thank you for bringing me the test kit and for telling me about Megan."

"I hope you will visit her. Like you, she's looking for answers, too."

"Only a different kind," Faith said to herself as she watched the other woman walk away. Megan wanted to bring back a past that she remembered. Faith simply wanted to remember.

IT HAD BEEN a long day for Adam. Despite appearing to be on the road to recovery, Megan was not yet out of danger. The infection from her ruptured appendix had her under close observation by the hospital staff. Although the doctor had assured him it wasn't uncommon for patients to suffer minor setbacks in recovery, Adam couldn't help but wonder if the emotional upheaval Faith's appearance had caused wasn't responsible for his daughter's slow progress.

He wished he could blame it all on Faith. It would make it easy to justify asking her not to visit Megan again.

Only, he couldn't justify keeping the two of them apart. He'd spent most of the day in Megan's room, watching her sleep. He wasn't sorry that the medication made her drowsy. When she was awake, the only subject she wanted to talk about was her mommy, her eyes moving often to the door, hoping that every set of footsteps she heard coming down the hallway would belong to the baby rocker.

Megan wasn't the only one who watched the door. He found himself turning at the sound of footsteps, expecting she was going to defy his request that she not visit his daughter. He was right. She did.

The following afternoon she appeared with a stack of children's books in her hands. When she came through the door, Adam felt a little catch in his chest. Dressed in a dark pair of slacks and the blue and green smock, and with her shoulder-length blond hair falling gracefully around her face, she had a shyness about her that made him think she was as wholesome as her appearance.

When she saw that Megan was asleep she looked at Adam and said in a low voice, "I'm on my lunch break and thought I'd stop in. I had hoped to read her a story but I can see she's resting."

"It's the medication. She's been sleepy all day," Adam explained as he rose from his spot next to the bed.

"That's good. She needs to rest to get better." She kept her voice barely above a whisper. "I'll come back another time."

She turned and would have gone out the door but Adam stopped her. "Wait." He moved toward her. "I need to ask you about the test sample. Did the courier pick it up?"

"Yes. Last night."

"Any problems?"

"None. He said we can expect results within three to five days."

He nodded. "I asked for rush service."

Faith glanced toward the bed where Megan was sleeping. "It's best to get this resolved as soon as possible. Will you tell Megan I stopped by?"

"Sure," he answered, knowing perfectly well he wasn't going to do any such thing. He didn't see any reason to encourage his daughter's fantasy as to who this woman was.

But before she could leave a tiny voice called out, "I'm not asleep."

Faith looked back over her shoulder and smiled. "Hello. How are you?"

"Better. I've been waiting for you to come." Seeing her standing in the doorway she asked, "Aren't you going to come in?"

Faith glanced at Adam. The look in her eye pleaded with him to let her stay.

"Faith has come to read you a story," he said. "That is, if you feel up to it. You look tired."

"No, I'm not tired," she denied, then promptly yawned. "I want her to stay."

He hesitated, wondering if he wasn't making a mistake. "All right," he finally conceded. The smile on his daughter's face told him he'd made the right decision.

When Faith would have taken the chair next to the bed, Megan asked, "Can you crawl under the covers with me? That's the way you used to read me stories."

"I think the nurses would scold me if I did that," Faith told her. "How about if I pull my chair up close to the bed so you can see the pictures?"

"Okay," she agreed.

"Which one would you like for me to read?" Faith asked, spreading the books out in front of her so that Megan could choose. Adam returned to his chair at the foot of the bed and watched the interaction between the two of them. The physical resemblance between them was so obvious that he was tempted to ignore everything the attorney had told him about the probability of Faith being Christie.

But the longer he stared at Faith the more doubts he had that she was the woman he'd slept with the night of the stag party. She had mannerisms that didn't fit with his memory of Christie—and it was hard for Adam to believe that this modest woman sitting next to his daughter could ever have been an exotic dancer. Having amnesia wouldn't change one's personality so dramatically...or would it? It was a question he should have asked Dr. Carson.

Whoever she was, he couldn't deny that she was very good with his daughter, revealing why the hospital staff held such a high opinion of her work in the children's center. Although Megan wanted to talk, it was obvious Faith didn't, which surprised Adam. He'd expected that she'd ask all sorts of questions hoping that the answers would jar her memory. However, whenever Megan mentioned her mother, Faith gently guided her attention back to the story she was reading. She treated Megan as if she were just another of the many hospital patients she visited.

Because she'd come on her lunch hour, her time with Megan was short, but she did promise she'd stop in before she went home for the day. When Megan spread her arms and asked if she could have a hug before she left, Faith didn't look to Adam for permission. She bent over and gently wrapped her arms around his daughter and told her to get well soon. Then with a quick glance in Adam's direction, she left.

"I wish she could have stayed longer," Megan said as soon as Faith was gone.

"How are you feeling?" he asked, changing the subject.

"I'm a little hungry," she admitted, then yawned. "Do you think I could have a snack?"

"I don't see why not. Would you like me to see if you can have some ice cream?" Adam offered.

"Yes, please," she said politely, then tugged her covers up close to her chin as she snuggled her head into the pillow.

"I'm going to go get you that ice cream. I'll be right back, okay?" He'd only taken a few steps down the hall when he saw his sister-in-law coming toward him.

"I just passed Faith in the hallway. Did she visit Megan?"

He nodded. "She read her a story."

"How did Megan react to seeing her today?"

"About the same as she did yesterday."

"I know you're worried about her, but she's going to get through all of this just fine."

"I hope you're right. I'll feel a hell of a lot better when we get the results of the DNA test and we can put an end to this, once and for all." He raked a hand over his head. "I just can't believe this is happening."

"It is a bit bizarre. If Faith turns out to be Christie, it has to make you wonder if she hasn't had the amnesia longer than she believes she has."

"She isn't Christie," he insisted.

"I know you don't believe she is, but I have to tell you, Adam, she does look an awful lot like the pictures I've seen of her."

He groaned. "Oh, not you, too. It's bad enough that Megan thinks she's her mother."

"I didn't say I believe she is Christie, but I think you need to be prepared for the possibility that the test reveals she is," she cautioned him.

"No, I don't because she isn't," he stated adamantly.

Lori held up her hands. "All right. She isn't," she conceded. "But don't you think it's odd that Megan wouldn't know that Faith isn't her mother?"

"She's confused."

"She seems lucid to me. Whoever this Faith woman is, I feel sorry for her. It must be terrible not knowing who you are."

"Yes, well you can feel as sorry as you like. I have my daughter to worry about."

Lori clicked her tongue. "What exactly do you have against the woman? Is it the fact that she looks so much like Christie?"

"No," he answered, which wasn't exactly the truth. Faith did evoke feelings in him that he'd rather not acknowledge, but he didn't even want to admit them to himself. He found her attractive. There was no point in pretending he didn't, but why he was attracted to her was a matter he didn't want to explore. "I'm just exercising caution, that's all. I mean, how many people have you met with amnesia?"

"None."

"That's my point. From everything I've read it's unusual to have the kind of memory loss she has."

Lori shrugged. "So she has a rare case of amnesia." She stared at him. "So what are you insinuating? That she's faking it?"

It was one of many thoughts that had crossed his mind in the past two days, yet hearing it aloud made him realize how ridiculous it sounded. "Amnesia or no amnesia, we know nothing about her past nor is there any way to check her credentials."

"You can speak to the doctor who's taken her into his home. He obviously trusts her."

Adam didn't want to admit that he already had. Or that he'd made inquiries at the hospital and come up with nothing that would confirm his suspicions that she wasn't being completely honest. He'd even thought about getting her fingerprints and taking them to a friend who worked for the police department.

"I'm just wondering if maybe she isn't hiding something," he suggested.

"How can she hide something she can't remember?" She glanced at her watch. "I only have a couple of hours so I'm going to go in and sit with Megan."

Which was his sister-in-law's way of saying she'd

lost patience with him, something that was occurring more frequently now that he was a new father.

"I have to look out for Megan and act in her best interest," he told her before she went into his daughter's room.

"You *are* acting in her best interest. You're letting her see Faith."

Yes, he was, and it was only because Megan cried when he suggested it might be better if Faith didn't visit that he encouraged her to return. She came every day, bringing more books and producing smiles and laughter from his daughter. During the visits when Lori was present, the three of them chatted as if it were the most natural thing in the world, leaving Adam to feel like an outsider.

On the sixth morning of Megan's hospital stay he was at home eating breakfast when a courier delivered the results of the lab test. With his heart pounding in his throat, he tore open the envelope and pulled out the report. He didn't realize he was holding his breath until he exhaled a long sigh.

Faith's DNA did not match Megan's.

CHAPTER SIX

ADAM DIDN'T BOTHER to finish his breakfast but went straight to the hospital, relieved that he could put an end to the speculation that Christie was still alive. For the past five days, a dark cloud of uncertainty had shadowed their lives. Now a refreshing wind had arrived in the form of a DNA test that would clear the air. Brighter days were ahead.

He'd intended to go straight to Megan's room, but as he waited for an elevator, he saw Faith coming through the main entrance. She walked briskly, her cheeks flushed from the cold, her blond hair peeking out from under a red woolen hat.

At first she didn't notice him, but when she passed the bank of elevators, her eyes met his. She didn't acknowledge his presence, but quickly averted her gaze, acting as if she hadn't seen him.

He knew she had. It was there on her face as she headed down the corridor leading to the child-care center. She'd noticed him but hadn't wanted to talk to him.

He knew it shouldn't bother him, but it did. On this day of all days when he had something of extreme importance to tell her, she had looked straight through him as if he didn't exist. A bell chimed, indicating an elevator car was available. He should have stepped inside and gone up to Megan's room.

He should have, but he didn't. He went after Faith.

"Good morning," he said as he caught up to her.

She kept on walking, tossing a "good morning" at him with a sideways glance.

"I need to talk to you," he said, matching her stride.

"I'm short on time this morning. Can it wait until I visit Megan this afternoon?"

"That's why I want to talk to you. You don't have to visit her again. I have the results from the DNA test." That brought her to a halt. "You're not Christie Anderson."

The color drained from cheeks that had been pink from the cold. "Megan was wrong?" It was more of a shock to her than he'd expected it to be.

He handed her the report. As she read the test results, she reminded him of the way Megan had looked the first day he'd brought her to his house. Lost. Vulnerable. And just as he had with his daughter, he found himself wanting to comfort her. "I'm sorry this isn't the news you wanted."

Her eyes sparkled with emotion. "But it is the news that you wanted, isn't it?" She shoved the report back at him and took off down the hall.

"Faith, wait!" he called out, but she didn't stop. He easily caught up to her again, stepping in front of her so that she had to stop or walk around him. She stepped around him.

"Can I talk to you, please?" he said, keeping pace with her.

"I think you've said all there is to say."

He wanted to reach out and stop her, but he knew better than to put a hand on her arm. As he watched her scurry into the child-care center, he wished he hadn't said anything to her at all. What had he been thinking? Of all the places he could have told her the test results, he'd chosen the middle of a hospital corridor at a time when she was already feeling stressed. He shook his head and stared at the paper in his hand, wondering what had happened to that wonderful sense of relief he'd felt only a short while ago.

Now he was faced with the task of telling Megan the news. He braced himself for what he knew would be an emotional scene. When he arrived at her room, he was glad to see that Lori was at her bedside. She always seemed to know what to say and do to reach his daughter when his attempts failed.

"This is a surprise. I thought you weren't coming until noon today," his sister-in-law said as he approached the bed.

"Change of plans." When he looked at Megan he couldn't help but notice how her hair was nearly the same shade of blond as Faith's. It was a meaningless comparison now. "Feeling better today?" he asked her.

"Yes," she replied politely. "I ate all my breakfast."

"The doctor was here earlier and he thinks she'll be going home soon," Lori added.

"That's good news." Adam pulled up a chair and moved it close to the bed. "Don't you think so, Megan?"

She shrugged her tiny shoulders. "I can't go to school until I'm all better."

"That's all right. I'm going to arrange for someone

to stay with you," he announced to both of them. "Her name is Gwen and she's a very nice lady."

Megan crossed her arms. "Not another nanny."

He glanced at Lori who could only lift her eyebrows in agreement. He knew the reason for his daughter's remark. In the time she'd been living with him he hadn't had very good luck with baby-sitters. He'd tried several different arrangements. None had lasted. It was only because of Lori's willingness to rearrange her work schedule and take responsibility for Megan's care that he'd had any peace of mind.

"She's not from the agency. She's a friend of mine," Adam said calmly.

Megan rolled her eyes.

"You'll like her. She's nice," he assured her.

"Why do I have to have a nanny? Why can't I just stay with Lori?" she asked.

Lori looked as if she wanted to speak, but deferred to him. "I'm sure Lori would love to have you stay with her, but in a few weeks she's going to be having a baby."

"I'm going to help her with baby Matthew." She looked at her aunt. "Aren't I?"

Lori squeezed her hand. "Yes, you are."

Megan looked back at him. "See. You don't need to hire anybody."

He sighed. He hadn't come here to argue about hiring a nanny. "We can talk about this later. Right now I have something very important I want to tell both of you." He pulled the DNA test results from his pocket.

"Remember when I told you about the test that could be done to see if Faith is your mommy?" When she nodded, he continued. "The lab sent me the results. They're right here in this envelope," he said, holding it in the air.

Megan immediately lowered her eyes. "I'm tired. Can we talk about this later?" She turned away from him, burying her face in the pillow.

Lori placed a hand on her shoulder. "You can rest in a minute, sweetie. Don't you want to hear what your dad has to say?"

The "no" was muffled.

Adam exchanged glances with Lori who looked as anxious as he felt. "Megan, this is important." When she didn't respond he spoke as gently as he could. "I'm sorry. I know this is not what you want to hear, but Faith is not your mother."

He expected her to protest or to maybe even cry, but she simply kept her face to the pillow. Adam put a finger under her chin and forced her to look up at him.

"Megan, you have to accept that she's not your mommy. It's the truth," he said softly. "People don't come back from heaven. You believe me, don't you?"

She nodded soberly. Again she lowered her eyes, but not before Adam saw something there that made him suspect she wasn't as surprised by his revelation as he thought she'd be.

"You already knew Faith wasn't your mommy, didn't you?"

She kept her eyes downcast as her blond head bobbed up and down.

"When did you know?" Lori asked the question they were both thinking.

"That first day she came to see me," she said softly. "She didn't sound like Mommy."

Adam knew exactly what she meant. He'd had the same reaction upon hearing Faith speak, only it had been such a long time since he'd seen Christie, he hadn't been sure if there really was a difference in their voices or if with maturity had come a lower pitch.

"Why didn't you tell us you knew she wasn't your mother?" he asked.

"Because I thought if I said she wasn't, you wouldn't have let her come see me," she explained. "I like the way she reads to me. Mommy was always in a hurry to turn the pages. Faith likes to look at the pictures and talk about them with me. I hope she brings a story about Frog and Toad when she comes today. She said she would."

Adam had no choice but to tell her, "She's not coming today, Megan."

"Why not? Is she sick?" Blue eyes gazed up into his.

"No, she's not sick," he answered.

"Then why isn't she coming?"

He shifted uneasily on the chair, wishing he hadn't made such a mess of his conversation with Faith earlier that morning. "I thought the reason she was coming to see you was because we didn't know if she was your mother or not. Now that we know she isn't, there really isn't a reason for her to come."

"Yes, there is. I like her and she likes me and she likes reading to me," Megan said with an innocence only a child possesses. "She told me so. And sometimes when I close my eyes and listen to her, it's like hearing the flowers talk."

Adam didn't agree with her simile. To him, Faith's voice was more like hearing the water lap against the side of a boat. Smooth, with the power to hypnotize.

"I'm sure Lori would read to you if you asked her," he suggested. He looked at his sister-in-law. "Wouldn't you?"

"Sure. You know what a bookworm I am," Lori said with a grin.

"But I want to see Faith," Megan insisted.

Adam exchanged glances with Lori who shrugged in helplessness. He needed to change the subject. "So the nurses tell me we need to think about you going home. That's good news."

Megan, however, wasn't about to be distracted. "Maybe I should call her." She reached for the phone on the tray next to her bed. "Do you know her number?"

Lori saved him from having to answer by taking the phone out of Megan's hand. "She's at work so it probably wouldn't be a good time to try to reach her."

"Okay," Megan said meekly. "Do you think Faith can come to our house and see me?"

"Maybe," Lori answered.

Adam knew that if his sister-in-law had witnessed the conversation he'd had with Faith earlier she might not sound quite so optimistic. Seeing Megan yawn, he pushed back his chair and stood. "You need to get some rest and I need to go talk to the doctor and see how you're doing."

"I'll come with you," Lori said. As soon as they had

left the room and were far enough away so that Megan wouldn't hear, she asked, "Did Faith say she wouldn't come see Megan again?"

"Not exactly," he hedged.

"What did she say when you told her about the DNA?"

"Not much."

"She wouldn't. She's so quiet. Maybe I'll stop in and see her at the child-care center," she said with obvious concern in her voice.

"Why?"

"Because I'm worried about her. She seems like a really nice person and I feel badly that we put her through all of this."

He stared at her for a moment before saying, "What is it about this woman that makes you feel as if you need to be her advocate?"

She shrugged. "I don't know. Maybe it's because her amnesia makes her so vulnerable right now."

"Megan is vulnerable, too, which is why I was initially against Faith visiting her. And I had good reason to be concerned." He jerked his head toward the room they'd just left. "You heard what she said. She knew Faith wasn't her mother, yet she let us believe she thought she was."

"Because she was worried you wouldn't let Faith visit her if she told you the truth."

"What does she think I am? An ogre?" He asked the rhetorical question, then groaned as six weeks of frustration at not being able to figure out what his daughter needed from a father escaped like steam out of a boiling teakettle.

Lori wisely didn't answer, but slipped her arm through his. "Come. Let's go. I'll buy you a cup of coffee." She pulled him in the direction of the lounge.

"Now what do I do? She's become attached to that woman," he pointed out.

"I wouldn't exactly say she's attached. She's responding the way any normal child would react to an adult who obviously loves children—and Faith is very good with children. It's no wonder they have such a high opinion of her in the child-care center."

"And what makes you think they do?"

"Because I've talked to the director."

"And you call me suspicious?" he asked with an exaggerated drawl.

"That's not the reason I inquired about her." They'd reached the lounge and, after buying a coffee for Adam, Lori sank down onto one of the chairs with a sigh.

He took the chair across from hers. "That's good news about Megan getting released."

"Aren't you going to ask me why I went to the child-care center supervisor to ask about Faith?" she asked.

"No, I have more important things on my mind than to discuss a woman we hardly know." He reached into his pocket for a piece of paper.

"What's this?" she asked as he handed it to her.

"A list of child-care providers. Those are the names of people I've already contacted. Each one has said she'd be interested in the job but I wanted to go over it with you before I select one. Megan didn't sound very enthusiastic about my friend Gwen."

"She probably remembers what your friend Erica

was like as a baby-sitter," Lori said dryly. "It's not a good idea to hire ex-girlfriends to baby-sit your children."

He ignored her sarcastic comment. "All of those people are affiliated with agencies."

She took one glance at the list and gave it back to him. "You don't need this."

"And why is that?"

"Because I'm going to take care of Megan."

He didn't put the list back into his pocket, but kept it in his hands. "I thought you weren't comfortable being her full-time caregiver. You said you only wanted to be the backup."

"Yes, but I've been thinking about it a lot lately—and not just because I feel guilty over her appendix rupturing. Megan's a joy to have around and I want to continue having her with me."

He glanced at her belly, which looked like a balloon that was about ready to pop. "Have you forgotten you're pregnant?"

She chuckled. "That's a little hard to do considering I'm lugging this around," she said, pointing to her stomach.

"So what happens when the baby comes? You're going to be in the hospital a few days and you're going to need some time once you get home to adjust to life with a newborn."

"I plan to get someone to fill in for me."

He waved the piece of paper in his hand. "Then you'll need this."

She held up a hand. "Nope. I've already decided who I want. I've checked her references and they're good."

"So are you going to tell me the name of this someone?" When she hesitated and began fidgeting, he grew uneasy. It was not like Lori to be nervous about anything. "Just who do you have in mind?"

She lifted her eyes to his and said, "Faith."

"You're not serious."

"Yes, I am. She'd make a wonderful nanny, Adam. She's proven that she's great with kids and Megan already is fond of her. Dr. Carson has nothing but good things to say about her and she gets glowing reports from the staff at the child-care center."

He shook his head. "Not a good idea." And not for the reasons his sister-in-law suspected.

"Why not?"

"Because it isn't. The circumstances are too…awkward," he said for lack of a better word. *Awkward* described the tension that existed between him and Faith. "She has amnesia."

"What does that have to do with her taking care of Megan?"

He took a sip of coffee before saying, "We have no idea who she is, what her background is, where she came from, what's in her past."

"I thought you told me you'd talked to enough people to feel assured that her story is legitimate."

"That doesn't mean I want her to be a nanny to my daughter."

"She's only going to be a backup for me. It could be that she only spends two or three days with Megan. I don't know how I'm going to feel after Matthew is born. I could bounce back quickly."

"I'd rather you use someone off the agency list. Megan's already formed an attachment to Faith. What happens when Faith's memory returns and she leaves? Megan will be heartbroken."

"Adam, there's no guarantee that anyone you hire to take care of Megan will stay for as long as you want them to." She leaned forward, resting her arms on her knees. "I know you'd like to protect her from everything that could possibly cause her pain, but you can't protect her from life."

"I can try," he said soberly.

"There's a difference between people dying and people moving away. And it's not like Megan doesn't have a female role model in her life. She has me. It's just that I'm going to need help if I'm going to manage a baby and a six-year-old."

"There are professional nannies."

"Yes, I know. You've been through three of them in six weeks," she reminded him, holding up three fingers on her right hand. "Plus an old girlfriend," she added with a cheeky grin.

"Reliable help is hard to find."

"Yes, it is. So is finding someone you trust and who Megan feels comfortable with. She has enough to cope with already...her mother's loss, adjusting to a new family, changing schools. It's no wonder she doesn't want to spend a good portion of her day with a nanny who's a total stranger."

"Faith is a stranger," he pointed out.

"In your eyes, maybe, but not in Megan's. She regards her as a friend," Lori argued. "I've watched the two of them together and it's easy to see why Megan warmed to her so easily. Faith is a lovely person. Besides being very kind, she's not the least bit pretentious and I like the fact that she's quiet. She has a soothing presence, don't you think?"

Soothing was hardly the adjective he'd use when describing the effect Faith's nearness had on him. Provocative would be more accurate. Whenever she came near him, something definitely stirred inside him.

"We don't know very much about her," he said in defense of his reservations.

"I'm wondering if she wasn't raised on a farm," Lori said thoughtfully.

"What makes you say that?"

"When she was reading Megan a story about life on a farm, Megan commented on how her mom took her to see the pigs at the county fair and they smelled bad. Faith told her there's a sweetness to the smell of cows, chickens and even hogs. Said each has its own essence."

"Essence?" Adam wrinkled his brow.

"Yes, and when a picture showed cows being milked by machines, Faith told Megan that hands work just as well and that sometimes small hands work better because they can grasp the cows' teats without pinching them."

"What did you say to all of this?"

"That it sounded as if she had firsthand experience. She looked at me and simply shrugged, as if bemused that she even knew such a thing."

"So you think because she may be a farm girl she'd make a good nanny?"

"No, but don't you think there's a wholesomeness to her?"

Adam couldn't deny that she looked the part of a nanny. "What makes you think she'd even be interested in taking care of Megan?" he asked, intrigued by the possibility despite his reservations.

Lori shrugged. "I don't know that she is, but we can ask her. I do know that she loves her volunteer position here at the hospital. Why wouldn't she want to have a job that paid her for doing something she enjoys?"

He could think of a pretty good reason why she wouldn't. The fact that he was Megan's father was probably enough to deter her from taking the job.

"So what you think? Should I ask her if she's interested?" She looked at him eagerly.

He paused for only a moment before saying, "No, I'll do it. I just hope I don't regret it."

FAITH WOULD HAVE WORKED through her lunch hour if Mrs. Carmichael hadn't insisted she take a break. The best way not to think about the DNA test results was to stay busy.

She should have been prepared for the news that she wasn't Christie Anderson. Despite Megan's insistence that she was her mother, Faith had had a feeling that it wasn't true. She'd hoped that the DNA test would at least give her an identity if not a memory. It had done neither. Now she was back to square one and without any real clues to her past. The only thing that had changed was that she'd met a sweet little girl who tugged on her heartstrings and an attractive man who stirred emotions she didn't want stirred.

Ever since Adam Novak had walked into the child-care

center, she'd been having trouble putting him out of her thoughts—and not just because he could have provided a connection to her past. There was something about the way he looked at her that made her pulse race and her insides scramble. She was surprised he was still single—something she'd learned from Megan, who had also revealed that he had lots of girlfriends. It shouldn't have surprised Faith. There was a lot to like about Adam Novak.

If there was one good thing to come out of the results of the DNA test it was that she wouldn't have to see him again. Unfortunately it also meant she wouldn't see Megan, either.

Adam had made it clear that there no longer was any reason for her to visit Megan, yet she wanted to continue bringing her stories to read. While on her lunch break she purchased a get-well card from the gift shop and found a quiet corner in the cafeteria where she sat down to personalize it. She was in the middle of composing her message when she heard a man's voice next to her.

"Hello, Faith."

She glanced up to see Adam Novak standing beside her. As usual, her body reacted to his presence with a pleasurable shiver.

"May I join you?" He had a lunch tray with a salad and a cup of coffee on it. She was about to say no when he said, "I'm sorry about this morning."

"Why? All you did was tell me the truth."

"I didn't have to tell it in quite that way. Can I sit down? I'd like to talk to you."

"My lunch break is almost over," she told him, hoping he would take the hint and leave.

He didn't. "This will only take a few minutes. It's about Megan."

Reluctantly she gestured for him to take the chair across from her. As he set his lunch on the table she noticed for the first time how long and slender his fingers were. Megan had said her father built boats, yet Faith saw no callused skin on his hands. They looked large and capable, and she found herself wondering what it would be like to feel them wrapped around hers.

Because she sat at a very small table, his knees bumped hers when he sat down. He murmured, "Sorry," and smiled apologetically. Between the woodsy scent he wore and the closeness of his body she was acutely aware of his presence and knew it was going to be an uncomfortable few minutes. She leaned back, hoping to put some distance between them.

He unfolded his napkin onto his lap. "I really am sorry about this morning. I didn't mean to upset you."

She shrugged. "It's over and done with now." He looked tired, and she wondered if Megan had taken a turn for the worse. "How's Megan?"

"She's fine"

"Have you told her about the DNA test results?"

He nodded. "This morning. She took it better than I expected. Much better, actually."

She thought he would eat, but he didn't. He sat staring at her with those intense brown eyes of his. It took a lot of willpower for her not to squirm under his gaze.

"She wasn't surprised, was she?"

He shook his head. "Apparently she knew the first day you met you weren't Christie."

"I thought maybe she did."

"Then you knew she was pretending when she said she believed you were her mother?"

"It seemed likely. There are quite a few differences between me and Christie." She wished he would start eating so his focus would be on something other than her face, but he continued to stare at her, as if he were noticing those differences for the first time.

When she shifted nervously in her chair he said, "You were right. It was good that you spent some time with her so she could see those differences."

"I enjoy being with her. She's a delightful child."

"She enjoys your company, too, which is one of the reasons why I wanted to talk to you. She's been a rather unhappy child since she came to live with me. It was a big change for her—going from a small town to a big city, from a mother who's now gone to a father she hasn't known for very long."

She nodded in understanding. "She's had a lot to cope with." And Faith had been around the two of them enough to see the strain the changes had caused in their relationship.

"You're very good with children, Faith...but you don't need me to tell you that, do you?" He smiled and took a sip of his coffee. Noticing the greeting card in front of her he asked, "Is that for Megan?"

Faith nodded. "I thought I'd send her a get-well wish."

"Wouldn't it be better to do that in person?"

"I didn't think you wanted me to do that." She saw no reason to pretend.

"I'm sorry about this morning," he apologized for a second time. "What I meant was you didn't need to feel obligated to visit Megan."

"She was never an obligation, Mr. Novak."

"Call me Adam," he said with a smile that made her heart skip a beat. "And it's nice to hear you say that because Megan's become very fond of you, which is the second reason why I wanted to talk to you. She's going to be discharged from the hospital in a couple of days and she's already asking if you're going to still be her friend."

"Are you asking me to stay in touch with her?"

"Would you consider it?"

"Sure. She can call me at the Carsons. Or I could write to her," she offered.

"Actually I had something else in mind. With Lori due to have her baby shortly, I need someone to look after Megan when she's not in school. It would be a temporary position. Lori's not sure how much time she'll need after the baby is born, but she's optimistic it won't be more than a couple of weeks."

Faith thought she must have misunderstood him. "Are you offering me a job?"

"Yes."

When he asked her what she would require for an hourly wage she shook her head. "I can't work for you."

"Is it that you can't or you don't want to?"

It was both, but she didn't tell him that. "I don't think it would be wise considering everything that's happened."

"Megan knows you're not her mother."

"Yes, but I still have my amnesia. I don't know what

I'm going to be doing three weeks from now. Chances are I'll still be here with the Carsons, but if I woke up tomorrow and remembered I had a family in another town or even another state…"

"You'd be gone," he finished for her. "That's what I told Lori."

She should have known. It was Megan's aunt who was responsible for him offering her the position. It wasn't simply that he'd noticed how good she was with his daughter. His sister-in-law had convinced him she'd make a suitable nanny. She didn't want to feel disappointed, but she was.

"Look, it's a temporary position. If your memory does return and you're no longer interested in the job, all you have to do is call Lori. You've already had amnesia for what…a month? Chances are you could have it another month or two."

"You're asking me to make a plan based on the probability that I'll have my amnesia a month from now."

"Isn't it better to have a plan and not need it, than to not have one and need it?"

Faith knew he had a point, and the thought of having a paying job was an appealing one. It would make her feel like less of a burden on the Carsons' generosity. She was tempted to say she'd consider the proposition. Tempted. Only one thing stopped her. The man sitting across from her. Did she really want to put herself in a position where she would see him on a regular basis?

"I haven't mentioned this to Megan because I didn't want her to get her hopes up until I talked to you," he told her.

"But you've discussed it with Lori."

"Yes. She wanted to be with me when I talked to you. I guess she thought she'd do a better job of selling it to you than I could do, and she's probably right," he admitted with a half grin that Faith found extremely charming. "Or are you going to tell me you're interested in the position?"

She lowered her eyes. "I don't think it would be wise for me to accept your offer."

"I'll tell you what. Don't give me an answer today. Think about it for a couple of days, or at least overnight. That'll give you time to talk it over with your supervisor in the child-care center and with the Carsons. Fair enough?"

Reluctantly, she agreed. "All right."

"I'll have Lori give you a call in a few days if I haven't heard from you," he said. "You probably should talk to her anyway because she's the one who can better tell you what it involves."

A glance at the cafeteria clock had her scooping up her things. "My lunch hour's nearly over. I need to be going."

He stood as she rose to her feet. "I'm sure Megan would rather you deliver that card in person."

"I will," she told him, then hurried out of the cafeteria.

As she made her way back to the child-care center she thought about his job offer. Part of her wanted to accept the position, yet another part of her warned her that it would be a mistake. She wished that someone else would make the decision for her, then immediately chastised herself. She was not a woman who needed others to tell her what to do.

It was a realization that startled her. Why did she come to that conclusion now, of all times? Who was she? She closed her eyes and with great concentration willed her memory to return. And as had been the case so often these past few weeks, her efforts were in vain. She couldn't recall who she was or why she knew that she didn't want anyone making decisions for her.

That included Adam Novak. She would weigh all the aspects of the job he'd offered and make her decision based on what was right for her. She was her own woman. It was a thought that sent her home with a smile in her heart.

CHAPTER SEVEN

WHEN FAITH STOPPED BY to see Megan that afternoon, she discovered that Adam was wrong about his daughter. Megan was very much aware that her father had asked Faith to be her nanny to help during Lori's pregnancy and did everything she could, including make all sorts of promises as to how much fun they would have, if she would only say yes.

But it was Lori who helped her reach a decision. She explained that even though Faith would be taking care of Megan, she should think of herself as Lori's assistant. She was, after all, the one who needed help. After talking with both the Carsons and Mrs. Carmichael who assured her she could still volunteer at the child-care center on the days she wasn't working for the Novaks, Faith accepted the job.

Although Lori wanted to provide transportation for her on her first day, Faith insisted she could take the bus. With the help of Marie and Avery, who took her on a tour of the city in order that she could become familiar with the route the bus would take, she had no trouble finding her new place of employment.

Located in a wooded neighborhood not far from the hospital, the house was a collection of stacked rectangles and squares with more glass than stucco. There were so many windows that when Faith stepped inside she felt as if she were still outdoors. Sunlight streamed through the skylights in the roof and the floor-to-ceiling windows brought nature inside in a contemporary fashion that fit Lori's sunny disposition.

"Let me take your coat," Lori said, helping her out of her winter coat as Faith gazed in amazement at the wide open spaces in the multilevel home.

"There are a lot of windows." Faith stated the obvious.

"That's because I'm a person who needs lots of light. The more there is, the better I like it," she said, looping her arm through Faith's. "Come and I'll give you a quick tour. Adam's going to call us when he and Megan get back from her doctor appointment. Until then, we'll have a cup of tea and chat."

Faith followed her employer as she led her through the various rooms of the house. Although the house had several levels, she discovered that most of the rooms were on the first floor, with much of the second- and third-story space used to create vast, open ceilings. The rooms that were on the upper levels were more like lofts that overlooked the living area below.

"I saved the best for last. This is my favorite spot," Lori told her as she spun around with arms outspread in the sunroom at the back of the house. "No matter how cold and nasty it is, I can come in here and feel as if I'm outside. I'm an outdoor person. Actually, we all are. What about you?"

Faith shrugged. "I don't mind winter the way some people do."

"Do you ski?"

"I'm not sure."

Lori placed a hand on her arm. "I'm sorry. I shouldn't have asked such a stupid question."

"No, it's all right. I don't understand myself why it is that I know some things without having a memory and other things I don't."

"It must be confusing."

Faith nodded, not wanting to talk about herself. She glanced out the window at the birdbath where a small basin of open water had attracted a male cardinal. It sat perched on the edge, gingerly hopping in and out of the water, flapping its red wings.

"The water's not frozen," she noted.

"It's heated. You can't see it because of the snow, but there's a cord going up through the base that connects to a heating element hidden beneath the surface of the basin," Lori explained.

Faith glanced around the yard and saw numerous platform feeders scattered across the yard. "You must feed a lot of birds."

"My husband's the one who could tell you which ones are still around in winter. He's the birder in the family. He likes this room as much as I do. When we remodeled we had the architect design those loft offices I showed you, but we often end up down here with our laptops, especially in the summertime. I love to open the windows and listen to the water running over the rocks." She nodded toward the garden where a series of waterfalls had been landscaped into the hillside.

"This doesn't look much like the city," Faith commented as she surveyed the forest surrounding them.

"That's what attracted us to this area. You feel like you could be living in the country. If it were summer and the leaves were on the trees, you wouldn't even see the neighbors' houses. See that gray roofline over there?"

Faith followed the direction in which her finger pointed.

"That's Adam's garage. His house is just to the left behind that group of evergreens," she explained.

"It's close by."

"Not as close as you think. The distance is deceptive and there's a pond between us. If you're going to walk, you need to take the street. Today the windchill is too cold to be outside for more than a minute or two, so we'll take my car."

Lori led her back into the kitchen where a large vase of cut flowers graced the oblong table giving the room a hint of spring despite the wintry weather outside. Over tea Lori handed her some notes she had made regarding Megan's schedule. Faith noticed she had listed "Make Adam and Megan's dinner" as one of her duties.

After looking it over she glanced up at Lori. "Do Adam and Megan usually eat dinner with you and Greg?"

"Sometimes. Usually Megan ends up eating with us because Adam works late." She rubbed the small of her back. "I am so glad you're going to be helping me with her. Even the smallest of chores are becoming difficult to do lately. You don't mind cooking, do you?"

"No, not at all," she answered, wondering if Adam knew that she would be fixing his dinner.

It wasn't much later that he called to let Lori know that he and Megan were home from the doctor's office. Faith knew the moment had come when she would have to come face-to-face with him again. It had been several days since she'd last seen him and her stomach did a small flip. She tidied up the kitchen, then pulled on her coat and climbed into Lori's Audi for the short ride to the Novak home.

Except for the fact that it was large, the house was nothing at all like Lori's contemporary residence. It was a large brick two-story that looked like something Faith had seen in one of the home and garden magazines on Marie's coffee table.

Lori didn't knock, but went straight into the house. They were not met by Adam, but by Megan, who wore a pink sweater with rhinestones in the shape of an *M* on the front. She smiled shyly at Faith.

"Look at you. You must be feeling better. You're up and moving around," Faith commented as she unbuttoned her coat.

Megan came closer. "I can do some stuff but I still have to be careful not to hurt this." She pointed to where her incision had been. "I can't play outside."

"You probably wouldn't want to today. It's very cold," Faith told her.

"I'll second that," Lori said as she hung up their jackets in the entry closet. "I'm sure we'll have lots of fun staying inside."

"Can we make cookies?" Megan asked.

"I think before we make any plans we better talk to your dad," Lori answered. "He said your teacher had sent home some work for you to do."

"She's already done her schoolwork." Adam's deep voice echoed in the tiled entry. "She worked very hard so that she would be finished by the time you came." He glanced at Faith, pinning her with his intense gaze. "How are you this morning?"

"I'm fine, thank you," she said, hoping her voice didn't sound as breathless as she felt. Wearing an off-white sweater and dark brown corduroy slacks, he was even more attractive than she remembered, and he had that look in his eye again—the one that made her feel as if they shared a secret.

She was glad when Lori drew his attention by asking, "What did the doctor say?"

"To keep up the good work. Because she's been following his orders, she's making very good progress," Adam answered. He wagged a finger at her. "Remember. No jumping."

Megan nodded dutifully.

He walked over to the closet and pulled out a leather jacket. "I need to get to the office. Can you show Faith around?" His question was directed to his sister-in-law.

Megan stepped forward. "I will." She extended her small hand to Faith.

"Will you be home for dinner or should I take Megan to my place?" Lori wanted to know.

"I should be home," he answered.

As he slipped his arms into the sleeves of the jacket, Faith couldn't help but notice how broad his shoulders were. There were too many things she had been noticing about him. All of them making her aware of just how attractive a man he was. She was relieved when Megan tugged on her hand.

The little girl shyly looked up at Faith. "Will you make cookies with me?"

Faith glanced at Lori who nodded in response to the unasked question.

"Sure, we can do that. Or we can play some games."

"Or you can read more stories," Lori suggested. "Megan has quite a collection of books." She looked at her niece and said, "Why don't you show Faith your room and she can see for herself just how many books you have?"

Megan looked at Faith. "You want to?"

"I'd love to see your room."

"Okay. It's this way," she said, and would have led her away except Adam's voice stopped them.

"Hey. Do you have a hug for me?" he asked, stooping to Megan's level.

Faith released her hand and gently urged her toward her father who gave her a squeeze. Then with a "See you tonight" he was gone and Megan was leading her down the tiled hallway toward the staircase, acting as a tour guide.

"That's the living room and there's the kitchen." Her tiny arm went first in one direction then the other. "The bathroom's in there in case you have to go," she said, pointing to a closed door to the right of the staircase.

"Thank you. I'll remember that," Faith told her.

"There are more bathrooms upstairs, but that's my favorite one because it's not so big."

It didn't take Faith long to see that most of the things

in Adam's home were big. He definitely liked large furniture. As they passed the living room she saw oversize leather chairs the color of dark chocolate. The house wasn't airy and open as Lori's house had been, yet it didn't feel dark, either. It felt warm and inviting.

"I'm not supposed to go up the stairs fast," Megan explained as she methodically climbed the steps. "I have to be very careful."

"It's always a good idea to use caution on stairs," Faith agreed.

When they'd reached the top landing, Megan continued her tour of the house. "That's a guest bedroom and that's a guest bedroom," she said pointing at closed doors as they walked down the hallway. "That's Adam's room," she said, aiming her finger at the double doors at the end of the hall.

"It must be big if it has two doors," Faith murmured, wishing she wasn't curious about the man's room, but she was.

"It's huge. He has a really, really big bed," she said, spreading her arms wide. "You want to see it?" She ran over and placed a hand on one of the knobs.

Although she was curious to see Adam's bedroom, Faith didn't want to invade his private domain. "No, it's all right. I'd rather see your room."

"Mine's prettier," Megan said, slipping her hand in Faith's and pulling her along.

Faith could see why Megan was so proud of her room. The walls were white with a border of pink flowers at the ceiling. Lacy white curtains covered the windows and on the floor was a soft yellow rug with a border of pink and blue daisies. It was the bed, however, that was the centerpiece of the room. It was an old-fashioned canopy draped in sheer pink curtains.

"This is a lovely bedroom," Faith told her, thinking the six-year-old lived like a little princess.

"It's not as nice as my room at home, but it's bigger."

Faith didn't miss that she still thought of the house where she'd lived with Christie as being home. It was a reminder of everything Megan had been through the past six months, something Adam had alluded to but had never actually talked about with her.

"See all my books," she said, posing in front of a bookcase that ran the length of one wall. She dropped to her knees and spread her arms as wide as possible across the lowest section. "These are the ones from Mommy."

They looked worn and used, compared to the newer books on the second shelf. Faith understood why. As she fingered the titles her heart ached for the woman who no longer had the joy of reading to such a precious little girl.

Megan went over to the bed and grabbed a cloth doll whose pink dress was stained and tattered. "And this is Mrs. Giggles. She used to laugh when you tipped her like this." She turned the doll upside down and then right side up again. "But she doesn't work anymore. Mommy says sometimes stuff just gets worn out and there's nothing you can do."

"That's true," Faith concurred, noticing that several other dolls, all shiny and new, sat in a corner looking rather neglected. It was only Mrs. Giggles who looked as if she'd had the attention of small hands.

Faith watched as Megan lovingly set the doll back in its coveted spot. As she did, Faith noticed a small picture frame on the nightstand. The photo was of Christie with Megan, her arms wrapped around her daughter lovingly. They were both happy. You could see it not only in their smiles, but in their eyes. Faith reached for the photo to get a closer look at the woman she was supposed to resemble.

"That's me and Mommy." Megan stated the obvious.

Faith didn't say anything, but stared silently at the photograph, trying to see some resemblance between herself and Megan's mother. She didn't see it, but then she wasn't the most objective person to be making that comparison. She wanted to ask Megan, "Do I look like this?" but she couldn't.

"Do you want to see my closet?" Megan asked, unaware of the thoughts racing through Faith's mind.

"Yes, I would." She set the photo down.

"It's over here," Megan told her, motioning for her to follow. What looked like a cranny was actually a walk-in closet. All of the racks and shelves were at a level designed for a child's reach.

"Oh! So many clothes for one girl," Faith exclaimed.

"Lori likes to shop...a lot!" She rolled her eyes.

"I can see that."

"I didn't have this many clothes when I lived with Mommy." She fell to her knees and reached for a large square box. She tore off the lid saying, "And these are my new ice-skates. I haven't got to use them yet because of my operation." She lifted the small pair of figure skates for Faith's inspection.

"They're very nice," Faith noted.

"Maybe we can go ice-skating when I'm better."

"Maybe we can," Faith said, not wanting to curb her enthusiasm. "Did your mother teach you to skate?"

"Uh-huh. She was really good. We used to skate in the backyard."

"You lived on a lake?"

"No. Uncle Tom made us a skating rink using the hose. I asked Adam if we could make one in his backyard but he said no." Again Faith noticed that she referred to her father by his given name and that the house was "his," not "ours." Clearly Megan didn't feel as if she belonged with him.

Megan stuffed the skates back in their box in the closet and continued with her show-and-tell tour of the room. There was a child-size table with four pink chairs, a dollhouse with miniature furniture and woven baskets filled with toys and stuffed animals. If the way to a little girl's heart was through a beautifully decorated room, Adam Novak would have certainly won Megan's. Judging by what Faith had seen, it wasn't material things his daughter needed.

"You can't just sit and pray for people. You have to go help them," a woman's voice echoed in her head. It startled Faith to hear it and she closed her eyes, hoping it would help her put a face or a memory to the voice.

"Why do you have your eyes closed? Are you sleepy?" Megan interrupted her thoughts.

Faith opened her eyes and smiled. "I was imagining all the fun things we'll be able to do now that you're out of the hospital and feeling better."

"Like bake cookies?"

"Yes, like bake cookies."

"I'm glad you're going to be my nanny."

Faith gave her a hug. "I'm glad, too."

ADAM DISCOVERED THAT not much of his daily routine changed with the hiring of Faith. He left Megan in Lori's care in the morning and when he returned in the evening it was his sister-in-law who greeted him. From Megan he learned that Faith came sometime during the day, juggling her hours at the child-care center with the responsibilities assigned by Lori.

Tonight when he stepped into the kitchen he found not only his sister-in-law and his daughter, but Faith, too. The three of them sat at the table playing Parcheesi. When they heard him enter, all three turned and stared as if he were a door-to-door salesman.

"What are you doing here?" Lori asked.

"Ah, I live here," he reminded her dryly, tossing his keys along with the mail onto the kitchen counter.

She clicked her tongue. "I know that, but you're never home this early."

"Your husband said you had dinner plans. I didn't want to be the one to make you late."

"If you had called I could have told you that there was no need for you to leave work early. Faith's here."

And looking very uncomfortable, Adam thought. He didn't miss how quickly she'd lowered her eyes once she'd seen who had entered the room. Now she sat looking down at the game board, avoiding any further eye contact with him.

He shrugged out of his leather jacket. "It doesn't matter. I was ready to come home. What smells so good?"

"It's stew," Megan chimed in. "I helped make it. I peeled the carrots, didn't I, Faith?"

"*Ja,* you did." Faith gave her an indulgent grin.

"And look. She braided my hair." Megan turned her head so Adam could see how her blond hair had been twined into a single strand. "And we made handkerchief puppets and we finger-painted. My picture's on the refrigerator."

Adam glanced over his shoulder and saw what looked to be a purple sun shining on three green stick people. He didn't ask who the people were, afraid he might learn he wasn't one of them.

"That sounds like an awful lot of activity for someone who's supposed to be resting," he commented.

"She took a nap this afternoon," Lori told him. "Besides, I wouldn't be a bit surprised if tomorrow when we go for her checkup the doctor says she's ready to go back to school."

Megan groaned and pulled a face. "Do I have to?"

Lori gave her braid an affectionate tug. "Yes, you have to. Your teacher and your friends are anxious to see you. Olivia Martin has called nearly every day wanting to know when the two of you can play together again."

"Kendra called me, too. She's having a birthday party next week," Megan announced cheerfully.

"See. If you're not in school you miss out on all those fun activities," Lori pointed out.

"But I like being with you and Faith."

"You'll still be with us after school." Lori glanced

at her watch. "As much as I'd like to finish this game, I need to go home." She gave her niece an apologetic grimace.

"But I only have one more elephant to get to the palace," Megan whined. "Can't we play just a little longer. Please?"

Lori scraped back her chair. "Sorry, sweetie, but I really should go home so I'm not late for this important dinner with Uncle Greg."

"But we need one more player," Megan said.

"Maybe your dad will fill in for me." She glanced at Adam, one eyebrow lifting slightly.

Before Adam could utter a sound Megan folded her arms across her chest and said, "He won't. He never plays games."

"It's not like I've had a lot of free time lately," he said in his own defense, but it was as if no one was listening.

Lori patted Megan's hand. "It's okay. You and Faith can take my turn and move my pieces for me."

Faith didn't look any more enthused about the game than he did. "Maybe I should go home with you," she said to Lori. "You probably have things for me to do there, yes?"

Lori waved away her concern. "No, you stay here and play with Megan."

"But I'm supposed to be working."

"You are working. You're making dinner for Megan and Adam."

"She doesn't have to feed us," Adam interjected. "I'll take care of dinner."

Lori waved him off with a flap of her hand. "Don't

be silly. Faith has already started it and she wants to do it, don't you, Faith?"

Adam had serious doubts about that, but he'd come to the conclusion that it wasn't in Faith's nature to be contrary. That's why he wasn't surprised when she told Lori, "I'll make sure that everything is on the table before I go."

"I'd appreciate that," Lori said, giving her arm a gentle squeeze. She pushed herself out of the chair, exhaling a long sigh as she placed a hand on her protruding stomach. "I'm not sure I'm going to be able to make it a couple more weeks. It's getting harder and harder to do even the simplest of things."

"Your time is close," Faith said in a comforting tone.

"I hope you're right." Lori held her arms open to Megan. "Give me a hug, sweetie." Megan obliged her and then popped back onto her chair, eager to resume the game.

Lori then turned to Faith. "You've been a peach all week. Thank you," she said, giving Faith a quick hug, too. "I'll see you in the morning. Same time, same place." As Lori passed Adam she whispered, "Didn't I tell you she'd be great?" and then she was gone.

Adam had known from the start that eventually, this situation would arise. Technically Faith may have been Lori's employee, but she was in his house taking care of his child and cooking his dinner.

As soon as his sister-in-law was gone he turned to Faith who had stood and was pulling on two large oven mitts. "No matter what my sister-in-law says, you don't need to wait on us. I know she thinks I'm incompetent in the kitchen, but I do know how to feed myself."

"I don't think it's you she worries about," Faith said, bending over to open the oven door and peek at the contents inside.

"No one's died of malnutrition under my watch yet," he said dryly.

She looked as if she wanted to club him with one of the giant oven mitts, but struggled for self-control. He had to hide his smile.

When Megan asked, "What's malnutrition?" he realized that his daughter was following every word of their conversation. He picked up the stack of mail he'd set on the counter and handed it to her. "Would you do me a favor and put this on my desk in my office?"

"Okay," she said in a dutiful voice and scrambled off the chair and out of the room.

When she was out of hearing he said to Faith, "You don't need to stay and feed us."

"You want me to go." It was said matter-of-factly as she pulled the earthenware pot from the oven and set it on top of the stove.

"I'm offering you the opportunity to leave early. I would think you'd be happy to have the time off."

"Why would you think that?"

"Because most people are eager to leave work at the end of a day."

She turned her attention back to the pot, stirred it, then slid it back into the oven saying, "Work isn't something to be avoided."

"You're not avoiding it. I'm giving you the time off," he said on a note of frustration.

"But Megan is expecting me to finish the game."

"As Lori pointed out, you can do that tomorrow."

"She's hoping we'll finish today…that we'll both play the game with her."

He shook his head. "I'm expecting a couple of important business calls. I don't have time to be playing a game."

"That's too bad, because it brings a sparkle to Megan's eyes. Her eyes haven't sparkled much lately."

If it was her intention to make him feel guilty, she succeeded. He sighed. "All right, then I'll play with her, but after dinner."

"*Gut.* She'll like that."

It sounded to him as if she'd said *gut,* the German word for good. Ever since he'd met her he'd been trying to figure out her accent. Now he wondered if it wasn't German. He would have questioned her about it had Megan not come bouncing back into the room.

She climbed back up on her chair. "Can we *please* finish this game?" she asked, impatience lacing her words. "My poor little elephant wants to go to the palace." She stared up at Adam beseechingly.

Automatically his eyes met Faith's. He expected to see an "I told you so" there, but all he saw was concern.

Megan picked up the dice. "Who's going to take Lori's turn?" She looked first at Faith and then at him.

It was an appeal he couldn't resist. He motioned for Faith to sit down, then took the chair next to hers at the table.

"What am I?" he asked, noticing the different animal pieces scattered across the board.

"You're the blue ones—the water buffalo," Megan

said. "I'm the green elephants and Faith is the red tigers. Do you know how to play?"

"I think I remember," he answered, surveying the board. "Your uncle Greg and I spent many hours bent over this game when we were kids, but I don't remember ever having a water buffalo for a game piece. I wonder when they redesigned it."

He glanced up at Faith who didn't say a word but simply shrugged as if saying, "Don't look at me. I can't even remember my childhood."

"You shake the dice and move your animals, like this." Megan cupped a pair of dice in her hand and rolled them out onto the table. "See? I get to move six spaces. You want to get all of your animals to the palace up here," she said, pointing to the area in the center of the board. "You're blue so you go to the blue palace."

Adam nodded, eager to take his turn and have the game come to an end. He rolled a four so he picked up one of the tiny water buffalo and counted off four places, landing on the same rectangle as a tiger—one of Faith's animals. He glanced up and found both Megan and Faith staring at him expectantly.

"What?" he asked, puzzled.

"You can't have two animals on one space," Megan chastised him. She picked up his water buffalo, clicked it against the tiger, muttering "bye-bye" as her tiny fingers sent the tiger prancing back over the board to a large circle of the same color on the opposite end.

Adam looked at Faith. "Sorry."

As he expected, she didn't say a word, but she did do something that caught him off guard. She wrinkled her nose at him. It was a gesture he found quite amusing and at odds to her usual sober demeanor. It made him wonder what sort of mischievousness lurked beneath her cool exterior.

She sat quietly, seldom speaking except when she'd roll the dice and she'd announce the number of spaces she was to move her piece. Megan chattered enough for all three of them, happy to be on the fast track to victory. When she moved the last of her pieces into the green palace, she let out a whoop of delight.

"I won!"

"Yes, you did. Good job," Adam congratulated her.

When he would have picked up the game pieces she stopped him. "We need to see who's the second winner."

He was saved from having to disappoint her with a refusal by the ringing of his cell phone. A quick look at the screen told him it was one of the calls he'd been expecting.

"I need to take this," he announced. "Megan, you're going to have to put the game away. When you've finished doing that, get your jacket and your mittens. As soon as I've taken care of this business call we're going to take Faith home."

That brought Faith's head up with a jerk, but she didn't argue with his statement. It was Megan who asked, "What about supper?"

"There'll be plenty of time for supper after we take Faith home," he said firmly, leaving the room so as not to allow any further discussion on the subject.

While on the phone, he heard footsteps on the stairs and knew Megan had done as he'd requested. After a brief conversation with his client, he returned to the kitchen to find Faith hadn't been as impressed by his authoritative tone as Megan had been. She had tied a dish towel around her waist to act as an apron and was at the stove, getting his dinner. On any other woman he knew the dish towel would have looked absurd. On her it went along with the simple charm she seemed to exude. A charm he was having trouble ignoring.

When she saw him she gave him a polite smile before turning her attention back to the dinner preparations. She was either stubborn or conscientious. He guessed she was the latter, with a dash of defiance.

"I said I would take care of dinner," he reminded her.

"Lori told me you would be stubborn about accepting help," she said calmly.

"I'm not stubborn. I simply prefer to do it myself."

She turned to face him. "If you don't want me here, just say so and I will respect your wishes, but don't pretend that you like cooking dinner when Lori has already told me that she does it for you nearly every evening."

He wondered what else his sister-in-law had told her about him.

She didn't say another word, but began to sing as she moved about the kitchen. She opened a can of sliced peaches, which she poured in a bowl and set on the table that was now covered with a pale yellow linen cloth he didn't even know he owned. Next she cut bread and stacked it on a plate, setting it beside a jar of jam she'd already pulled out of the refrigerator. For someone who'd only seen his home for the first time a few days ago, she moved with surprising ease about his kitchen, efficiently putting the meal together.

"I can't very well take you home when you have all this food already on the table," he told her.

"You don't have to take me home. I'll take the bus," she told him, not bothering to look up at him as she continued to go about her work.

"You take the bus to Lori's every day?"

"Yes."

He frowned. He didn't even know where the bus stop was in his neighborhood and he certainly didn't like the idea of her standing outside in the cold and the dark waiting for a bus to come along. "My car's more comfortable than a bus."

"The bus is not a discomfort."

"It won't be tonight because I'm giving you a ride."

She glanced at him when she said, "That's not a good idea."

He shoved his hands to his hips and asked, "Why not?"

As she lined up the forks and knives next to the plates she said, "Because your food will be cold when you return."

"You said it's stew. Why can't I just leave it in the oven until I get back?"

"It's not good to leave the stove unattended."

He frowned. "Then I'll turn the oven off, put the stew in the refrigerator and zap it when I get back." When she stared at him in confusion he added, "In the microwave."

She gave him another blank look before turning her attention to setting the table. Megan came bouncing into the kitchen dragging her fur-trimmed parka behind her. When she saw what was on the table she said,

"Yum. I haven't had peaches in a long time." She let her jacket slide to the floor and climbed up onto the chair. "Is this the bread we made yesterday?" she asked Faith, helping herself to a slice.

"Megan, mind your manners. We're not sitting down to eat just yet," Adam reprimanded her.

She shot him a wounded look, then snatched her hand back and slumped down in the chair. "I'm hungry," she said in a very small voice.

"It won't be much longer now," Faith said over her shoulder.

Whether or not Adam liked it, dinner was being served. It annoyed him. Tonight he didn't want anyone waiting on him, much less Faith, who managed to get everything on the table in a very short time and look charming as she did it.

"There," she announced with satisfaction as she set the earthenware pot on a trivet in the center of the table. "Is there anything else I can get you?" With the oven mitts on her hands and the dish towel around her waist, she looked the picture of domesticity. And so very unlike any of the women he'd dated.

As he stood gazing at her he realized that what he wanted was for her to stay and have dinner with them. "You can get another plate and join us."

Megan gasped in delight. "Are you really going to eat with us?" she asked, her eyes widening at the possibility.

"I'd like to but the Carsons are expecting me," she answered.

"Can't you call them and tell them you're eating here with us? You can sit by me. Please say you will?" Megan turned her baby-blue eyes on Faith with an appeal most adults would find hard to resist.

Faith was no exception. After only a moment's hesitation, she gave Megan an indulgent grin and said, "All right. I'd like that." The glance she shot in Adam's direction, however, didn't have even a hint of a smile. It was a look that made sure he understood that she was only staying because of Megan.

As she sat down, Megan jumped up to turn on the television.

"What are you doing?" Faith asked.

"We always watch the news during dinner," she answered.

Faith shot Adam an inquisitive look. "How can you have any conversation?"

He didn't want to tell her that there wasn't much talk between him and Megan even without a television running. "Leave it off, Megan. We don't need to watch the news."

When he would have reached for a slice of bread, Megan said, "Wait!" She looked at Faith and asked, "Are we going to do patties down?"

This time he was the one shooting Faith the inquisitive look. "What is patties down?"

"You put your hands down and bow your head and say a silent prayer of thanks," Megan told him.

He pulled his hand back from the bread tray and said, "Sure. We can pray."

As he watched his daughter at the dinner table he realized that in a very short time Faith had already been an influence on her. With him Megan was usually subdued and polite, but with Faith she blossomed into a talk-ative, playful little girl. Adam didn't understand why. Faith led a simplistic life and had a quiet disposition.

Yet there was no denying that she'd had a positive in-fluence on Megan. Lori said it was because she pos-sessed a gentle soul. Connecting with people came naturally to her. Adam knew that was true. He'd seen examples of her compassionate nature in Megan. Last night when his daughter had overheard him refer to one of the neighbors as an idiot, she'd said, "You should al-ways speak kindly of others."

Faith was kind. Lori hadn't been wrong about that. As he watched her help Megan butter a slice of bread he no-ticed how with a tender touch or a brief word she had an unobtrusive way of lending support. He wished he knew more about her past. What was it that she had left behind? Or whom? He glanced at her left hand and saw no ring on her finger. He knew that didn't necessarily mean she didn't have a husband waiting for her somewhere, al-though he didn't understand why any man involved with her wouldn't have filed a missing-person report when she'd disappeared. Her description had matched none of those on file with local police, yet he knew it would be unusual if there wasn't a guy waiting for her somewhere.

She was the kind of woman a man settled down with—the kind *he* avoided and shouldn't be thinking of in that way right now. It was purely sexual. It had to be because she *was* nothing at all like the women he dated.

As if she sensed what thoughts were running through his head she looked at him. He didn't need to smile, or cock his head, or give her that look a guy gives a woman he's interested in getting to know. She saw it in his eyes and he saw it in hers. There was no point in pretending that they weren't attracted to each other because they were.

She quickly lowered her eyes and turned her attention back to Megan, a blush turning her creamy white cheeks a delicate pink. Normally he found shyness in a woman annoying, but in her it was charming. She appeared to be as innocent as Megan, yet he knew she couldn't have reached adulthood without there having been a man in her life.

He was sorry to see dinner come to an end. When he offered to help with the cleanup, she turned him away. Megan, however, she allowed to stay. While he waited for them to finish, he went into his study and worked. From his desk he could see the two of them at the sink standing side by side doing the dishes. He liked the picture they made.

He thought she would refuse to accept a ride home but she once more surprised him by accepting his offer. She sat in the back seat with Megan, making him feel like a chauffeur as he drove his Lexus SUV through the city streets. He found himself glancing in the rearview mirror to catch glimpses of her.

How he ever could have mistaken her for Christie amazed him. With the exception of superficial similarities, she was nothing at all like the stripper. She intrigued him in a way the other woman hadn't. Maybe it was because she was a mystery to be solved.

By the time they reached the Carsons' Megan had fallen asleep and snow was falling. Adam climbed out of the car saying, "I'll walk you to the door."

She didn't wait for him to come around, but shoved the door open and jumped out, making a dash for the house. She hadn't gone but a couple of steps when she went sprawling to the ground.

He hurried to her side. "Why didn't you wait?" he asked as he bent down to help her.

She didn't respond, but grimaced as she tried to get to her feet. "Ouch!"

"Are you all right?"

"Yes, I'm just wet," she said, spreading hands that were covered with snowy slush.

He pulled a handkerchief from his pocket and began to dab at them. "You should have been wearing your gloves." He expected her to snatch her hands away or make some quiet remark, but she did neither. She sat perfectly still, staring off into space.

"Faith?" He called her name. Startled, she looked at him. "Are you all right?" he asked for a second time.

"Yes, I…" She trailed off, her face pale.

As she appeared unable to get up on her own, he put his hands beneath her arms and hoisted her to her feet. She didn't object.

Still looking dazed, she stared at him. "I had a memory flash."

"What did you see?"

"It was bitterly cold and I was hanging laundry out on a line. I could barely get the sheets pegged to the line before they became frozen stiff. My knuckles were red." She wrapped one of her hands around the other, trying to warm them.

He covered her hands with his and brought them

close to his face so he could blow warm air on them. Staring into eyes filled with confusion, he asked, "What else do you remember?"

She shook her head. "Nothing." Frustration replaced the confusion. She squeezed her eyes shut, as if by doing so she could will her mind to remember more, but after a few moments she opened them again and slowly shook her head. "That's it. One brief picture." Her shoulders sagged and a solitary tear escaped down her cheek. "When will the darkness go away?"

It was such a sad lament that all he could think about was comforting her. Still holding on to her hands, he lifted them to his lips and planted a kiss on them. "You have the most beautiful blue eyes. Don't cry. Everything will be all right."

As if suddenly aware of their closeness, she cast her eyes downward and snatched her hands away from him, wiping at the tear with the back of her hand. "I've got to go." She walked away without looking back at him.

He didn't try to stop her.

CHAPTER EIGHT

MARCH IN MINNESOTA CAME in like a lamb, leaving the bitterly cold windchill factors of winter behind. The mild temperatures and sunny skies were perfect for adults and kids alike who welcomed the opportunity to enjoy the outdoors, except for Megan who could only kneel on the sofa, her arms draped over the back and watch with envy as other children in the neighborhood frolicked in the snow.

"Am I ever going to be able to go outside and play?" she asked Faith with a sigh of exasperation.

"As soon as it's okay with your father," she answered, her hands pushing a needle and thread into a pair of Megan's pants that had come apart at the seam. Although Megan had been allowed to return to school, she still had limits on her physical activities, much to her dismay.

Megan let the curtain fall back into place and slumped against the sofa. "The snow will be all gone by then."

"I doubt that."

She sighed. "Can't I just go out for a little while? I won't go sledding." She cast an appealing glance in Faith's direction.

"If I let you do that, your dad would be very angry with me."

"We don't have to tell him."

"Oh, yes, we do," Faith corrected her. "How about if we work on your numbers instead?"

Megan groaned. "But I want to do something fun."

"Numbers can be fun."

"No, they're work. You always say work is fun."

"Because it is."

Megan folded her arms across her chest. "I hope I never grow up because I don't want to work all the time."

Faith set aside her mending. "Grown-ups don't work all the time."

"Adam does."

It was hard for Faith to argue with that statement when the only reason she was with Megan on a Saturday was because her father was working. A boat show at the convention center had all of the Novak family members in attendance, including Lori.

"I wish I could go home."

"Megan, you are home," Faith said gently.

"I mean to my house in Silver Bay. Uncle Tom doesn't work all the time."

"I thought you told me he goes away for months at a time on a ship."

"In the summer he does but in the winter he plays with me. We have snowball fights, and one time he made me a fort that was this tall." She stood and lifted her hand high above her head.

"You miss him, don't you?"

"Mmm-hmm. He's going to come see me when he

gets his car fixed. I hope he comes when the snow is still here so you can see how he makes a fort. Adam said he can sleep in the blue bedroom."

"Megan, why do you call your father Adam instead of Daddy?"

"Because."

"Because why?"

She kept her eyes downcast. "Because that's his name."

"Most children call their fathers Dad or Daddy."

"I know."

"Then why don't you?"

Megan came over and sat down beside her, lowering her voice to a near whisper. "If I tell you something, will you promise not tell anybody?"

"If you want me to keep it a secret I will." When Megan didn't speak, Faith reached for her hand. "Do you need me to keep a secret?"

The little girl nodded, then with a very serious face she whispered, "He's not really my daddy."

"Who told you that?"

"I heard Uncle Tom's girlfriend, Mandy, talking about it. She said she didn't believe Adam is my real daddy. I don't believe he is, either, because Mommy told me my real daddy is in heaven and people can't come back from heaven. Just ask Adam."

Faith frowned. She thought back to when Adam had explained DNA testing to her. He'd told her the results would confirm or deny that she was Megan's biological mother. Not once had he mentioned whether or not *he* was her biological father. Faith had simply assumed

he was, and no one had ever given her any reason to believe he wasn't—at least not until now.

With a couple of innocent statements, Megan had
raised all sorts of questions in Faith's mind. Like why
hadn't Adam seen Christie in over six years? Had they
ever been married, or had Faith simply assumed they
had been because he'd told her from the start that he was
Megan's father? What exactly had been his relationship with Christie? Was it possible that he wasn't Megan's biological father? If he wasn't, why would Christie
name him Megan's guardian? They were questions she
didn't want to ask a child, yet she had a feeling that the
answers were the key to Megan's relationship with her
father.

"Are you sure you didn't misunderstand what your
uncle said?" Faith asked.

Megan shook her head. "Uncle Tom wanted to be my
guardian but the judge wouldn't let him. Mandy said it
was because Uncle Tom doesn't have a lot of money.
That's why the judge made Adam my daddy."

Suddenly Faith felt as if she'd ignored a No Trespass-
ing sign and was now in the middle of some very private property. She'd entered the zone of family matters
and had no business being there, yet something com-
pelled her to stay.

"But I've heard your aunt Lori say you look like a
Novak," Faith commented.

"She just says that because she has to pretend, too. Do
you want to see a picture of my uncle Tom?" Megan asked,
changing the subject. She didn't wait for an answer but
went scrambling up the stairs calling out, "I'll go get it!"

While she was gone Faith thought about what Megan had told her. She knew there were two sides to every story and she'd only heard one side that might not even be accurate. She wished that she felt more at ease around Adam so that she could talk to him about Megan's misconceptions—if indeed that's what they were. More than anything she wanted to ease the pain the child still felt from the loss of her mother.

Within a few minutes Megan was back clutching a large photo album that looked as if it had seen better days. The edges were frayed and when Megan opened the cover, a sheet of plastic fell out.

"That looks old." Faith watched as Megan slowly flipped through the pages.

"It was my mommy's. Here. This is him." She pointed to a snapshot of a sandy-haired man wearing jeans and a sweatshirt, sitting on the deck of a boat with a fishing rod in his hand.

"I bet he likes to fish, doesn't he?" Faith noted.

"Sometimes he takes me with him." She carefully turned the pages, but still some of the photographs slipped out of the plastic holders.

"Maybe you should put this away," Faith suggested. "It looks rather fragile."

"First I have to show you my house." She kept flipping through the album until she found the photograph she wanted. "There it is."

Faith stared at the rustic-looking cottage built on a hill overlooking Lake Superior. It was badly in need of paint but the yard was neat with marigolds lining the walk. The fact that Megan liked it better than Adam's expensive home with all the modern comforts only showed that it wasn't the material things that made the house feel like home to Megan.

"It looks like a nice house," Faith commented.

"And here's me swimming," she said, showing Faith another picture, this one of her splashing in a shallow plastic pool molded in the shape of a fish.

"You don't swim in the lake?"

She shook her head. "Uh-uh. It's too cold." She shivered and rubbed her arms. "Brrr. I went in one time and it was so cold my teeth chattered."

Faith noticed a picture of Megan wearing grown-up clothing. She had on a pair of pajama bottoms with the cuffs rolled up, a T-shirt that said, Born to Boogie on it and a feather boa wrapped around her neck. On her head was a baseball cap with Cutie Pie embroidered across the top, and a pair of large rectangular sunglasses hid her eyes.

"When was that taken?" Faith wanted to know.

"That was when I was feeling really sad because Angela Dolemeyer wouldn't let me play house with her and Emily Butcher. Mommy said the best way to get over feeling bad was to dress funky and dance. Do you put on funky clothes and dance when you feel sad?"

"No, I don't think I do," Faith answered.

"You should. It makes you feel better."

Faith doubted that any of the clothes hanging in her closet at the Carsons would be classified as funky. "I'm not sure I know how to dance."

"I can teach you," Megan offered eagerly, closing the book and setting it on the end table. "Should I put on some music?" She bounced between the sofa and the floor with an abundance of energy.

"Not just now. I need to finish mending your pants."

Megan groaned and went back to the window. "It's snowing again. Big giant flakes. I like to catch them with my tongue cuz they taste good. Oh, please can't I go outside?" she begged. "Just for a little bitty bit. Please?"

Faith could feel her resolve weakening. Despite what Adam said, she didn't think that Megan could do any more harm to herself being bundled up in a snowsuit and playing in the snow than she'd done running around inside the house.

"I'll tell you what. If you promise to be very careful, I will let you go outside, but there will be no sledding, and no jumping off snow piles. Got it?"

Megan nodded excitedly. "Will you come with me?"

"Yes. I like catching snowflakes on my tongue, too."

"WELL, LOOK AT THAT. Someone made a snowman," Robert Novak exclaimed as Adam turned his SUV into the driveway. "Megan must be feeling better."

"Not well enough to build a snowman," Adam told his grandfather, wondering if the neighbor kids had been playing in his yard. Upon getting out of the vehicle, he took a closer inspection, however, and saw a pink-and-white-striped scarf wrapped turban-style around the snowman's head, purple sunglasses resting on a plastic pig nose and a mouth made out of radishes. He was certain that all of the trappings, including the blanket draped like a serape across the bulk of the body, had come from his house.

"Very clever," his grandfather said, giving the snowman a poke with his cane. "Looks like you won't have to shovel the walk. Somebody did it for you."

Adam frowned. He should have known Faith would take care of it. She was always cleaning or straightening or moving something. His sister was right. She certainly didn't shy away from work.

"I suppose it's too late for me to see my great-granddaughter," Robert said as he climbed the steps to the front door. "As usual, we stayed longer than we intended to at the boat show."

That was why Adam had insisted his grandfather come spend the night with him rather than drive all the way back to his home on the St. Croix River. Many of the secondary roads hadn't been plowed from the recent snowfall and Adam worried about him driving alone at night.

"Megan's probably asleep, but you'll be able to see her in the morning," Adam said as he unlocked the front door.

"She'll be up before we leave?"

"Oh, yeah. She'll be up." He pushed open the door and stepped inside ahead of his grandfather so he could turn off the security system. He discovered, however, that it wasn't on. A ripple of annoyance wrinkled his forehead. He'd told Faith he wanted the security alarm on at all times.

"Where's this new nanny Lori was talking about?" Robert asked as Adam helped him off with his coat.

"She's probably in the living room. Come, I'll introduce you to her."

They found Faith curled up in one of the large oversize leather chairs, her eyes shut. The book she'd been reading had fallen to the carpet. She wore a plain white blouse with a navy blue cardigan over it and a pair of dark pants, yet she didn't look in the least bit ordinary to him. She looked beautiful.

"She's a pretty little thing," his grandfather whispered, echoing Adam's sentiments.

Adam would have agreed with him but he didn't want to give him any reason to think he was attracted to her. "She's not exactly little, Grandpa," he whispered back.

"No, but she sure is pretty. Guess I'll have to wait until morning to talk to her, too."

"She's not going to be here in the morning."

"No? Why not?"

"Because I'm going to take her home tonight. Lori's not going to the boat show tomorrow so she's going to come stay with Megan," he explained.

"Then I'd better get upstairs. I don't want to be in the way of you talking to a pretty girl." With a wink he was gone.

Adam could imagine his grandfather smiling smugly to himself. He should have known he would make some wisecrack about him making the most of his opportunity with a pretty girl. It was what he'd been doing ever since Adam's voice had changed and he'd started sprouting hair on his chin. Adam usually shrugged off his comments with a grin, but tonight, seeing Faith sleeping like a kitten in his living room, he didn't see it as a joke. He liked the way she looked asleep. Warm. Soft. Approachable. It was a stark contrast to the message her body language usually gave him—*Don't Touch*.

She stirred and her blouse separated in the front, giving him a glimpse of a plain white bra beneath the cotton cloth. He should have known she wouldn't have lacy, feminine undergarments. She had a simplistic style that fit her personality. Nothing fancy. Nothing colorful. As if she could feel his eyes on her she stirred, her eyes fluttering open.

Startled, she pushed herself upright. "Oh. I must have fallen asleep."

"All that shoveling must have worn you out," he said with a grin. "Or was it making the snowman?"

"Megan wanted to go outside," she said defensively, a sparkle in her eyes. "I watched her carefully to make sure she wasn't overdoing it."

He liked that for once the hint of color in her cheeks wasn't from modesty but from defiance. "I'm not complaining. Shoveling the walk, however, is not part of your nanny duties."

"I don't mind."

"But I do."

She shrugged in acquiescence.

"Did everything go all right while I was gone?" he asked.

"Megan went to bed at eight. You had several messages—I left them next to the phone in the kitchen," she said as she slipped her feet back into her shoes. "We ordered pizza, as you suggested. The leftovers are in the refrigerator."

"All right," he said, trying not to notice how sexy she looked tousled from sleep.

"Is the taxi here?"

"No, I'm going to take you home."

"But Lori said I should take a taxi so you wouldn't have to wake Megan. She needs her sleep."

"I don't need to wake her. My grandfather is spending the night. He's upstairs and will hear her if she needs anything. Are you ready?"

She nodded and headed for the foyer. She didn't wait for him to help her with her coat, but pulled it on then stood next to the door while he punched in the code for the security alarm.

"You didn't have this on when I came home," he mentioned.

"I must have forgotten to turn it back on when we came in," she said quietly. "I'm sorry."

"It's for your own protection."

"From what?"

"Not from what but from whom. The criminal element of society that has no respect for other people's property," he told her.

She gave him a blank look and he wondered if her lack of concern was due to her memory loss or the possibility that she lived in a place where residents didn't feel a need for security alarms.

She said very little on the way to the Carsons'. As he pulled into the doctor's driveway, he expected she'd jump out of the Lexus as soon as they stopped.

To his surprise, however, she turned to him and said, "I'm glad we have this time alone."

"You are?"

She took a deep breath and straightened her shoulders. "Yes. I have something I want to say to you."

"All right."

He waited, but she remained silent. She fidgeted with the fingers on her glove and he wondered if she was nervous about what it was she wanted to say.

Finally he said, "I don't bite, Faith. Just say whatever it is that is on your mind." Curiosity had him imagining all sorts of things, including the possibility that she was tired of pretending they weren't tap dancing around the sexual tension that kept getting thicker and thicker every time they were in the same room together.

He wanted to place a hand on her shoulder but he didn't want to risk her flinching. Instead he said, "Maybe if you gave me a hint as to what it is you want to say I could help you out."

The shy glance she tossed his way nearly had him reaching for her cheek, but she took a deep breath and said, "I'm concerned about something Megan said to me."

So it wasn't about what was—or wasn't—going on between them. It was about his daughter. "What did she say?"

"It's hard for me to tell you because she told me in confidence. I said I would keep her secret, but it's something you need to know."

"Does she still think her mother might return from heaven?" he asked, his heart growing heavy at the thought.

"No. We've talked about that and I believe she now understands that's not going to happen."

"Then what is it?"

Faith licked both her upper and lower lip and cast a sideways glance at him as she said, "Megan thinks you don't want to be her father."

"What?"

"She thinks you don't want to be her daddy," she repeated.

Stunned, he asked, "She told you that?"

She nodded. "She believes you're only her guardian because the court ordered it."

"That's ridiculous. Where would she get such an idea?"

"Apparently she overhead a conversation between her uncle and his girlfriend in which her paternity was questioned."

Paternity. The word resonated in him like thunder rumbling in a dark sky. "Are you saying my daughter doesn't think I'm her biological father?" He knew his voice rose with emotion.

She nodded. "Are you?"

"Yes, and Tom Anderson knows it," he stated in no uncertain terms. "So should that flaky girlfriend of his, because there's a DNA test on record that proves it." He didn't add that the reason it was on record was because he had been the one to request it.

"Does Megan know this?"

"About the DNA test? No. At the time I didn't think there was any need to tell her. However, had I known she would be running around thinking I'm only pretending to be her father, I certainly would have explained it to her." He couldn't understand how she could have become so suspicious of him. "No wonder she's been so unhappy living here."

"She's had a lot to cope with since her mother died."

"I know she has, which is why I'm doing everything I can to make her feel at home here. She goes to a good school, she doesn't have to go to day care, she has a brand-new wardrobe—and you've seen her room. It has everything a kid could want."

"Maybe *things* are not what she needs right now," Faith suggested.

"As soon as she's well we'll get away for a vacation. We both could use an escape."

"Real pleasure is not about escaping. It's about togetherness. Megan needs to feel as if she is a part of your world. Can't she help you with your work?"

"My work?" Was she serious? "I'm an engineer. How is she going to help me design boats?"

"I'm talking about the work at home. She may be small, but there are chores she can do. Dusting the furniture, sweeping the floor, folding the laundry. If you show her what needs to be done by doing the work with her, you'll not only spend time together but she'll see how fulfilling work can be."

For a moment he thought he'd fallen into a time machine and he was sitting opposite June Cleaver or Donna Reed. "I don't have time for housework. It's why I have a cleaning lady."

"I know. And you don't have a close relationship with your daughter."

So Faith had noticed the strain in their relationship, too. It shouldn't have surprised him. It was obvious to anyone who spent any time with them that he hadn't figured out how to be a father. He didn't think, however, it was because he hadn't shown Megan how to mop a floor.

"Look, I appreciate you wanting to help me find a way to reach Megan, but it isn't as simple as you think.

Until six months ago Megan didn't know she had a father and I didn't know I had a daughter."

He could see the curiosity in her eyes. He waited for her to ask the question he knew had to be foremost in her mind, but she didn't. She simply looked at him with sympathy in her beautiful blue eyes.

"Her mother chose not to tell me I had a daughter," he continued, trying not to sound bitter, even though he was. "And apparently whenever Megan would ask about me, Christie would tell her that I had died and gone to heaven."

"I know. Megan told me her mother had done that. It's one of the reasons she's confused about her feelings toward you."

"I've tried to explain that her mother made a mistake, that I never went to heaven, but I'm not sure she believes me." He chuckled without humor. "Of course she doesn't believe me. If she doubts that I'm her real father, it probably doesn't matter what I say."

"Why did her mother tell her you had died?"

"I don't know," he answered. He'd spent a lot of time speculating as to why she wouldn't have wanted him to know he'd fathered a child and there was only one reason that made any sense. "Obviously she didn't want me in Megan's life. Maybe she thought I wouldn't be a good father."

"If that were the case, why would she name you as Megan's guardian?"

He shrugged, staring out into the darkness. "I'm afraid that is something we'll never know, and I guess it doesn't really matter what her reasons were. I'm just grateful I now have Megan with me and sorry that I missed out on the first six years of my daughter's life."

"Megan missed out on something important, too." The tenderness in her voice had him turning to look at her. The face staring back at him was beautiful and filled with compassion.

"I'm going to make it up to her," he vowed, admitting something he would never have said to any of the other women he'd dated.

But then, Faith wasn't a girlfriend; she was his daughter's nanny. It was something he needed to keep in mind, especially when every nerve in his body screamed at him to look at her simply as a woman.

"If you don't want to work, you can sing with her," she said, her mouth breaking into a partial grin.

"I have a terrible voice."

"All fathers make sweet music to their children's ears," she insisted.

He stared at her for a moment, wondering again who she was and what was in her past that had shaped her into the woman she'd become.

"When I look at Megan I see a little girl who wants very much to belong somewhere. I know that feeling," she said quietly.

He wondered if that was why she and Megan had connected the way they did. They both had lost a part of their past.

Silence stretched between them but it wasn't an uncomfortable one.

"I appreciate you telling me about Megan. I'll have a talk with her first thing in the morning."

She looked at him. "You'll remember what I said—about it being her secret she shared with me?"

"I'll find a way of bringing up the subject without involving you."

She nodded and reached for the door handle.

"Wait," he said to her.

She gave him one of her shy glances over her shoulder and it did in his self-control. He leaned across the seat and placed his lips on hers. He expected she would pull back before he could get much of a taste, but she allowed his mouth to coax a sweet response from her before easing away from him. The look in her eyes told him that she'd been caught off guard but pleasantly so.

"That was rather nice, wouldn't you say?" he asked, but she'd returned to her shy self and lowered her eyes.

"We can't be doing that," Faith said as she fumbled for the handle.

"Why not?" he asked, making no attempt to stop her.

"Because I have no past." She pushed the car door open.

"I'll walk you to the door."

"No, it's all right," she said, getting out. "Good night." And before he could utter another word she was gone.

CHAPTER NINE

Two things caused Faith to lose sleep Saturday night. One was knowing that she'd broken a confidence and divulged Megan's secret. The other was Adam's kiss. The former she could justify because she had done what was in the best interest for Megan and her father. The kiss, however, she was having a hard time rationalizing. Just because it felt good didn't make it right.

But it had felt really good. Adam had called it nice. Faith would have described it in a different way. Incredible. Delicious. Exciting. Sweet. The list of adjectives was long. What it boiled down to was that he was a good kisser and Faith wanted more of his kisses.

That was the problem. She had no right to want more—at least that's what her conscience told her. Where that idea came from she wasn't sure. Not knowing what people and events had filled her life before the accident was reason enough for her to believe she shouldn't get involved with Adam Novak. And she wouldn't. She'd decided that sometime in the wee hours of the morning just before falling asleep.

Finding her in the kitchen Sunday morning Marie said, "I didn't expect you to be up so early this morning."

Faith shook her head. "I couldn't sleep."

"Anything you want to talk about?"

"No. I'm just feeling restless." She wasn't ready to tell anyone about her feelings for Adam. "Maybe I'll go for a walk. Would you like to join me?"

"I would but Avery and I are working the pancake breakfast at church this morning. He helps out in the kitchen and I wait tables," the older woman said with a grin.

Faith returned the smile. If there was one thing that she'd learned about the Carsons it was that their generosity didn't just extend to her. They volunteered their time in many different places and never seemed to tire of giving of themselves.

"You make it sound like fun," Faith remarked.

"It is. If you want to join us, we can always use more volunteers."

It only took a moment for Faith to say yes. When she got to the church basement and saw the number of people waiting to be served, she was glad she'd agreed to help. It made her feel as if she was repaying some of the kindness that the Carsons had shown her.

By the time the last of the diners had filed through the serving line, Faith's feet and back ached, but the sense of accomplishment she felt made it all worthwhile. While she waited for Avery and Marie to finish the paperwork they needed to take care of before they could leave, she decided to look around.

When she'd first moved in with the Carsons, they'd invited her to attend church services with them on Sunday, but she had declined. Praying silently by herself was one thing; praying with a crowd something altogether different. The thought of going to a religious ceremony and not knowing what to do or whether she even belonged there made her reluctant to accept their offer. Although Avery had said that like any other experience she may have, she could discover that she knew exactly what to do in a church, something stopped her from finding out.

Now, with time to explore without worrying about any people being around, she climbed the steps and went to see if anything looked familiar. She paused at the large double doors leading into the church. She pushed one open and peeked inside. It was empty.

Slowly she entered and ambled down the center aisle, taking in the interior of the church. Nothing about it looked familiar. Not the stained-glass windows filtering the early-afternoon sun, not the rows of wooden pews, nor the altar draped in a white cloth.

She sat down in one of the pews, pulling a red hymnal from the book rack. She opened it, flipping through the pages and glancing at the titles. None of them evoked tunes in her head. She put the book back and sat quietly, her eyes shut, trying to call up any memory at all that would connect her to such a place.

She heard the door open, voices speak softly and the door shut again. When she turned around, there was no one behind her. She got up and walked back toward the entrance. Standing outside were Avery and Marie with several other people.

"We didn't mean to disturb you," Marie apologized.

Faith shook her head. "You didn't. I was just sitting in there. It's very peaceful."

"Yes, it is," Marie agreed. "Faith, I'd like you meet a dear friend of ours, Bishop Foster."

Faith smiled at the gentleman beside Avery. It was a dark-haired woman, however, who extended her hand upon hearing Marie's introduction.

"You're a woman," Faith said, then blushed. "I'm pleased to meet you."

"And I've been wanting to meet you."

She didn't hear what followed because as she shook the bishop's hand, she had a memory flash. She was in a dimly lit room where a woman sat on a bed brushing waist-length hair saying, "You must confess in front of the bishop."

Startled, Faith found herself at a loss for words and was grateful when Avery said, "As much as I enjoy talking to all of you, we need to think about getting home. They say freezing rain is headed this way."

As the small group dispersed, Marie said to Faith, "You weren't expecting the bishop to be a woman, were you?"

She shook her head.

Avery slung his arm around her shoulder and gave her a squeeze. "Don't feel bad. You're not alone in your reaction. The bishop is used to people being surprised."

Faith smiled politely and followed them out to the car, debating whether or not she should tell the Carsons about the flashback she'd had, but something held her back. Maybe it was the feeling of guilt that had washed over her upon remembering that moment. She wondered what she could have done that would cause someone to tell her she needed to repent.

It was a question that was on her mind all the way

home. And she didn't doubt that it would have been in her thoughts the rest of the day had there not been a voice mail message waiting for her when she arrived back at the Carsons. It was from Lori asking her to call as soon as possible. Her voice sounded strained.

Faith immediately dialed Adam's number. Megan was the one who answered.

"Hi, Megan, it's Faith. Can I speak to Lori, please?"

"Hi, Faith. Are you coming over to take care of me? Lori's sick and tired and needs to go to bed," the child blurted out.

Faith frowned. "Can she talk on the phone?"

"I'll check." Faith heard a swoosh as the six-year-old hurried into the other room with the phone. It seemed as if several minutes passed before she heard Lori's voice.

"Faith, hi." She sounded subdued—nothing at all like her usual bubbly self.

"Megan said you're not feeling well. Is everything okay?"

"Everything's fine. I'm just tired. I spent way too much time on my feet yesterday at the boat show and I'm feeling it today. The baby's pressing on everything he can press on."

"I'll come take care of Megan so you can go home and rest," Faith offered.

"Are you sure you don't mind?"

"No, I'd love to do it. I don't have any plans for this afternoon."

"That would be good. What time should I pick you up?"

"You're not picking me up. I want you to stay off your feet. I'll either catch a taxi or have Avery give me a ride. I'll leave as soon as I change my clothes. In the meantime, put Megan back on the phone for a minute, will you?"

Megan's voice came on the line. "Are you coming over, Faith?"

"Yes. Until I get there I want you to do me a favor. Make sure that Lori gets to rest, okay?"

"Okay. Should I make her lunch? I know how to make a peanut butter samwich."

"Maybe you should wait until I get there."

"Okay."

There was one other thing she needed to ask her before she hung up. "Did you talk to your dad this morning before he left?"

"Uh-huh. He wasn't mad that we went outside. He liked our snowman. So did Great-Grandpa. He stayed overnight because he was going to the boat show again today and he didn't want to drive all the way back to his house because it's far away."

"Then it's a good thing he could stay with you and your father."

"He tells funny stories. And he likes to play checkers. Guess how many times I won?"

"You can tell me all about it when I get there. I'm going to hang up now so I can get there as soon as possible, okay?"

"Don't forget to bring an extra pair of mittens so when we play outside your hands won't get cold," Megan said before hanging up.

Faith didn't want to tell her that the forecast was for rain, not snow. From their brief conversation she assumed that Adam either hadn't brought up the subject of her paternity or if he had, he'd managed to keep Megan from connecting Faith to it. By the time she'd changed her clothes, it had already started to rain. As she expected, Avery and Marie insisted they drive her to the Novaks.

When she arrived, she found Megan had done just as she had been told. Lori was stretched out on the sofa, a pillow beneath her head and a lap robe over her. On the coffee table was an assortment of food items including cookies, crackers, red licorice and an apple.

Noticing Faith's eyes on the food, Lori said, "Megan wanted to make sure I wasn't hungry."

"I pulled the curtain so she could rest, but she won't close her eyes," Megan told Faith.

"I couldn't," Lori told her. "I'm too uncomfortable."

"Uncomfortable how?" Faith asked, taking off her jacket.

"My back aches, my side aches, my feet ache…" She sighed. "You don't need to hear me whine. I should go home."

Something told Faith that she shouldn't be alone. "Are you sure you want to leave? It's nasty out there. It's a sort of an ice-and-rain mix."

"I'll be fine," she said with a flap of her hand.

Faith wasn't convinced. "Why don't you stay here until Greg comes home?"

"We'll take good care of you," Megan said, pushing Lori's hair back from her face in the same manner as her aunt had done for her when she'd been in the hospital.

"But I'm not much fun when I feel like this," Lori told her.

"You don't have to entertain us, does she, Megan?"

Megan shook her head. "We're going to go outside."

Faith let that comment slide and looked at Lori. "How about if I make you a cup of tea?"

"I'd like that," Lori said with a grimace.

It was while Faith was heating the kettle on the stove that Greg called to confirm what Faith had already suspected—Lori should stay put because of the weather. Megan and Faith kept her supplied with magazines and food, but she grew restless. She swung her legs down, forcing herself into a sitting position. She placed a hand on her enormous stomach. "I don't know what this kid is doing in there, but he's way too close to my bladder." She stretched out her hand. "Help me up, will you?"

Faith did as she requested and pulled her upright. "The baby looks awfully low."

"You're telling me. I have so much pressure I feel as if he could fall out. That's one of the reasons I've been off my feet as much as possible."

"Your time is getting close."

Lori shook her head. "Not close enough. When I was at the doctor's on Friday he told me it would be at least another week yet." She grimaced as she waddled toward the bathroom.

"You don't look like you're going to make it another week."

"Believe me, today I don't feel like it."

"You're not having contractions, are you?" Faith asked when she saw how slowly she was moving.

"I don't know. I have so much discomfort I'm not sure what it is. I just feel weird."

"Weird how?"

"Like I just peed my pants." She glanced down. "Omigosh. I did pee my pants." She shot a look of panic at Faith.

Faith looked down and saw wet stains down the legs of Lori's slacks. "Your water is leaking."

She stood staring at Faith, as if in shock. Suddenly a rush of water fell onto the hardwood floor and she gasped in horror.

"Correction. Your water broke," Faith said calmly, stepping gingerly around the puddle of water. She took Lori by the arm and turned to Megan. "Run and get me a couple of big towels, would you?" The little girl took off up the stairs.

"Omigosh! Now what do I do?" Lori screeched. "What a mess!"

"I'll clean it up. You go take off those wet clothes." She gave her a gentle shove in the direction of the bathroom, then called out to Megan who was upstairs. "Megan, does your father have a robe Lori could use?"

The six-year-old came hurrying to the top landing carrying a stack of towels. "It's on the door. Should I get it?"

"Yes, please," Faith answered, giving Lori another gentle shove. "I'll take care of the floor. You take care of you."

Lori didn't move, however, but stood watching as Megan handed Faith the towels and began soaking up the water on the floor. "The doctor said the baby wouldn't be born for another week!"

"Looks like the doctor was wrong." Faith quickly cleaned up the mess, drying the floor as best she could. Megan returned with a thick navy-blue velour robe that she gave to her aunt.

"Go change," Faith ordered once more.

This time Lori did as she was told, coming out a few minutes later with Adam's robe draped over her pregnant body. It hung nearly to the floor and held a hint of the woodsy cologne he wore.

"Smile," Faith told her. "You're going to be a mother."

"But I'm not ready," Lori said on the verge of tears.

"Sure you are. Now who are you supposed to call?"

"Oh! Greg!" She looked around frantically. "Where's my phone?"

Faith noticed her purse on the floor and reached for it. "It's probably in here."

Lori dug through the leather shoulder bag mumbling, "I know I didn't leave it at home. I've used it since I've been here."

Faith glanced beyond her to the coffee table and saw the cell phone sitting there. She picked it up and handed it over.

Lori tossed her purse on the sofa and punched the speed dial. Faith listened as Lori told her husband what had happened.

"He's coming home right away to take me to the hospital but I wonder if I shouldn't call an ambulance," she fretted.

"Maybe you should call your doctor first," Faith told her, and watched a nervous Lori fumble with the phone a second time.

During her call to her doctor, some of her anxiety eased. Faith watched the panic slowly be replaced by a desire to do what was best for her baby.

As she snapped the phone shut she said to Faith, "I feel better. The doctor told me I don't need to worry about getting to the hospital as long as I'm not having any labor pains, so I can wait for Greg. She told me to relax and time the contractions when they start."

"Is Greg going to stop at your house and pick up your things?" Faith asked.

Lori rubbed her fingers across her brow. "You're right. He needs to get my stuff. I've got my bag packed." She reached for the phone again.

Faith listened to the harried conversation, noticing that Lori grimaced several times as she spoke to her husband. When she had finished Faith asked her, "Are you in pain?"

"I had a couple of cramps while I was talking to Greg," she answered. She wrinkled her face. "Oooh— there, I had another one."

Just then the Novak phone rang. Faith answered it and took it into the kitchen.

Her heart missed a beat when she heard Adam's voice. "Greg filled me in on what's happening. Is everything all right?"

"Yes. Lori has spoken to her doctor and she's just waiting for Greg to get here." Her heart continued to pump irregularly. "You don't need to worry about Megan. I can stay with her for as long as you need me."

"I appreciate that. You shouldn't have to be there too much longer. We're heading out now."

"You're coming home with Greg?"

"I'm driving him. He's so nervous I don't trust him behind the wheel of a car, especially not in this weather. What does it look like there?"

Faith pushed the curtain aside and glanced out the window. "Icy. It was raining when I came, but it looks like it's freezing on the ground. There's a glaze of ice over everything."

"That's what I was afraid of."

"You think you'll have a problem getting home?"

"No, but it may take us longer than usual. You have my cell phone number. Call me if anything changes, will you?"

"Yes."

He was about to hang up when he added, "I'm glad you're there, Faith."

She stared at the receiver for several moments before hanging up. Then she heard a wail from the other room. She rushed into the living room and found Lori grimacing in pain.

"My back hurts so bad I can't stand it," she cried.

"Turn around and I'll massage it for you," Faith said, hoping to ease her discomfort.

Although she found some relief from the pain, Lori continued to shift from standing to sitting to lying down. When an hour had passed and there still was no sign of Greg and Adam, she began to fret.

"I'll call and see where they are," Faith told her, calling Adam on his cell phone. To Lori's dismay, the two men had made little progress. Poor visibility and ice on the roads forced them to reduce their speed, increasing their driving time.

When Lori grunted and cried out once more in pain, Faith asked, "How far apart are the contractions?"

"They're not apart at all. They're one after another," she said, her face twisting in distress. "Faith, I'm scared. I think I'm having the baby."

Faith put her hand on Lori's stomach to feel the contractions. Lori was right. They were coming one on top of another. She reached for the phone and dialed 9-1-1, requesting immediate medical assistance.

"I thought I was waiting for Greg to take me to the hospital." Fear widened Lori's eyes.

"No, that's not a good idea." Faith dialed Adam's number again. Just as she had done with the 9-1-1 dispatcher, she spoke calmly. "I wanted to let you know that I've called an ambulance to take Lori to the hospital."

Adam didn't question why. It didn't surprise Faith. There was no way he could not hear his sister-in-law's cries in the background. "If the ambulance has as much trouble getting to you as we're having getting home, it'll be a while before it gets there," he warned her.

"Is driving that bad?"

"The roads are glazed ice. We're crawling at speeds under ten miles per hour and we've had to take at least half a dozen detours because of accidents blocking the roads. Faith, are you going to be able to handle things there?"

"Yes," she answered confidently. "Tell Greg everything is under control. I'll call you as soon as the ambulance arrives."

"How bad is it out there?" Lori demanded as soon as she'd hung up.

"We're having an ice storm. I already told you that. It's so typical of March, isn't it? Warm one day, freezing rain the next," she stated nonchalantly, although she was feeling anything but unaffected by the storm.

"Why isn't the ambulance crew here yet?"

"Because we just called them." Faith put a cold cloth on Lori's forehead, then placed her hand on her stomach. Something was telling her the baby was not far from being born. "Lori, where do you think you'd be most comfortable having the baby?"

"I chose a birthing room. They just remodeled the OB wing at the hospital and—"

"No," Faith interrupted her. "I mean, where do you want to have it here? In the house. Do you think you can make it upstairs to one of the spare bedrooms?"

Lori panicked at the realization that she wasn't going to make it to the hospital. "I can't have it here! My doctor's not here! Greg's not even here!"

"You don't need them. You're the one who's going to do all the work and I'm going to be here to catch it. I know how to do this, Lori. You have to trust me."

A strong contraction temporarily halted Lori's panic. When it had passed she said, "I don't think I can walk up the stairs."

"Then we'll do it right here. It's nice and warm with the fire."

It was then that Faith realized Lori wasn't the only one with a look of panic on her face. She turned to Megan and said, "I need you to go upstairs and play in your room for a while. Will you do that for me?"

"But I want to help."

"I think Lori would be more comfortable if you were in your room, wouldn't you?" Faith looked to the other woman, expecting her to agree, but she didn't.

"No, it's all right. If I were in the hospital she'd be able to come into the birthing room." She reached for her niece's hand. "You can be my coach until Greg gets here, okay?"

Megan nodded, her face showing how seriously she took the role.

Faith looked at Lori, then at Megan. "All right. I don't want to leave you alone, but I've got to round up a few things. I'm going to take Megan with me, okay?"

They went first into the kitchen where Faith put two pots of water on the stove to boil. Then they rushed through the house gathering items such as scissors, clean sheets and washcloths. A visit to the medicine cabinet yielded a syringe and a package of sterile gloves.

"We need a couple of clothespins," Faith told Megan as she opened and closed drawers quickly. "Do you think your father has any?"

"He doesn't do the laundry. Jill does."

Jill was the cleaning woman who came once a week. She had her own workroom in the basement. Faith ran downstairs and rummaged through the cabinets of cleaning products but found no clothespins. She did, however, find a metal clamp, which she tucked into her pocket.

Faith knew she had little time and went back up the stairs two at a time. With Megan's help, she set up Lori's birthing area in front of the fireplace. "Megan, come with me and we'll wash our hands," she told the six-year-old.

They soaped up and rinsed off several times before

Faith opened the package containing the sterile gloves and slipped them on. With each item she carried into the living room, she listened for the doorbell to ring announcing the arrival of the paramedics.

Soon she stopped looking at the door and focused on Lori as she prepared for delivery. "Let your body do the work."

"I can't do this. It's too hard," Lori told her, fatigued.

"Yes, you can. It's the hardest pain you'll ever have, but the easiest to forget." The phone rang and Faith instructed Megan to answer it.

She heard the little girl say, "She can't come to the phone. Lori's having the baby!"

"Who was it?" Faith asked.

"It was Uncle Greg. He said they're almost here."

Neither Faith nor Lori had time to comment. The top of the baby's head began to crown. Faith put her fingers on the cap to keep it from coming too quickly. "Stop pushing and pant, Lori."

Lori did as she was told and the baby's head rotated. Faith could see his forehead and then the rest of his face. "One more push, Lori, and you're done."

Lori pushed one more time and the infant's body slid into Faith's hands. She felt as if a jolt of electricity had traveled through her. He started crying right away and she held him up for Lori to see.

Tears of joy spilled onto Lori's cheeks. "He's beautiful. He's so beautiful."

Faith cleaned the fluids out of his nose and mouth with the syringe. Then she took the scissors and cut the umbilical cord. "Hand me that clamp," she told Megan, who did as requested. Faith wrapped Matthew Novak in a yellow terry-cloth towel and gave him to his mother just as the doorbell rang.

Megan ran to open the door and the paramedics came rushing in. Faith gladly stepped aside and allowed them to take over. Following on their heels were Adam, Greg and a gray-haired gentleman.

Within minutes Lori, the baby and Greg were in the ambulance on their way to the hospital. Faith began to dismantle her makeshift delivery room.

"Lori peed on the floor," Megan told her father as he surveyed the living room.

"No, she didn't," Faith corrected her. "Her water broke. I wiped it up."

"She puked one time, too."

"Not on the floor," Faith inserted.

"I never expected my nephew would be able to say he was born in my living room," Adam said with a be-mused shake of his head. "The paramedics said you did the right thing, Faith."

"Yeah, I know. They told me that, too. I really didn't do much of anything though. Lori was the one who did all the work."

"We just caught the baby, didn't we, Faith?" Megan boasted.

"Megan saw the whole thing?" Adam asked.

Megan nodded, wide-eyed. "You should have seen it! First the head came out, then the shoulders, then the belly and finally the tiny little feet. He was all full of gooey stuff," she said, wrinkling her face. "And he had stuff in his nose that Faith had to suck out with a—"

Adam held up a hand. "It's all right. I get the picture."
He bent down to pick up the pillows from the floor.
"How about helping put some of this stuff away?"

"All right."

"We'll launder these right away," Faith told him,
gathering up the linens. She cast a glance at Megan that
told her she expected her help.

"Just put them in the laundry room. I have a cleaning woman who will do it," Adam told her.

"It's better if we launder them right away," she advised him. "Otherwise the stains will set."

"Listen to the young lady." The gray-haired gentleman who'd been standing off to one side came forward.
He extended his hand to Faith and gave her a grin. "You
must be Faith the Fantastic. I'm Megan's grandfather...or I guess I should say great-grandfather."

Faith took the wrinkled hand in her grasp, surprised
by the firmness of his handshake.

"I've been hearing all kinds of good things about you
from this little one here." He tugged on Megan's braid
with his left hand. He looked at Adam and added, "As
well as from a few of the grown-ups in this family, too."

"It's nice to meet you," Faith said. "Megan has been
saying nice things about you, too."

"Megan, why don't you and Grandpa go into the den
and play a game while Faith and I clean up?" Adam
suggested.

Not wanting to be alone with Adam, Faith was
tempted to ask if Megan could help her, but she didn't
want to deprive Adam's grandfather of time with his
great-granddaughter simply because she was worried

Adam would mention what had happened last night when he'd taken her home. To her relief, he said nothing about the kiss, but went about helping her pick up the living room.

After they finished gathering the soiled linens, Adam led the way down the stairs to the brightly lit laundry room. He opened one of the wall cabinets and pulled out a bottle of detergent. He punched a couple of buttons on the washer, dumped a capful of detergent into the machine and took the sheets from her hands. He stuffed them into the washing machine, then closed the lid.

"I do know how to launder sheets if necessary," he told her, standing far too close to her for comfort. He looked down at her blouse. "You should probably wash that, too."

She glanced down and saw blood stains on the sleeves.

"I have a shirt you can borrow," he offered.

"It's all right. I'll wash it as soon as I get home."

"That might not be for a while. I feel very fortunate to have made it home without smashing up my car. I would prefer not to leave again until I know that I'm not going to slide through every intersection I approach."

"But the ambulance…"

"Had a newborn and a mother who needed medical attention. They'll get through."

Faith took a tentative step toward the door. "I can probably catch a bus."

"Be my guest. I don't think you'll get past my driveway without falling. As I said, it was a miracle Greg and I even made it here. The highway department is advising no travel until sanding crews have been able to get out, and until it stops raining ice, they won't be doing that."

She shoved her hands to her hips. "Are you saying you think I should spend the night here?"

"Would that be so horrible?"

Horrible, no. Uncomfortable, yes. She had no change of clothes, no personal care items. And every time he looked at her she felt as if she had Jell-O for legs. And then there was the matter of the kiss—a kiss they still hadn't acknowledged today. She hadn't forgotten and by the look in his eyes, he hadn't, either.

"I have two guest bedrooms and a six-year-old daughter," he told her, as if he could read her mind.

She blushed.

"Every time you do that I want to kiss you," he said, enjoying her discomfort.

"Well, don't." She had to step around him to get to the door and by the mischievous look on his face she had a feeling he was going to extract a price for her exit. "We should go back upstairs."

"In a minute. I want to thank you for being here for my family," he said with a sincerity that darkened his eyes. "You did a remarkable thing and you did it right."

"I'm not sure how I knew what to do," she admitted.

"Maybe you're a nurse."

She shrugged. "I don't know. When I saw Lori having those contractions, I knew what I had to do."

"Well, it's a good thing it was you here and not me. I'm not sure I would have been as calm as you were about the whole thing. So thank you."

He leaned toward her and Faith had a feeling he was

going to kiss her, but Megan's voice called out to them. "Hey, I'm up here with Great-Grandpa. Did you guys forget us?"

"We'll be right there," Adam called back. "So should I bring you a shirt?"

"I don't really have much choice, do I?"

"No." The grin he gave her was one of satisfaction.

CHAPTER TEN

As ADAM SAT at his desk, savory aromas drifted into his office. He tried to ignore them, but he knew their source and couldn't resist the temptation to see what Faith was up to in the kitchen. He'd offered to put a couple of frozen pizzas in the oven but she'd insisted on making dinner for the four of them. Now she and Megan stood side by side working together and singing some silly little song about oats.

Because her clothes were in the wash, Faith had borrowed one of his white dress shirts and a pair of his burgundy silk pajama bottoms. She'd rolled up the sleeves on the shirt and the cuffs on the pajamas, but they still made her look as if she were a child playing dress up with an adult's clothes. What amazed him was that without any effort on her part at all she could look so sexy.

"I'll do the cucumber," Megan announced from her perch on the step stool.

Adam expected Faith to give her an easier chore, but to his surprise, she simply handed her the vegetable peeler. Megan beamed a smile in her direction and began to skin the cucumber to another song he didn't recognize.

When Faith noticed him standing outside the doorway she said, "I thought you said you had work to do?"

He shoved his hands into his pockets. "Just checking to see if you need anything."

"No, we're fine." She turned to Megan, "Aren't we?"

Megan gave a cheerful "Yup" and resumed her singing.

Adam nodded and went back to his desk, but he had difficulty concentrating. He couldn't stop thinking about Faith. Instead of looking at diagrams on his laptop he wanted to be watching her move about the kitchen. Actually he wanted to do more than watch her, and after last night, that urge was greater than ever.

He was grateful when one of the Novak sales reps called and he was forced to turn his attention to business matters. By the time he'd finished the conversation, Megan was at his office door.

"Faith said to tell you to come now. Dinner's ready."

"Did you tell Great-Grandpa?"

"Yup," she said then skipped away.

When Adam walked into the kitchen there were four place settings on the table, but enough food to feed twice as many people.

His grandfather must have thought the same thing because when he strolled in he said, "What a spread!" He nudged Adam with an elbow. "Looks like your little lady knows how to do a proper Sunday dinner, linen tablecloth and all."

Adam wished his grandfather wouldn't refer to Faith as his little lady. She was hardly small and she certainly wasn't his.

"Faith is teaching me how to cook!" Megan boasted. "I peeled the cucumbers by myself."

His grandfather eyed the vegetables appreciatively. "That's exactly how I like them. In cream. It's how your great-grandmother served them. She could have easily set this table." His eyes took in the mashed potatoes and gravy, the bread, the platter of chicken and the assortment of salads and vegetables and he sighed appreciatively. "Now there was woman who could cook. She could get me to eat anything—even creamed celery."

"Ah, the wedding food," Faith stated with a knowing smile.

"Why is it a wedding food?" Megan asked.

Faith lifted her eyebrows. "I don't know. It just is."

As soon as everyone was seated and had filled their plates, Adam's grandfather picked up his fork. He was about to begin eating when Megan stopped him.

"Patties down, Great-Grandpa!" she admonished him.

When he gave her a puzzled look Adam said, "Megan, you need to tell Great-Grandpa what 'patties' down means."

"Put your hands in your lap away from your food, bow your head, close your eyes and thank God for the good food. Privately." She held her finger to her lips.

His grandfather set down his fork. "Forgive my manners, but it's been a while since I dined with company at a Sunday dinner table."

Adam could say the same thing. He usually worked at home on weekends, squeezing meals in between projects. Unless Lori invited him and Megan over for dinner, they either ate frozen foods he'd zap in the microwave or had something delivered from one of the local restaurants.

Like his grandfather, however, he hadn't forgotten the Sunday afternoons he'd spent at his grandmother's house as a child. They were some of his fondest memories of his youth. It was true his grandmother had been a good cook, but it wasn't the food that had drawn him there. It was knowing that after dinner his grandfather would take him into his shop and show him the latest boat he was designing.

"Well, ladies. This is very good," his grandfather said, lifting his fork in appreciation.

Megan beamed and Faith simply murmured a polite "Thank you."

Then his grandfather turned to Adam and said, "If you were smart, you'd snap her up." He used his knife to point in Faith's direction. "It's about time you got one that could cook. That last one thought mashed potatoes only came out of a box."

Confused, Megan asked, "What last one?"

Adam cringed. He should have known that his grandfather would either say something about a past girlfriend or hint that Faith should be his current one. He'd managed to do both.

"Grandpa's referring to a friend of mine," he said smoothly, not missing the spark of amusement in Faith's eyes. He decided a change of subject was in order. "If Lori wants company we'll go visit your new cousin tomorrow."

"At the hospital?" Megan wanted to know. "Can I miss school?"

"No, we'll go after you get home from school," he told her.

"But I don't want to wait." She sighed and leaned her chin on her hand. "Why do I have to go to school anyway?"

"So you can learn the three R's—reading, writing and 'rithmetic," his grandfather said with a grin.

"Faith can teach me numbers and she reads to me, too," Megan told him.

Faith, who had been silent, spoke up. "That's true, but school is where you learn to cooperate with others."

Megan wrinkled her nose. "What's cooperate?"

"To get along with other people. That's why you need the other scholars so you can learn how to work together," she answered.

"What's a scholar?" Megan asked.

"I think Faith means a student, don't you?" Adam glanced in her direction.

"Yes."

He thought it unusual that she would refer to elementary school students as scholars and wondered if it wasn't another indication that she wasn't from the Twin Cities area. From the first day she'd spoken to him he'd noticed her language seemed a bit formal at times. There was also a hint of an accent that he'd been unsuccessful at identifying.

It wasn't Faith, however, who did most of the talking at dinner, but Megan. She took great pleasure in entertaining her great-grandfather with stories of her hospital stay. Adam didn't mind because it kept the conversation from dissolving into a discussion of his personal life—a subject dear to the old man's heart.

He thought he was going to be spared comments about his love life, but then Faith served dessert. When she placed the apple dumpling in front of Robert Novak, his eyes lit up.

"You must be a mind reader," he said with an ear-to-ear grin. "This is another favorite of mine. Faith, you are one special lady, and if this big feller here—" he jerked his head in Adam's direction "—can't see that, then he deserves to eat his food out of a box."

Adam glanced at Megan who was engrossed with dipping her fingers in the whipped cream on her dumpling and wasn't paying attention to what her great-grandfather was saying. Faith, he could see, understood the implication of his words, a mischievous light sparkling in her eyes.

"I believe he likes eating out of a box," she said, giving Adam a look that said they shared a secret and it wasn't about food.

"Ah, he won't live long," his grandfather said in between bites of his apple dumpling. "Single men don't make it as long as the married ones. It's why I've been thinking I should get back out there in the game."

"What game?" Megan asked.

"The game of having fun," Robert said with a wink.

Adam chose to remain silent, knowing that anything he might say would more than likely encourage his grandfather to talk about his single status—a subject he didn't want to discuss in front of Faith or his daughter. Fortunately Megan's thoughts were on her new baby cousin and they finished dinner without any further reference to his love life.

He knew, however, that sooner or later, his grandfather would want to give him his advice on women because his grandfather *always* gave him advice on women. That's why Adam wasn't surprised when after dinner his grandfather suggested the two of them have a brandy in the living room.

The first thing he said to Adam as he settled himself in one of the large leather chairs was "Take the advice of an old man who knows what's important in life. That little lady in the kitchen is one heck of a gal. You let her get away and you're going to have missed out on something special."

"Grandpa, she's an employee," he told him, pouring brandy into two glasses.

Robert Novak brushed away Adam's comment with a wave of his wrinkled hand. "I don't want to hear any excuses. You always manage to find something wrong with every girl you date. I'm telling you. This one is special."

"And you know all of this after only one hour of dinner conversation and one of her apple dumplings?" Adam teased.

"Go ahead and snicker all you want, but I'm telling you, she's made of good stuff. You forget. I spent all day yesterday with Lori. I know more about that little lady in the kitchen than you think I do."

Adam handed him a snifter of brandy. "Here. To another prosperous year at the factory." He lifted his glass to his grandfather's.

"I'll second that." After a sip he said, "Megan's talking more."

Adam nodded. "I think she's feeling more comfortable here." He swirled the brandy in his glass. "I'm thinking maybe I should bring her to the factory…you know, show her what we do there."

"You started coming along with me when you were smaller than she is," he reminded him.

"I know. She might not be interested—" he began, but his grandfather cut him off.

"Oh, she'll be interested. And it'll be good for her to see where you work."

He smiled. "So I've been told." He didn't tell his grandfather that it was Faith who'd put the idea in his head. Although she'd suggested he show Megan work around the house, Adam wanted to show her the work he loved.

"Now tell me what you thought of that folding catamaran we saw at the boat show."

If there was one subject that was dear to both of their hearts, it was boats, and they spent the rest of the evening talking about them. Adam discovered, however, that he couldn't put Faith totally out of his mind. An occasional noise in the kitchen would remind him that she was out there in his shirt and pajama bottoms.

As much as he hated to admit it, all evening long he'd been thinking thoughts similar to his grandfather's. She was one fine woman. So fine that not even the possibility that she could have a husband and kids waiting for her could keep him from wanting her.

When he'd invited her to stay the night he hadn't realized how difficult it would be to have her only a couple of doors down the hallway from his bedroom. Even though he worked until after midnight, sleep eluded him when he went to bed. Every time he closed his eyes he imagined what she must look like lying in bed, her blond hair fanning across her cheek. He wondered if she was tossing and turning, trying not to think about him as he was trying not to think about her?

He eventually did fall asleep only to be awakened by the sound of a woman's scream. He jumped out of bed and reached for his robe; only, it wasn't behind the door. Wearing only a pair of silk pajama bottoms, he crossed the hall to the bedroom where Faith slept and knocked on the door.

"Faith, are you all right?" he called out in a voice that was just barely above a whisper.

It was several moments before he heard a muffled "yes."

"Are you sure?" When she didn't answer he was tempted to open the door, but she did it for him. Just as he was about to knock another time it flew open and she was there, wearing only the shirt he'd given her earlier in the evening. It was the first time he'd seen her legs bare and he saw how shapely they were. She stood trembling, her arms wrapped around her midsection.

"What happened?"

"I had a dream. I'm sorry if I disturbed you," she said quietly.

"Was it about your past?"

She shrugged. "I'm not sure. I hope it wasn't." She rubbed her arms, as if to ward off a chill. A lone tear rolled down her cheek and then another.

"Faith, why are you crying?" he asked, fighting the urge to take her in his arms.

"Because I'm tired of being alone," she said, turning away from him.

He gently wrapped his arms around her and pulled her back toward him. "You're not alone, Faith."

"Yes, I am. I don't fit in anywhere." She quietly sobbed against his shoulder.

"You fit in with us…with me and Megan and Lori and Greg." He stroked her hair, trying to comfort her.

"I don't belong here," she said between sobs, "but I don't belong there, either."

"Where is there, Faith?"

"It's someplace awful."

"Why do you say that? Is it because of your dream?"

With her face pressed close to his shoulder, he could feel the warmth of her breath on his bare skin. When she didn't answer him, he lifted her chin with his finger and forced her to look at him. "Talk to me, Faith. Tell me why you're still trembling even though you're awake."

She straightened and he saw her blue eyes were glossy with tears and saw her pulse was throbbing at her temple. "The doctors say that sometimes memory loss can occur because a person doesn't want to face the past."

"Yes, and you've been through a trauma. You were assaulted and left on the roadside. It's no wonder your mind doesn't want to remember the details." A wave of repulsion echoed through him at the thought of what someone had done to her.

She shook her head. "I'm not having dreams about that night."

"What are you dreaming about?"

She bit down on her lower lip. "A place that's dark, where there are angry voices."

"Whose voices are they?"

"I don't know. While I'm dreaming I see things so clearly, yet when I wake, all I have is this horrible feeling that I can never go back to wherever it was I came from."

"It could be your fear of not finding your memories, Faith."

"I don't think so. It feels too real. The few words I do remember from those dreams are always the same. It's a man's voice saying, 'Get out and don't come back.'" She shuddered as she said them.

"I can't imagine any man ever saying those words to you. You're a good person, Faith. Anyone who spends even a few minutes with you can see that. You're kind and compassionate. I can't believe you would ever do anything that would warrant such words to be said to you."

Again she turned away from him. "You don't know me."

"Yes, I do," he argued. "I may not know your past, but I know what kind of person you are. You couldn't hurt anyone."

Her silence told him she wasn't convinced of that. He wanted to pull her back into his arms, but he could see by the tightness of her shoulders she wouldn't welcome his touch.

"You're tired. Why don't I get you some warm milk?" he suggested, wanting to take care of her.

"I can get it."

"No. You wait here." Seeing that she still trembled, he pulled the down comforter from the bed and gently draped it around her unsteady body.

"I'll be right back," he told her before hurrying downstairs where he heated a mug of milk in the microwave.

When he returned to her room she was sitting on the edge of the bed in the soft glow of the bedside lamp. With her tousled hair and troubled eyes, she looked hauntingly beautiful. He handed her the mug and watched her take a sip.

"Thank you. I think I will be all right now," she told him, avoiding his gaze.

"You sure?"

"Yes." She kept her eyes downcast. "You shouldn't be in here. It's not proper," she stated primly.

"We're not doing anything but talking," he said, amused by her modesty. Usually when a woman told him he shouldn't be in her bedroom it was to be provocative, not principled.

Silence stretched between them as she sipped the milk. When she'd finished, she looked up at him over the rim of the mug. "Thank you. That was *gut*."

It was the second time he'd heard her use the German word for good. "Do you realize that you just said *gut* instead of good?"

She hadn't. It was apparent by the look on her face. Nor did she seem to care that she'd used it. She was more interested in getting him out of her room. "You should go now. I'm fine." She set the mug down on her nightstand and tightened the comforter around her, avoiding his eyes.

"Okay, I'll go," he conceded, although it was the last thing he wanted to do. "You sure you're going to be all right?"

"Yes, I'm fine, thank you."

"Good." He stood there staring at her, watching her eyes study the pattern on the comforter rather than look at him. He wanted to see those eyes. He put a finger beneath her chin, and when she looked up at him, he saw what she'd been trying to conceal. Desire.

He leaned over to brush his lips over hers. She tasted of warm milk. His intention was to give her a quick kiss then leave, but the soft warmth of her mouth was far too tempting. Their mouths met in a series of kisses that resembled two dancers learning to tango. Back and forth, touching and releasing, becoming more passionate as the music played on.

Only there was no music, just the beating of their hearts and the sounds of expectation and satisfaction. A sigh here, a moan there. When he slipped his hand inside the down comforter she pushed him away.

"We shouldn't…." she said breathlessly.

Even though her words said one thing, the look on her face said another. She wanted him as much as he wanted her. It was there in her eyes.

"I'm sorry—" she began, but he silenced her.

"You have nothing to be sorry about," he said, dropping down onto the bed beside her.

"It's just that I'm not sure this is right."

He could have told her that her body had responded as if it was, but he didn't want to make her uncomfortable. Instead he said, "We're two adults, Faith."

"I'm also a woman who has no idea who she is or what's in her past," she reminded him.

Which was her way of saying she didn't know if she

was free to pursue a relationship with him. "You're worried there could be a man in your past?"

"It's possible."

He shrugged. "I can't argue with that, but there's also a chance that there isn't one."

He didn't want to admit that the former was probably more likely than the latter. She was beautiful inside and out, possessing a tranquil attraction that made people want to be around her. How could there not be a man in her life? She was, as his grandfather had said, something special.

"But until I know…" She left the rest of her sentence unsaid.

Adam knew what it meant. Until she was certain she didn't have someone waiting for her, she didn't feel she had the right to get involved with him. "You don't want to do anything that might hurt someone."

She nodded.

"Then I'd better go," he said, and rose to his feet.

THE AROMA of freshly brewed coffee greeted Adam when he walked into the kitchen the following morning. It wasn't the only sign that Faith was already at work. A light glowed in the oven. When he glanced inside, he saw a coffee cake baking on the middle rack. Faith, however, was nowhere to be seen.

He knew she wasn't in her room because he'd passed it on his way to the kitchen. He made a quick survey of the first floor but it was empty. Then he noticed a light in the stairway going down to the laundry room.

A few seconds later he heard footsteps on the stairs

and Faith appeared. In place of his white shirt and pajama bottoms were the pink blouse and dark pants he'd seen her in yesterday except the stains from delivering Lori's baby were gone. Hair that had swung loosely about her shoulders was pulled back and secured with a clip. Today she looked like Megan's nanny rather than the woman who'd cried on his shoulder last night, and he felt a pang of regret.

When she saw him, she said good morning and blushed.

"It certainly is," he said, thinking how nice it was to wake up and find her in his house.

"What would you like for breakfast? Pancakes? Eggs?"

She was all business and he wondered if that was to make sure he understood just what their relationship was.

"You don't need to cook for me this morning," he told her.

"Yes, I do. It's my job."

"Says who? Lori?"

"When she hired me she said I was to fill in for her. Coffee?" She reached for a mug from the shelf.

He took the mug from her hand. "What you've been doing here the past two days is not filling in for Lori."

She mistook his comment as a criticism. "You're not satisfied with my work?"

"Yes, I'm very satisfied, but you were hired to be Megan's nanny, not the housekeeper."

She shoved her hands to her hips. "You're complaining because I'm doing too much work?"

"I'm not complaining exactly," he argued, although he really was. It bothered him to see her doing chores around his house because he didn't want her to be his housekeeper. He wanted her to be his girlfriend.

"It sounds to me like complaining." She turned away from him to open a cupboard and pull out a pan. When she saw him eyeing the cooking utensil she said cheekily, "For Megan's pancakes. You do allow nannies to cook for children, yes?"

There was an impish light in her eye which he found intriguing. He had seen hints of this side of her personality before, but the thought of discovering more was a tempting one. Before he could respond, however, Megan came bouncing into the kitchen in her nightgown. Her left hand supported her right elbow, her hand in the air. Around one of her fingers was a piece of plastic that looked as if it were some kind of bandage.

"What's with your finger?" he asked her.

"Faith is getting rid of my sliver," she answered. She thrust her hand in front of the two of them. "Do you think it's done?"

"It should be," Faith answered. "Bring it over to the sink and we'll see." Megan did as she was told, setting her hand on the counter for Faith's appraisal. She watched as Faith unwrapped the plastic from her index finger revealing a sandy-colored soggy mass.

Adam grimaced. "What is that?"

"It's bread and milk," Megan answered as Faith carefully removed the wad and tossed it into the garbage. "Faith put it on last night before I went to bed."

"You slept with that on your finger?"

"Uh-huh. I had to. It hurt real bad."

Faith ran Megan's finger under the faucet before

holding it up to the morning sunlight streaming in through the window. "I think it's gone," she said as she examined it closely. "What do you think?"

Megan looked at her finger, gingerly pressing on the tip. Her eyes widened. "It *is* gone! It doesn't hurt anymore! Thanks!"

"Works every time," she said with a grin.

"I've got to go tell Great-Grandpa. He didn't believe me when I told him bread takes away slivers." She went racing out of the kitchen.

Faith called after her, "Don't take too long. You need to get dressed so you're not late for school."

"Did she really have a sliver?" Adam asked.

"Yes. You don't remove them by soaking your finger overnight?"

"Ah…no. I usually use a needle and a pair of tweezers," he told her.

"It's less painful to soak it. All that jabbing and picking…" She shuddered and he had to suppress a smile. She'd just helped deliver a baby yet the thought of a tender finger could bring a chill.

When she pulled the eggs and milk from the refrigerator Adam said, "Megan usually just has a bowl of cereal in the morning."

She paid no attention, tying an apron around her waist before getting started on the pancake batter. "She asked me if I'd make her pancakes today. Are you sure you won't have some? You can serve yourself," she said with a playful grin that made him want to pull her into his arms and kiss her.

"I'll leave the pancakes to my grandfather and my

daughter," he told her, watching her whisk the eggs in a large bowl.

"Suit yourself." As she measured the ingredients into the bowl, she said over her shoulder, "I need you to tell me what you want me to do."

"About what?"

"Megan's care. Now that Lori's had the baby, will you want me to come directly here in the morning?"

He wished she never had to go home at night, but didn't voice that sentiment aloud. "There's no reason why you have to be here when she's at school. Lori's probably going to need your help during that time. You're familiar with Megan's school routine—I take her in the morning and Lori picks her up in the afternoon?"

"Yes, but there's a problem. I can't drive."

"That's something I'm going to check into. I'll call the Department of Motor Vehicles to see what you need to do to get your driver's license replaced. You may have to retake the driver's exam but it would be worth it. I have a second car in the garage you could use," he suggested.

"You have two cars?" She looked at him as if it was a luxury few people shared.

"It's a convertible that I mainly use in the summer, but there's no reason why it can't be driven in the winter."

"But I'm not sure I know how to drive a car."

He frowned. He was thirty years old and the only adult women he knew who didn't drive were of his grandfather's generation. "That seems unlikely. Have you tried driving?" When she shook her head he said, "I'll tell you what. After all the Novak employees have gone home for the day, I'll take you to the factory parking lot and we'll see how you do."

"But what about the slippery roads?" Alarm flashed in her eyes.

"It's warmed up enough that yesterday's ice is no longer a problem," he told her. "Novak Boats has a big parking lot. It's a good place to practice because you won't have to worry about running into anything if you find out you're not familiar with the controls. We can do it this evening if you can stay an extra hour or so?"

She looked apprehensive. "Even if I do know how to drive, maybe it's been a long time since I've practiced."

"That's all right. I believe it's like riding a bike— once you learn, you don't forget," he said. "You'll quickly get the hang of it again."

"And if I haven't ever learned?"

"Then I'll have to give you lessons. In the meantime, I'll make sure that Megan gets to and from school this week. Since Lori is still in the hospital you might as well take this morning off. Would you like a ride back to the Carsons'?"

"No, that's not necessary."

He thought about arguing with her but knew it would more than likely do no good. When she poured the pancake batter into the frying pan, he heard a sigh of satisfaction.

"Don't you need a recipe for those things?" he asked, realized she'd made the batter without the help of a mix.

"I guess one thing I haven't forgotten is how to make pancakes," she answered.

She hadn't forgotten quite a few things. Like how to

make puppets out of handkerchiefs and how to remove slivers from fingers. Using a poultice of bread and milk might not be folklore remedy, but it was another piece of information about Faith he found intriguing.

After feeding both his grandfather and his daughter, she restored the kitchen to the same pristine appearance it had been in last night when he went to bed. It was the first morning since Megan had come to live with him that Adam didn't feel as if they were racing the clock to get out the door on time.

When Megan turned on the television to catch a few minutes of an animated children's program, Faith deliberately turned it off again saying, "You have no time for TV this morning. *Es ist Zeit zu gehen,*" then hurried to the entry closet where she pulled out her coat.

Adam looked at his daughter. "What did she just say?"

"That I have no time to watch my show," Megan answered, lugging her backpack behind her.

"No, after that."

"I don't know. She says things that don't make sense sometimes."

Because she was speaking a foreign language. He walked over to her. "Faith, what did you just say to Megan in there?" He jerked a thumb toward the living room.

"I told her she couldn't watch television because it's time to go."

"You said that in English?"

She gave him a puzzled look. "What did you think I said?"

"I'm not sure."

He would have said more, but his grandfather came

toward them saying, "Time's a-wasting. Are we going
to leave or aren't we?"

Adam had no choice but to postpone any further conversation on the possibility of Faith being bilingual. It
was just one more thing to add to the growing list of ob-
servations he hoped would someday help solve the mystery of her identification.

CHAPTER ELEVEN

"IS THAT ALL he does—sleep?" Megan asked as she gazed at her cousin swaddled in a blue blanket in the bassinet next to Lori's hospital bed.

Lori smiled. "I think he has his days and nights mixed up. He was awake last night and has been sleeping most of today."

"Better get that switched around before you leave this place," Adam warned his brother with a grin.

"Oh, we will," Greg assured him.

"He has a dent in his chin," Megan pointed out.

"That's called a dimple. Uncle Greg has one in his chin, too."

Adam didn't miss the way Megan's eyes went from Matthew's chin to her uncle's.

Lori reached over to carefully lift the baby out of the bassinet. "Let's see if we can get him to wake up." She tickled his cheek with her finger, gently calling his name, and his tiny mouth began to move.

Megan leaned forward to get a closer look. "Does he have any hair?" she asked as Lori tried to coax the baby awake.

"Yes. It's blond, just like yours. See?" She removed the tiny blue knit cap from his head, revealing what

Adam thought looked like peach fuzz. "You probably didn't notice it yesterday because it was all wet from his birth."

Adam saw Megan look from Lori to Greg and then back to the baby. "How come his hair's not brown like yours and Greg's?" she wanted to know.

"I guess because he's a Novak," Lori answered. "Your dad and Uncle Greg both had blond hair when they were born."

Skepticism furrowed her brow. "They did?"

"Mmm-hmm. Haven't you seen any pictures of them when they were babies?" she asked, and Megan shook her head.

Adam wasn't sure that a photo would convince his daughter that he was her biological parent, but he did see this as an opportunity to reaffirm that he was her father. "Not every kid has the same color hair as his mom and dad," he pointed out.

"And hair color can change," Lori added, unaware of her niece's doubts about Adam. "Sometimes babies start with one color and end up with another."

"Yeah, so don't be surprised if one day you wake up and you're staring at a brown head," Greg said with a grin.

"Or you might always be a blonde—like your mom was," Lori told her.

Adam could see that while the talk turned to other topics common to newborns, Megan continued to compare the newest member of the family to his parents. When she continued to ask questions about him on the way home from the hospital, he decided to stop at an ice-cream shop and set the record straight.

After ordering each of them an ice-cream cone, he sat down across from her in a small booth with leather padded seats and contemplated a way to bring up the subject. She gave him the opening he needed when she said, "Lori said new baby girls get little pink hats at the hospital. Do you think I had one when I was born?"

"I don't know," Adam answered honestly. "I wasn't at the hospital. Do you know why I wasn't there?"

She shook her head, then her tongue snaked out to lick the cone.

"I didn't know you were born," he said quietly.

"Because you were in heaven?" she asked in between licks.

"No. I was never in heaven, Megan. We've talked about this before. People don't come back from heaven once they go there. You believe that, right?"

"Yes," she said on a sigh. "But I wish they could."

"It would make it easier, wouldn't it," he said in understanding.

"Uh-huh."

"Megan, if someone had told me you were born, I would have been at the hospital. I would have been like Uncle Greg, studying your little face and trying to see what part of me you inherited."

She didn't say anything, but kept licking her ice-cream cone. He knew that he needed to get to the heart of the matter.

"When the lawyer contacted me and said your mother had died and that I was your father, I wasn't sure it was true. I thought maybe there had been a mistake."

She paused in licking her cone to stare at him. "Maybe it was a mistake," she said in a tiny, uncertain voice.

"No, it wasn't," he stated firmly. "Do you know how I know that it wasn't?" When she shook her head he said, "Because I did a DNA test."

"Like the one Faith took?"

"Yes, only mine came back positive. You and I are a match. That test proved it. I am your father," he said emphatically. "That's why the judge said you had to come live with me instead of your uncle Tom. And you know what? I'm really glad he did because I wanted you to be my daughter."

"Even if it means you're never going to get married?"

He frowned. "Why can't I get married if I have a daughter?"

"When Erica was baby-sitting me I heard her talking on the phone and she said you'd soon find out that no woman wants to marry a guy who already has a kid."

Adam groaned inwardly, wishing he had listened to Lori when she'd advised him about letting an ex-girlfriend baby-sit Megan. "Well, Erica's wrong—just like your mother was wrong when she thought I was in heaven."

Her eyes widened and she pointed to his ice cream, which was melting down over the edges of his napkin. "You'd better lick fast or you're going to lose it."

Adam did as she suggested. When he'd eaten enough that ice cream no longer ran down the edges, he asked, "Just out of curiosity, would you like me to get married?"

"Yes, but Great-Grandpa says I shouldn't hold my breath waiting because you wouldn't know a good woman if she jumped up and bit you in the face," she said in a tone that sounded very much like the Novak patriarch.

Adam chuckled and said, "Don't be so sure of that," then finished his cone.

FAITH KNEW THAT HAVING a driver's license would make her job easier. If she wanted to continue as Megan's nanny and help Lori with the new baby, she needed to be able to pick up Megan after school. Until Adam had suggested she use one of his cars, she hadn't thought about whether or not she knew how to drive. Ever since she'd moved in with the Carsons she'd either taken the bus to work or relied on Avery or Marie to give her a ride.

Because she'd met few adults who didn't drive, Faith assumed that she probably had a license, but without a name, it was impossible to know from which state it had been issued. However, once she climbed into the driver's seat of Adam's Lexus, she discovered she didn't know the first thing about operating a motor vehicle.

True to his word, Adam had taken her to the Novak factory parking lot for a test drive. He'd pressed a button, magically moving her leather seat forward so she could more easily touch the foot pedals of the luxurious SUV. Next he'd adjusted the rearview mirror and pointed out the location of the strategic controls. Brake pedal, gas pedal, shift knob, turn signal.

She'd listened intently to his instructions, keeping her left hand on the steering wheel while she used her right one to shift the vehicle into Drive. Carefully, she'd moved her foot from the brake to the gas pedal and had slowly pressed it toward the floor.

Unfortunately it hadn't been slow enough. The car had shot forward at an alarming speed that had Adam screaming, "Hit the brakes." It had taken her a moment to realize that by brakes he meant the brake pedal. During that moment the Lexus had come dangerously close to hitting a lamppost, prompting him to bark out a second command, "Turn the steering wheel!"

The vehicle had spun around and come to a screeching halt without hitting anything. Stunned, she'd managed to say in a breathless voice, "I don't think I've done this before."

"Obviously not," was all he had said before trading places with her.

He'd been so quiet on the way home that she'd thought he was angry with her, but when she'd apologized for nearly smashing up his car, he'd simply said, "No damage was done and at least now we know you need lessons."

Only she had soon learned that it wasn't simply a matter of Adam teaching her how to drive. In order to get a learner's permit she needed identification or proof of residency. Without a clue as to her past, she had no documentation that would satisfy the Department of Motor Vehicles regulations. She'd hit a roadblock.

Even though she couldn't get her driver's license, Adam had brought home an instruction manual, telling her that he wanted her to be prepared for the day when there would be no obstacles in the way. "You can get to know your car even if you can't get behind the wheel," he'd said with a gleam in his eye. She'd known that he wasn't only talking about driving.

There was no point in pretending they weren't attracted to one another. She couldn't think about him without her heart missing a beat, or be in the same room with him without her body aching with awareness. She knew that he was as affected by her presence as she was by his. It was there in his eyes whenever he looked at her and in his voice whenever he spoke to her.

The feelings he aroused in her felt new, causing her to wonder if she had ever been in love before or if it simply felt like the first time because she had no memory of past relationships. Because she could remember the knowledge she'd gained and was able to perform activities she'd learned in her past, she didn't understand why she should feel like such a novice when it came to kissing, unless she'd had little experience doing it. When Adam had pressed his mouth to hers, she'd felt totally unprepared for the emotions that took over. Yet kissing was like driving. How could she not have any experience when it seemed as if every other adult woman around her knew what to do?

They were questions she doubted she would find an answer to until she found the key that unlocked her past. Until she did, she knew it would be wise to avoid spending any time alone with Adam. Because even though her brain told her it would be foolish to think of him as anything other than Megan's father, she wanted him to teach her about more than just driving.

"DO YOU HAVE PLANS for Saturday night?" Greg asked, poking his head inside Adam's office at Novak Boats.

"Yeah. Dinner and a movie," he said, leaning back in his chair and stretching his arms behind his head.

"Are you and Naomi back together?"

He chuckled. "Hardly. Ever since I had to cut short my Miami trip she's refused to talk to me."

"So who are you seeing?"

"I didn't say I had a date. That's me fixing dinner for Megan and the movie will be some children's flick. If anyone tries to tell you that men with children are babe magnets, don't believe them."

His brother grinned smugly. "I'd like to feel sorry for you, but you've had more than your share of women over the years. And you will again. You just need to learn how to juggle being a father and being a player."

"Yes, well, right now I'm concentrating on the father part."

"I'd say you're making progress in that department. Lori said Megan's been referring to you as her daddy instead of Adam."

"Yeah. Finally." He sighed. "Considering everything that's happened in the past six months, I guess I should be happy that we're doing as well as we are. So why did you ask about Saturday night?"

Greg had stepped into the office and stood in front of Adam's desk, his hands in his pockets jiggling change. "A couple of Lori's college friends are in town so she thought she'd have a small dinner party."

"How small?" Adam asked with a raised eyebrow.

"Five or six people."

"Is that five as in one couple, three singles or six as in three couples?"

"She's not setting you up on a blind date," he was quick to assure him.

"Good, because I may not have seen a lot of action in the past few months, but I can still get my own dates."

"It'll probably be three guys and three woman, but Lori and I will be the only couple. It all depends on whether or not Faith comes."

"Faith?"

He nodded. "When Lori invited her she told her she'd rather baby-sit Matthew, but Lori explained no one has to baby-sit because we'll be there. By the way, you can bring Megan and she can spend the night."

"Do you think Faith will be there?"

Greg shrugged. "It's hard to say. She's something, isn't she?" It was a rhetorical question. "I've never met a woman who had so little interest in material things. Lori's always trying to give her things but Faith won't take them. At first I thought it was because she was proud and she didn't want to be considered a charity case, but I think she simply isn't impressed by the things most people regard as status symbols. You don't suppose she's a nun, do you?"

"A nun? Don't be ridiculous!"

"What's so ridiculous about that? Maybe that's why she wears a bracelet that says faith on it. She has faith. Get it?"

No, he didn't, and he didn't want to even contemplate such a possibility.

"It would explain why she doesn't really seem to care about money," his brother went on. "Don't nuns take a vow of poverty? And look at how she's always wanting to help someone out. She's humble and she has a simple lifestyle—" He was building a case Adam didn't want to hear.

"That doesn't make her a nun," he interrupted, wishing his brother had kept his thoughts to himself. It was one thing for Adam to think that he may be competing with another man in Faith's past and quite another to think she'd taken a vow of chastity.

Greg eyed him curiously. "No, it doesn't, but it wouldn't hurt to explore the possibility. There can't be that many convents in this area."

"I would think if one of their members had disappeared they would have filed a missing-person report on her," Adam remarked.

"You're probably right." He cocked his head to one side. "Hey—she isn't the reason you haven't been seeing any action, is she?"

"Why would you ask that?"

"It's just something Lori said."

"And what was that?"

He shrugged. "It was something about the way you look at Faith when you think no one else is looking. You know, all the chick stuff us guys never pay attention to," he said with a grin.

Adam should have known his sister-in-law would notice that he was having trouble keeping his eyes off Faith. He tried to dismiss her comments with a chuckle. "We don't need to even open our mouths and they think they know what we're thinking."

"I mean it's not like Faith is anywhere near your type," Greg noted.

"No, it's not."

He chuckled. "I mean…she likes to cook, she likes to sew and she likes kids…." He shook his head. "She's the kind of woman a man settles down with, definitely not the type usually found leaving your house on a Sunday morning."

"There haven't been any women leaving my house on a Sunday morning since Megan has been with me," he reminded him.

"I know, and I respect you for that."

Adam acknowledged the compliment with a nod. "So what time is this dinner party on Saturday?" he asked.

"Does that mean you'll come?"

He was tempted to say, "Only if Faith is there," but held his tongue. He shrugged and said, "Sure, why not."

"Good. I'll see you at 8." Greg turned to leave but paused in the doorway. "Can I give you a word of brotherly advice?"

"Sounds as if you're going to, whether I want it or not."

"I am, but knowing you, you won't take it anyway. You never have."

"You're my younger brother. I'm not supposed to listen to you," Adam said lightly.

"I know, but this time you should."

Adam rolled his eyes with mock impatience. "All right. What is it you want to tell me?"

"Be careful with her, Adam."

He knew it would do no good to pretend he didn't know to whom he referred. "She's Megan's nanny."

"Yeah, I know, and I also know you and beautiful women. If she is a nun, she could be very inexperienced when it comes to men. She might not know that a guy says things he doesn't always mean."

"Will you stop with the nun talk?" he demanded, his voice rising with impatience. "Contrary to what you might think, I don't promise women things I can't give them, which is probably one of the reasons I'm still single."

Greg held up his hands in mock surrender. "I'm sorry. Forget I said anything."

"No, it's all right." He didn't mind the advice. He just didn't want to be reminded that Faith could be someone who'd chosen a life that didn't include men. "I know Lori is very protective of Faith, but you have to know that I'm not going to do anything stupid. I don't want Megan to get hurt because of something I do."

"No, of course you don't," Greg said. "Forget I said anything."

"Sure," he replied, but it was easier said than done.

For the rest of the week Adam tried not to think about the possibility that Faith could be a nun, but it bothered him enough that he spent an entire afternoon calling convents in the five-state area. None were missing any of their members. He knew that just because she didn't belong to any of the local orders of sisters it didn't mean she couldn't be a nun in another state or even another country.

On Saturday night when he arrived at Greg and Lori's and found her in the living room wearing a simple black dress, he tried not to imagine her in a nun's habit, but he couldn't stop the image from invading his imagination. It didn't help that at one point Greg whispered in an aside meant only for his ears, "Sister Faith looks lovely this evening, doesn't she?"

Adam could have given him a swift kick in the shins. To his relief, Lori put her husband to work serving beverages. That left Adam to entertain Lori's college friends who wasted no time in letting him know they were single. He, however, only had eyes for one woman and she was the one who made the least effort to capture his attention.

Throughout the evening he found himself assessing her behavior. When she didn't bow her head and pray silently before dinner, he saw it as a good sign. When she placed her hand over her glass so Greg wouldn't give her any wine, he saw it as a bad sign.

"You're not going to have a glass of wine with dinner?" Adam asked.

"It doesn't seem like I should."

"Why not?" he probed.

She shrugged. "I don't know. My first reaction was to say no…as if that was the natural thing to do."

Because she's a nun and she's not supposed to drink, a little voice in Adam's head said. "Not even a taste?" He tempted her in defiance to the voice.

Greg stood next to her, bottle poised to pour. To Adam's surprise, she pulled her hand back from the glass and said, "I might as well try it, right?"

"Might as well," Greg said, exchanging glances with Adam who was relieved when his brother moved on to serve wine to the next guest.

When Faith had taken her first sip, Adam asked, "Well, what do you think?"

"I like it."

He smiled, ignoring the little voice that told him he was corrupting a nun. By the time she'd finished her glass, he knew by the slight slurring in her voice that she wasn't accustomed to having wine with her meal.

The rest of the evening passed much too quickly for Adam and, despite his preoccupation with Faith's occupation, he enjoyed himself. When Lori asked Adam if he would give Faith a ride home, he didn't hesitate to say yes.

He was tempted to take her by the local Catholic church on the way to the Carsons and see if she genuflected in front of the statue of the Virgin Mary. She didn't say a word as he drove her home and he realized it was because she'd fallen asleep.

When he pulled up in front of the Carsons' he turned off the engine and leaned over her. "Faith." He gently repeated her name until her eyes fluttered open.

She wrinkled her nose. "Ooooh. I don't think I should have had that wine. It made me sleepy."

"Did you have a good time?" he asked, his face only inches from hers.

"Yes. Thank you for bringing me home. It was very kind of you," she said with a shy smile.

"I had an ulterior motive," he confessed.

"What?" she asked innocently.

"This," he said, then covered her mouth with his. Her lips parted beneath his as the light, friendly kiss became a hard, probing caress that surprised both of them with its intensity. When it ended she was trembling.

"I'd better go in," she whispered, her breath warm against his skin.

Reluctantly he released her and climbed out of the car to walk her to the front door. He was tempted to kiss her one more time but the porch light went on. Unaware of what he'd interrupted, Dr. Carson opened the front door and smiled.

"I thought I heard a car out there. Hope you kids had a nice time this evening," he said.

"It was fun," Adam answered. Seeing the doctor holding the door for Faith, he knew there was no point in hanging around on the front step so Adam looked at her and said, "I'll see you on Monday."

She nodded and slipped inside. All the way home he kept thinking one thought.

Please, don't let her be a nun.

"I AM SO GLAD you talked me into turning these old clothes into a quilt," Lori said to Faith one afternoon as she cut fabric patches with scissors.

"How's this?" Faith knelt beside pieces of cloth arranged in a diamond pattern on the floor.

"I like it!" Lori said enthusiastically. "It's a good thing I wear a lot of red and purple, isn't it?"

"Yes. Along with Greg's blues and greens they'll make for a colorful pattern." She sat back on her heels to admire the design.

"This is going to be a wonderful gift for Matthew, and it will have so much more meaning for him because he'll know every piece on it came from clothes his mom and dad wore," Lori noted.

"*Ja,* and at the rate we're going he'll be about twenty before it's finished," Faith said with a teasing grin.

"I know I'm slow, but it's the first time I've ever tried to make a quilt. Obviously it's not yours," she said, nodding toward the colorful squares Faith had arranged on the floor.

"Must not be. I feel very comfortable with a needle and thread and I like creating the patterns," she admitted. "You do know that this project would go a lot faster if we had more hands. Are you sure you don't have some friends who'd like to come spend a few hours each week sharing in our fun?"

"I don't think any of my friends even know how to use a needle and thread," Lori quipped. "They're much more comfortable with a spreadsheet and a PDA."

When Faith shot her a puzzled look, Lori added, "You don't know what I'm talking about, do you?"

Faith shook her head.

"I doubt you've worked in the corporate world, Faith. A spreadsheet is…" She began then stopped short and flapped her hand. "You don't need to know that stuff. It's really not important. These past few weeks have shown me that. What matters is that little guy over there." She glanced lovingly at the bassinet where her son lay sleeping only a few feet away.

"You like being a mother," Faith observed.

"I do and I can't imagine having to go back to work and leaving him every day. My maternity leave is going by so quickly. Before you know it, June will be here and I'll be back at work."

"I thought you said you could do your work from here?"

"I can, but I'm still going to have to go into the of-

fice occasionally, which is why I'm going to need someone to take care of Matthew for me. I'd like that someone to be you, Faith. I know this job was set up to be
temporary, but I'm hoping you'll consider changing
that."

"You want me to stay on full-time through the
summer?"

She nodded. "I know it's going to mean having two
children for the entire day once Megan's on summer
break, but I wouldn't expect you to work for the same
wages you've been getting. I'd increase your hourly
rate because of the added responsibility."

Money wasn't a factor as to whether or not she accepted Lori's offer. She loved working for Lori and
Adam, but she wasn't sure it would be fair to make the
kind of commitment they needed for the summer when
she didn't know what the future would bring.

"I'm sorry, Faith. I didn't mean to put you on the
spot," Lori said.

"You didn't put me on the spot," Faith told her. "The
day the Carsons found me I started over with a new life.
With every day that goes by I become a little bit more
confident in who I'm becoming and less fearful about
who I used to be." She paused, then asked, "Does that
make sense?"

Lori's voice softened. "Yes, it does. You shouldn't
have to put your life on hold, Faith. I know the most difficult part of this for you has been not knowing if you have
a family somewhere." Faith nodded and she continued.
"Maybe I can help you find the answer to that question."

"How?"

"I'm not really sure, but there must be a way of solving this puzzle…because it really is a puzzle. We know some things about you already, like the fact that occasionally you speak German."

"I do?"

"Mmm-hmm. You slip in words and phrases every now and then, and you don't even realize you're doing it, do you?"

She shook her head.

Lori got up and went over to the desk where she removed a manila folder from a hanging file. "I want to show you something." She pulled out a newspaper clipping and handed it to Faith. "This is a picture of a yacht we built for one of our German clients. He sent us this from his local paper."

Faith looked at the newsprint and saw a picture of a man on the deck of a large boat.

"Can you read what it says?" Lori asked.

Faith gasped. "I can. Can you?"

"No."

"But you speak another language besides English, right?"

Lori shook her head. "No, just English."

Faith handed her back the newspaper clipping. "Dr. Carson said I have a slight accent. You think English could be my second language?"

"It's possible, but I personally don't think it's true. You could have studied German in school or lived with someone who spoke German."

"But you've said to me on more than one occasion that you didn't think I was from this area."

"That doesn't mean I think you're not an American. Faith, this is just one clue that might help us determine who you are. The more you can tell me about yourself, the easier it will be to try to put the clues all together and come up with a possible answer to the question of who you are. Have you had more flashbacks recently?"

She shook her head. "Just the ones I already told you about, but I've been having a recurring dream. I'm lost in a maze of corn stalks, and just when I think I find a way out, I hear voices warning me that I'm going to get in trouble. They're boys' voices."

"Do they call you by your name?"

"No, but I hear things like 'You'd better come out now or you're going to be sorry' and 'He's really mad.'"

"Who's really mad?"

She shrugged. "I don't know."

"Are the voices speaking German or English?"

"I'm not sure. I think I'm a little girl in the dream, which doesn't make much sense, either."

"Dreams seldom do… At least mine don't. And I can tell you from personal experience I've had some pretty bizarre ones. I do find it interesting that you're dreaming about a cornfield though."

"You think it might mean I've lived on a farm?"

"That isn't the only reason. When you were reading that book about farming to Megan, some of your comments made it sound as if you had experience around farm animals. And the way you cook reminds me of my mom's friend, Martha Banning. Canned goods to her were the fruits and vegetables she'd preserved herself, not the stuff she bought at the grocery store. She's the only other person I've seen who bakes with lard, too."

Faith was silent for a moment before saying, "I don't know why I do things the way I do." She patted her head with her hands. "If I could only get this to work properly."

"You will," Lori stated confidently. "I told you. I'll help you. We'll keep putting the clues together until we find out where you came from."

"It might not be St. Paul or even Minnesota," she warned her.

"I know. That doesn't necessarily mean you'll leave. You might not want to return to the life you had before the accident."

It was a possibility Faith herself had been considering lately. It was much easier on her emotionally to regard her past as something that she had willingly left behind because it had caused her pain, rather than wonder if she had been taken away against her will. Because she knew in her heart that she would never leave her children behind, no matter how bad the situation had been.

"You're right. I can't keep postponing decisions with the hope that tomorrow I'll wake up and have my memory restored," Faith told her.

"Does that mean you'll take care of Matthew for me when I go back to work?"

"Yes."

CHAPTER TWELVE

TO FAITH'S DELIGHT, April showers brought May flowers. The spring rains also washed away all traces of winter, leaving in their wake a lush blanket of green lawns and colorful flower gardens. Faith welcomed the warmer weather, spending as much time as possible outdoors, taking the children on regular walks to the park where she would help Megan fly her kite.

Ever since she'd started working for the Novaks she had been treated more like a member of the family than as an employee, which was a comfort to her as the days stretched into weeks and there appeared to be no end in sight for her amnesia. Even though the list of clues to her identity grew longer, the answers to the questions of who she was and where she'd come from eluded them. The bits and pieces of memory that had flashed like snapshots in Faith's mind giving her glimpses of her past life had stopped abruptly, the last one occurring over a month ago when she'd been at Lori's helping her fold baby clothes.

She had run up the stairs to put them away when she paused at the top of the landing to catch her breath. Briefly she closed her eyes and in those few seconds she saw a room furnished simply with a bed, a chest of drawers and a table. On the bed was a quilt made of dark blues, greens and black. Next to the bed on the floor was a braided rag rug. The walls were gray, the curtains dark blue and gathered on a string. Whose room it was she didn't know, but she hoped it hadn't been hers. It was gloomy with too little light and such a sharp contrast to the brightness of Lori's home with its abundance of windows.

Lori had tried to coax her into remembering more of the details, but it had been a futile effort. In the weeks that followed, Lori often asked if she'd had any more memory flashes, but there had been none.

Without additional pieces to the puzzle, Faith knew she had very little chance of putting together a picture of her past. It made her wonder if Dr. Carson had been wrong about her being on the road to recovery. She'd read of patients who'd suffered from amnesia for as long as fifteen years.

It was a scary thought, yet it was a possibility she needed to face. When she'd first realized she had amnesia, she'd expected it to be gone in a matter of days. The days had turned into weeks and the weeks had turned into months. She wondered if the months wouldn't now turn into years.

If they did, she didn't want to live her life in fear of what could be in her past. If there was a reason to be pleased about the passing of time it was that now when she woke up in the morning she no longer saw a stranger in the mirror, but a woman named Faith who had a history—albeit a short one. The only life she could remember was the one she'd created as an accident survivor. She didn't know what kind of woman she'd been in her other life, but the longer she was Faith the survivor, the less she worried about her.

Yet she did worry that the past she didn't remember would haunt her future. As she watched Megan play hop-scotch with two of her friends on the front walk one warm evening, she thought about what a relief it would be to have no doubts that she'd be sitting on the porch a year or even a month from now. In a very short time Megan had become an important part of her life. The possibility of not being around to watch Megan's childhood was a sad one.

"Anything wrong?" Adam asked as he approached the porch.

"No, why?"

He sat down beside her on the wooden swing. "You look thoughtful…that's all."

A wave of desire swept over her as his thigh brushed hers. "Where did you come from?" she asked, not wanting to tell him what she was thinking. "I thought you were working late?"

"It was too beautiful an evening to spend it working." He placed an arm across the back of the swing. "I'm going to take Megan out for a hamburger and fries. Want to come?"

It was a silly question. He knew it was and so did she. They could pretend that they didn't want to be together, but they both knew that the attraction between them was almost electric. To Faith it felt as if the more they denied it, the stronger it became.

"No, I should go," she said, and would have risen to her feet but he stopped her.

"Don't run away, Faith," he said, his hand on her arm.

She glanced at him and the look in his eyes made her ache with longing. "I'm spending too much time here."

"You're not spending enough," he contradicted her. "Megan asked me the other day if you could move in with us."

"We can't play house," she said, looking out at Megan who was now crouched low on the lawn as if she were looking for something.

"Isn't that what we're doing now...only you and I aren't getting to enjoy our roles as we should."

That brought a blush to her cheeks. The tension was broken by Megan who came running over to the porch, her hands cupped and extended in front of her.

"I found one! I found one!" she called out victoriously, her two friends following behind her. When she reached the porch she placed her right hand, palm upward in front of him for his inspection. "Look, Daddy. I found a four-leaf clover."

"So I see," Adam said, peering at the tiny green plant.

"Now I get to make a wish and it will come true, right?" she asked.

"I'm not so sure about that," her father answered. "I believe four-leaf clovers bring good luck, not wishes."

Her face fell. "But Mommy said if I were lucky enough to find one my wishes would all come true. I only want one wish to come true."

The two little girls behind her giggled and one said, "We know what it is."

Megan turned to them and put her finger to her lips.

"Shh. You're not supposed to tell a wish or it won't come true."

One of the little girls snapped back, "Then *you* shouldn't have told it."

"But I didn't tell them," Megan said, pointing to Adam and Faith. Then suddenly realizing the error of her ways, she rolled her eyes. "Now I have to go find another one and next time I'm not telling anyone." She gave Adam the clover then went bouncing off the steps of the porch, the two little girls following her.

Adam stared at the clover in his hand. "This could be a good sign."

"Are you telling me that Adam, the practical engineer who needs to know the how and why things work, believes in good luck charms?" She could feel her lips twitch at the thought.

"It couldn't hurt to carry this in my wallet, could it?" he asked rhetorically. "Or maybe you'd like it?" He offered it to her.

She shook her head. "You keep it. I really do need to go." This time she didn't let him stop her from getting up.

"Before you do, I want to talk to you about something. My grandfather's birthday is the last weekend in June. Every year a big group of us gets together at his place on the St. Croix to celebrate. I'd like you to come with me and Megan this year."

"Saturday or Sunday?"

"Actually we celebrate the entire weekend. It's sort of a tradition."

"I don't want to intrude on a family party."

"You won't be intruding. When you see the number of boats you'll know what I'm talking about."

"Boats?"

He nodded. "Although my grandfather's house is large, most people prefer to spend the weekend on the river."

"So I'd be sleeping on your boat?"

"Yes."

"With you and Megan?"

"Yes."

She knew exactly what that entailed because she'd seen his boat. It was more like a luxurious apartment on water. An intimate apartment. It would be risky spending an entire weekend in such close quarters.

As she mentally debated the wisdom of such an arrangement, she heard a voice in her head. It belonged to a woman and said, "Follow your heart and let God do the judging." She closed her eyes, hoping to put an image to the voice, but nothing came.

Her heart was telling her to accept his invitation. Before she could lose her courage she said, "I'd like to spend the weekend with you on your boat."

ADAM GOT a speeding ticket driving home from Novak Boats on the Friday before his grandfather's birthday party. He didn't care. All that mattered was that he spend every minute of his weekend with Faith. He saw her acceptance of his offer as a sign that she was finally ready to take their relationship to another level.

The thought of such a possibility sent a rush of blood through him. He felt like a teenager anticipating his

first date. Never would he have expected someone so
shy and reserved could arouse such feelings in him.

When he arrived home he found her with Megan on the
patio. He paused for a moment at the gate watching them.

"You need to hold really still," he heard his daughter tell Faith as she applied polish to her fingernails.

"What color is this?" Faith asked.

"Purple passion," came Megan's reply.

Adam grinned. It sounded like the perfect selection
for the weekend.

Diligently and carefully, Megan worked at making sure
each one of Faith's nails was polished to her satisfaction.

When they heard Adam's footsteps on the patio, both
blond heads turned. "You're early," Faith said.

"What are you two doing out here? It's so warm I
thought you'd be inside in the air-conditioning," he said,
carrying his sport coat over his shoulder.

"We're painting our fingernails for Great-Grandpa's
party," Megan answered. "Look at the purple polish.
Isn't it pretty?" She lifted her hand to show him.

"Beautiful." Faith must have known he wasn't only
referring to their nails because she blushed. "I thought
we'd get an early start. Beat the traffic."

"Are we going to eat dinner on the boat?" Megan's
eyes widened at the thought.

He glanced up at the blue sky. "It's a perfect day,
don't you think? How long will it take for you two to
get ready?"

Faith held up her hand with the unpainted fingernails.
"We need to finish this…and change clothes."

His eyes roved over her shorts and T-shirt. "Uh-uh.

What you're wearing is perfect. Hope you didn't forget to pack a swimsuit. You do have one, don't you?"

Megan answered for her. "Lori helped her pick one out. It's a tankini." She turned her attention back to the unpainted fingernails.

Meanwhile images of Faith in a swimsuit danced through his head.

"I'm not sure I know how to swim, though," she said tentatively.

"You can just splash around in the water," Megan told her.

"We won't let you drown, will we, Megan?" Adam said with a grin.

"Uh-uh. I'm glad you're coming with us, Faith. It's really fun to sleep on the boat."

What he was thinking must have shone in his eyes because Faith blushed when she looked at him, then quickly averted her gaze. She began picking up the items on the patio table, shoving them onto a plastic tray.

"Don't forget your rosary," Megan's command caused Adam's eyes to dart to the table.

Sure enough. There was a blue string of rosary beads in front of Faith. *You don't suppose she's a nun?* For weeks he'd managed to tuck the possibility away in the back of his mind because he hadn't wanted to give it any further consideration. Now it was back staring him in the face.

"Where did that come from?" he asked, his mouth as dry as cotton.

"One of the volunteers at the hospital makes them so she gave me one," Faith answered.

"Why?" he wanted to know. "Are you Catholic?"

Faith shrugged. "I don't know. I suppose I could be. I expect I'm probably a Christian because I seem to have knowledge of the Bible and some of my flashbacks have had religious overtones."

"Is Faith going to sleep with me in my room on the boat?" Megan asked, bringing the conversation back to their weekend plans.

Even if Adam had entertained thoughts that she might possibly end up sleeping anywhere else, they were being pushed aside and all because of a string of glass beads someone had made for Faith. It didn't help that the subject of where she would sleep had put a look of uneasiness on her face.

"We'll decide that once we get to the boat." He finally answered his daughter's question.

"It's going to be so much fun!" Megan enthused.

Adam hoped she was right. When his daughter asked if they could have a picnic supper, he decided to stop at a gourmet deli on the way to the marina.

When they arrived at the boat, they dined on an assortment of sliced meats and pâtés, fruits and cheeses and a fresh baked baguette. They didn't swim, but they did stop to wade in the shallow water of a sandbar where they anchored for the night.

They sat on the deck watching the sunset until the mosquitoes drove them inside. After a game of Parcheesi, which Megan won, they made ice-cream sundaes and listened to the soundtrack from her favorite movie. When she fell asleep on the sofa, Adam carried her into her stateroom.

Faith followed him.

"You don't have to share a bed with her. You can have mine." Seeing the suspicious look in her eyes Adam added, "I'll sleep on the sofa. It converts into a bed." When she hesitated he added, "You should take me up on my offer." He jerked a thumb toward his daughter. "She sprawls."

"Are you sure you don't mind?"

"No, I want you to take the bed." He just wished he could take it with her. He led her to the forward stateroom where the master bedroom was located. He showed her where the shower was, how to use the remote for the entertainment center and where to adjust the temperature if the air-conditioning was too cool.

She glanced at the full-size bed. "Why don't I take the sofa and you sleep here? I don't need this big of a bed."

For weeks there'd been an unanswered question dangling between them. Tonight it looked as if they were finally going to confront it. He wanted her—probably more than he'd ever wanted a woman. And never had he waited so patiently for anyone. He was tired of waiting. He was ready to give in to the desires that had kept him lying awake thinking about her on many a night.

He'd been with enough women to know when they shared his feelings. She wanted him as much as he wanted her. He'd been waiting for her to make the first move but she hadn't. He suspected it was because of her shyness so he decided to give her some help.

"You do if you're sleeping with someone," he said in a tone that left no uncertainty as to his meaning.

The look in her eyes had him forgetting his resolve

to let her be the one to make the first move. He pulled her to him and kissed her with all of the pent-up passion he'd fought so hard to keep under control. Her body quivered with eagerness as his hands moved across her hot flesh. Each kiss was deeper and longer than the previous until they were both breathless. When he lifted his mouth from hers, she clung to him for support.

With one swift movement he pushed her back until he was lying over her on the bed. "You are so beautiful," he said, before claiming her mouth once more.

When his hand began to unbutton her shirt, she gasped.

He lifted his mouth from hers. "Yes, or no?"

"Yes," she said, her breath hot against his face. "It's just that…I don't think I've done this before."

It was the splash of cold water he needed. He rolled away from her onto his back, his arm draped over his eyes. All of the doubts that had kept his desire in check since he'd first met her came rushing back.

They didn't talk, but simply lay there. He stared at the ceiling. A sideways glance told him that her eyes were focused on it, as well.

She was the first one to speak. "It's not that it doesn't feel good. It does." She paused. "And I want to. I want to really badly." And she paused again. "But I don't think I know how."

Adam thought that with any other woman he would have been seriously doubting the sincerity of the words. But not with Faith. She had no reason to pretend with him. He truly believed she was an innocent.

He leaned over, pressed a butterfly kiss on her lips and left.

FAITH KNEW THERE WAS little chance that Lori didn't know that she was falling in love with Adam, not after his grandfather's birthday party. Although they'd never talked about it directly, Lori had hinted that she was aware that Faith had feelings for her brother-in-law. Now that they'd spent the weekend together on the yacht, Faith expected her to bring up the subject the next time they saw each other.

When she walked into Lori's backyard the following Monday morning, Lori greeted her with her usual cheerfulness. "This is a surprise. I didn't expect you today," Lori said, patting the blanket upon which she and Matthew rested.

Faith greeted the baby with her usual smile and kiss, then curled her legs beneath her. "Megan's at a birthday party for her friend Emily so I thought I'd stop in and see if you needed help with anything."

"Yes, I do. I need an opinion."

Faith looked at the magazine in Lori's hands. "On a bridal dress?"

"Bridesmaid dress," she corrected her. "My sister Julie is getting married and she's thinking about having us wear these horrible dresses. I have a picture of it somewhere. Believe me, they are not flattering to any figure. Anyway, she told me to look for something I would feel comfortable wearing so that's why I have these." She patted the stack of magazines at her side.

"You're one of the side-sitters?"

Lori's brow wrinkled. "The what?"

"Side-sitters. You know…attendants."

"I've never heard them called that before," Lori said,

her brow still creased as she made a notation on a piece of paper.

Faith shrugged. "Must be a farm thing," she quipped. That had become her pat answer to whenever she said something that wasn't familiar to the others. "What color does she have in mind?" Faith asked, opening a bridal magazine.

"Red. She's getting married on Valentine's Day. It's going to be so romantic."

"Weddings usually are," Faith said on a sigh. "Did you have a big one?"

Lori shook her head. "Greg and I were married on a cruise ship."

"You're kidding?"

She shook her head. "It was actually a lot of fun. Speaking of fun…" She changed the subject smoothly. "You and Adam looked as if you enjoyed Grandfather's party."

Faith couldn't prevent the blush. "Yes."

"You don't need to be embarrassed about dating my brother-in-law, Faith."

"We're not dating," she denied.

"No?" Lori shrugged. "Call it whatever you want, but you two are only kidding yourselves if you think you're just friends."

"You don't think it's foolish?"

"No! Adam's a great guy. He works too much, but then so do you, so that shouldn't be a problem," she stated.

"But I don't know who I am."

"Yes, you do. You're Faith…a woman of great compassion and kindness who is extremely good with children. What you don't know is what may have happened to you in your past."

She narrowed her eyes. "What if a husband happened?" Although after what happened with Adam on the boat, Faith now had her doubts.

Lori shook her head. "I don't believe it did."

"Why not?"

"Because he would have moved mountains to find someone like you," she answered, giving her arm an affectionate squeeze. "You've been missing for at least four months, maybe more."

She sighed. "I'm beginning to wonder if my memory is ever going to come back."

"Until it does, I suggest you enjoy being Faith."

She planned to do just that.

ADAM WAS IN his SUV on his way to an appointment to meet with a couple to discuss their plans for a customized yacht when his sister-in-law phoned.

"Are you already on your way to Rochester?" she asked.

"Yeah, why? The client didn't cancel, did he?"

"No. That's not why I'm calling. I saw something on TV last night that I can't stop thinking about."

"And what was that?"

"It was a program about the Amish. And, Adam, I have to tell you, it was fascinating. Hearing how they live, what they believe…"

"I'm sure it was, but what does this have to do with me driving to Rochester?"

"Because the Amish in Minnesota live just south of there around the area of Canton and Harmony."

"And I need to know that because…?"

"I know this is going to sound crazy, but the longer I watched that TV program last night, the more I began to wonder if Faith isn't Amish."

"You think Faith is Amish."

"Yes. She has stuff in common with them."

"Such as?"

"For one thing, they speak German in their homes. We both know she's bilingual."

"That doesn't make her Amish," he pointed out.

"No, but if you had seen this program describing their lifestyle you'd know what I mean. Adam, she doesn't drive. And remember how when she first started working for us we both remarked about how unfamiliar she was with modern technology? She didn't even know how to use a computer. And it's obvious she has some kind of strong religious background."

You don't suppose she could be a nun. "At least if she's Amish it means she isn't a nun, which is what Greg thought she might be. Amish women aren't celibate, are they?"

"No, but you might have a better chance of getting a nun to leave the convent than an Amish woman to leave her community."

It wasn't what he wanted to hear. "Have you mentioned any of this to Faith?"

"I'm going to go see her this morning, but I thought as long as you're already down in that area, you could stop and make a few inquiries."

"With the police? Faith said there were no missing-person reports filed anywhere in Minnesota."

"I know, but the Amish are not like us, Adam. They keep to themselves."

"If that's the case, then how would I find any information even if one of their members was missing?"

"I don't know. I just thought maybe you could do some nosing around down there."

"I'll see how my time goes," he said evasively.

"All right. I've got to go. Matthew's fussing. Take care and call me if you find out anything."

Adam thought about waiting until he'd talked to Faith about the possibility before going in search of answers, but when he'd finished his business meeting in Rochester, he found himself in his car driving south on Highway 52, not north.

He'd learned from his client that Harmony was the community where the Amish did most of their business. As he drove down Main Avenue he thought he could have been in any other small town in the Midwest. Small shops lined the block—a drugstore, a hardware, a bank. He pulled up in front of a gift shop that had a sign overhead that read Amish Country Tours and went inside.

At first he thought the store was empty, but then he saw the small man sitting at the end of the counter. From the lines on his face Adam knew the man had seen a lot of living and was probably around the same age as his grandfather. Actually he looked a lot like Robert Novak except his grandfather wouldn't have worn a county cap.

The man looked up briefly when he heard the door

open, narrowed his eyes as he peered at Adam, nodded, then turned his attention back to the project in front of him. He had a miniature screwdriver in one hand, a pair of glasses in the other.

Adam glanced around the gift shop. There were quilts and wall hangings, woven baskets and wooden kitchen accessories, all made by Amish crafters. A bookshelf caught his attention and he paused to glance at a history of the Amish in Minnesota.

"If you want to know about the Amish you should take the tour," the wizened little man said from behind the counter.

Adam turned around to face him. "You must know a lot about the Amish if you do business with them," he said, waving the book in the air.

"As much as any outsider can know," he said with a wary eye. "They're private people."

"But they let you give tours of their farms?"

"It's a cooperative business venture. They have stuff they want to sell."

Adam glanced around the store. "I can see that."

"Not just this." The man chuckled. "This is just a very small amount of what they produce. If you take the tour you'll see what I mean." He smiled and the pose he struck reminded Adam of a yard gnome.

"How long does it take?"

"Couple of hours…give or take." He held up his eyeglasses and peered at them before placing them on his nose. "You want to make a reservation?"

"Do I need one?"

"Sure." He climbed down from the stool and Adam

saw the man was even shorter than he first thought. "Fifteen dollars to go in the van, thirty if you want to take your car," he recited. "What kind of car you drivin'?"

"I've got an SUV."

He stepped over to the front window to look outside. "Pretty nice. Too bad I'm full for this afternoon. I wouldn't mind riding in that." He went back to the ledger on the counter. "I could take you tomorrow morning." He looked up with a hopeful light in his eye.

"You've got nothing for today?"

The man shook his head. "Booked solid. It's the height of the tourist season you know."

Adam glanced around the empty shop but didn't comment. "I'm only here for today."

The old guy shrugged. "Guess you'll have to settle for a book then."

Adam put his selection on the counter and reached for his wallet. While he waited for the shopkeeper to process the transaction, he asked, "You know most of the people around these parts?"

"Some of them."

"I'm looking for someone. A woman."

He cracked a wry smile. "It figures." He placed the book in a brown paper bag and handed it to him. "You think she's Amish?"

"Yes. I have a picture of her." He did. It was one he'd pulled out of a packet he'd recently had developed and still carried around in his briefcase.

The old man held up his hand and shook his head. "If you have a picture, she's not Amish. They don't believe in graven images."

"What about if she's someone who has left that way of life?"

He cocked his head to one side and nodded. He held out his palm and Adam placed the photograph on it.

The old man looked at it first through his glasses, then he lifted the frames and squinted to look a second time. Finally he shook his head. "No one I know." He handed the photo back to Adam.

"It's important that I find out whether or not she has family around here."

"Amish family?"

He nodded.

"The Amish are very private," he told Adam for a second time. "I wouldn't go barging in on them with that photograph."

"What would you do?"

"Maybe pay a visit to a shop on the other end of town," he said with a wave of a gnarly finger. "It's owned by a couple who left the Amish community. They might be willing to help you." He gave Adam the name of the store and directions on how to get there.

Adam extended his hand. "Thank you, Mr...."

"Just call me Earl," the old guy said as he pumped his hand.

"I'm Adam Novak. I appreciate your help."

"Hope you find what you're looking for. Come back when we're not so busy. I'd like a ride in that car of yours."

"I may just be back to do that, Earl," Adam said with a grin and went in search of the gift shop. On the way he spotted a horse-drawn buggy making its way down

the same road where cars zoomed by. When it pulled up
in front of an ice-cream parlor, Adam watched as a
bearded man wearing a straw hat and dark clothing
climbed out of the buggy. From the other side came several children, two boys dressed like their father and a
little girl wearing a long blue dress with an apron. On
her head was a black cap.

Adam wondered if that was how Faith had dressed
when she was young. As the family disappeared inside the
ice-cream parlor, Adam continued on his way to the gift
shop where he hoped to find an answer to his question.

Like Earl's Amish Country Tours, the small tourist
stop offered crafts and homemade items for sale. Adam
wondered if the proprietor would be bearded as the man
in the buggy had been, but when he stepped inside he
saw a clean-shaven face on the man behind the counter.
Dressed in a plaid shirt and a pair of jeans, there was
nothing about him that resembled the Amish man with
his children.

"Hello." The man greeted Adam with a friendly smile.

"You have a nice place here," Adam told him, glancing about the store.

"*Ja.* If you're looking for furniture, it's in the back
room." He cocked his head toward a doorway. As if on
cue, a woman poked her head out and smiled.

"Actually, I'm looking for information."

The woman disappeared and the man stiffened.
"You're not a reporter, are you?"

"No." Adam extended his hand and introduced himself.
"I design boats." That had the man's shoulders relaxing.

"What can I help you with?"

Adam pulled the snapshot of Faith from his pocket and held it up. "Do you recognize this woman?"

Without even looking at the picture he walked away shaking his head. "I'm afraid I can't help you."

"I'm sorry I had to take her picture. I didn't mean any disrespect," Adam said, following him down the counter.

"It's not that," he said, turning to lift a box off the shelf behind him.

"Then what is it?"

"Just because I'm not one of them anymore doesn't mean I don't respect their wish for privacy."

"Then she is Amish?"

"It's not for me to say." He walked over to a revolving rack and began restocking it with postcards.

Adam followed him. "What if I were to tell you this woman was in an accident and can't remember who she is?"

That brought his head around with a jerk.

"She's living in St. Paul, wondering whether or not she even has a family," Adam continued. "Everything that happened before her accident is a blank."

"She does not know whether she is English or Amish?"

Adam shook his head. "She's worried that people may be looking for her, wondering what happened to her…maybe even thinking that she's dead."

"Some believe to disobey the church is to die," he said cryptically.

Adam frowned. "Are you saying her family wouldn't want to know she's alive?"

"I'm saying family matters are private and we don't know the circumstances of her past."

"Then you do recognize her?"

It took a long moment, but he finally said, "It may be someone I have seen."

"Can you give me a name?"

He shook his head. "This is not your matter. She needs to be the one who asks the questions."

"If I bring her here will you give her the answers?"

"If she wants to know."

"She wants to know," he said, then thanked him for his time and left the shop.

"WHERE'S MEGAN?" Adam asked as he walked through the gate into the backyard.

Faith, who'd been weeding the garden, sat back on her heels. "She's over at her friend Emily's house. Is everything okay? You look so serious."

He smiled then and her heart did its usual flip-flop. "Come sit down. I need to show you something," he said, taking a seat at the patio table.

She pulled off her gardening gloves and sat on the chair next to his. It was then she noticed he had a book in his hand and what appeared to be tourist brochures. He handed the top one to her.

"'Welcome to Harmony, the biggest little town in southeastern Minnesota,'" she read aloud. Puzzled, she looked at him for an explanation.

"I picked that up today."

"You were in Harmony?"

He nodded. "It's just south of Rochester."

"I know where it is."

"You do?"

She nodded. "It was featured in an article in the travel pages a few weeks ago. They have a wonderful bike trail that follows the Root River. I believe there are also quite a few shops that sell Amish furniture. Is that why you went? To look for that new table and chairs you talked about getting for the house?"

"No, I was looking for you."

"But I was here," she said, then realized the implication of his words. A wave of uneasiness began to uncurl inside her.

He reached for her hand. "Faith, I think I may have found where you belong."

Her mouth went dry and her heart felt as if it had moved into her throat. "You found my family?" she whispered.

He shook his head. "No, but there's a good chance we will find them if we go back down to Harmony. I showed your photograph to a couple of people," he continued.

"And someone recognized me?"

"Not exactly. It's not easy getting information about the Amish. They're a very private people, but I did talk to someone who was a former member of their community and he gave me reason to believe that you're somehow connected to them."

The Amish? She unfolded the tourist guide and saw a horse-drawn buggy. "You think I'm Plain?"

"Faith, Plain is the term Amish use when referring to themselves."

"But you're familiar with it."

"Because I was just in Harmony. There are other things about you, Faith, that point in that direction."

She shook her head. "It can't be."

"Why not?"

"Because that lifestyle is not mine." She could see by the look on his face that he was wondering how she knew what kind of lifestyle the Amish led. "I have knowledge about a lot of things, Adam," she pointed out. "Things I read and learned at school are still up here," she said, pointing to her head. "I've heard about the Amish but I'm not one of them. I'm not."

"I know. I didn't say you are Amish. I just said there's a possibility. It would explain a lot of things…like why no one has looked for you."

She was quiet for a long moment as she digested what she'd just learned. "I need to find out…one way or the other."

"I know. Until we know for sure that you are a member of that community, we'll assume it's simply speculation."

"When will we know?"

"When do you want to go to Harmony?"

She was tempted to say never. She'd finally accepted that her past might be forever locked away. Now she was being told that everything she feared may be coming true. He didn't press her for an answer, but raised her hand to his lips and kissed it.

"How long will it take to get there?" she asked.

"Around a couple of hours."

She took a deep breath and said, "Then I'd like to go in the morning if Lori is able to take care of Megan for me."

"She will." He kissed her tenderly. "No matter what you uncover, I'm going to be there for you. I'll help you in any way I can. We'll get through this together."

Faith appreciated his strength and his concern, but deep down inside she knew that this was something no one else could do for her. She was the only one who could find herself, yet it frightened her to think of how unlocking her past could change her whole future.

She rubbed two fingers across her brow. "Maybe we could call and get the information."

"The Amish don't have phones and I really think this is something better done in person, don't you?"

She nodded. "It's just that…" She didn't finish, not wanting to tell him that she was scared. She didn't need to tell him that. She knew he could see it in her eyes.

He wrapped his arms around her in a reassuring hug. "I'll be there with you."

She pushed away from him and straightened. "All right. I'll do it. I'm ready to find the answers."

CHAPTER THIRTEEN

ADAM EXPECTED the drive from St. Paul to Harmony would take close to two hours. While he drove, Faith read the book he'd purchased at the gift shop. When he asked her, "Does any of that sound familiar?"

Her reply was "Yes."

Uneasiness rumbled through him. Despite the evidence to the contrary, he wanted to believe that he and Faith were on a wild-goose chase that would lead them nowhere.

When she closed the book and set it aside he asked, "What are you thinking?"

"That I don't want a life of self-denial," she answered candidly.

"You don't have to have one. They don't keep people hostage there."

"I don't want them to be my people. They're Old Order Amish, the least progressive."

He could hear the anxiety in her voice and reached for her hand. "I know. Maybe you don't belong there."

She didn't answer, but stared out the window at the rolling countryside. After a few moments she said, "Why wouldn't someone have looked for me?"

"We don't know that they didn't."

"They didn't file a police report."

It was the same question that had been troubling him. "Maybe because they live apart from modern society and independent of government."

"Or because they believe those who leave are fallen from God's grace."

Again silence stretched between them. After only a few minutes he realized that she'd fallen asleep. While she dozed he thought about that very question. Were the Amish that private a people that they wouldn't have asked for help in locating their missing daughter?

It wasn't long before Faith awakened from her nap, shooting forward with a gasp.

"Are you all right?" he asked.

She looked at him, then sank back against the seat with a sigh. "I'm okay. I—I must have been dreaming."

"About your past?"

"I don't know," she said.

"Tell me about it," he urged her.

"I can't."

He didn't want to press her, but he felt as if she were becoming Amish right before his eyes. Separating herself from him.

A few minutes later she said, "Oh, look!"

Traveling on one of the side roads beside the highway was a horse-drawn buggy. He didn't ask her if it looked familiar. She turned her head and stared at it long after he'd passed it by.

The closer they got to Harmony, the more he wanted to turn around and drive as far away as he could in the opposite direction. He knew running away wouldn't solve anything. Her memory could return tomorrow and they would still have to make this trip. He was surprised to hear she was thinking the same thing.

"It was inevitable—eventually I would have remembered who I am," she stated calmly.

"Do you really think you would have gone back after fifteen years?"

"I don't know that I'm going back now," she said quietly. "I'm just trying to find out who I am."

He could have told her he knew who she was. She was the woman who made his life complete, the woman who'd given hope to a six-year-old who, for months had been saddened by grief but now sang with joy. He said nothing, however, because he knew how difficult it already was for her to be taking this step.

As he lowered his speed to enter the business section of Harmony she said, "It looks like a nice place."

It *was* a nice place—it just wasn't the place where Adam wanted to be. When he parked the SUV he looked at her and said, "Ready?"

"No," she answered in her usual candid manner.

"Want to get a cup of coffee first? There's a café right around the corner."

She shook her head. "I'm fine."

He gave her hand a squeeze. "I'm right here with you."

As they entered the gift shop, a bell tinkled and from a back room came the same woman Adam had seen yesterday. Her smile froze when she saw Faith.

She disappeared into the back room and seconds later the man Adam had talked to yesterday came out.

Adam put a hand beneath Faith's elbow and led her over to the counter. "This is Faith," he announced.

When the man saw her, he called out to his wife who once more came out from the back room.

She muttered something in German, which caused the color to drain from Faith's face. "Does she recognize you?" Adam wanted to know, although it was obvious from the looks being exchanged that it was an unnecessary question.

Stunned, Faith answered, "She said I'm her cousin."

Adam's heart sank. So it was true. *Faith was Amish.* He watched her shock turn into relief as the couple spoke rapidly in German, gesturing with their hands. Any reservation they had had about speaking to strangers was gone as they talked to Faith. Adam saw no suspicious glances, only welcoming smiles.

As if suddenly aware that he was standing next to her, Faith turned to him and said, "I have a name. I know who I am." There was bewilderment in her eyes and joy in her words. "Can you believe it? I have an identity!"

"What is your name?" Adam asked.

"She's Esther Miller, Ebram Miller's daughter." It wasn't Faith who answered, but her cousin who introduced herself as Mary and her husband as John.

"Esther?" Adam looked at Faith.

She shrugged, as if saying, "What can I say?"

"What about family?" He felt his heart booming in his chest as he waited for her to answer that particular question.

Faith looked anxiously at Mary. "Do I have children?"

"No, you never married," she answered, and Adam's

chest felt like a balloon being deflated. She was single with no children.

Faith glanced at him then and he saw in her eyes the same relief he was feeling. "Does this Ebram live around here?" he asked.

"*Ja,* it's just south of here," John replied. "It's pretty easy to find."

"I could take you," Mary offered, but Adam wasn't ready to leave Faith in anyone else's hands.

When Faith suggested, "Maybe you could write down the directions," he shot her a grateful look.

Mary did as she requested, then gave the slip of paper to Faith who thanked her. "Remember what we told you," the woman warned her as Faith shook her hand.

As soon as they were out of the shop Adam asked her what the comment meant.

"They both warned me that my father doesn't like the English and that he especially doesn't like the English when they come to his place in automobiles," she said as they climbed into his vehicle.

"Do I need protection?" he quipped, but she didn't respond.

He started the car and headed toward the Miller farm following the directions, which were fairly simple. Faith acted as his navigator, watching for landmarks and road signs. Despite having said only hours ago that she didn't want to learn she was Amish, now that it had been confirmed, she looked more excited than dismayed.

"You don't look like an Esther," he said as he glanced at her sitting across from him.

"And how does an Esther look?" she wanted to know.

"I don't know, but you're not it. You'll always be Faith to me," he said, reaching across to give her hand a squeeze.

They reached a fork in the road, which indicated they were close to the Miller farm. Within minutes they were at a white farmhouse.

"I think this is it," she said as they approached the farmstead.

There wasn't much of a driveway, just some worn tracks that Adam guessed came from a buggy. The house was a two-story with a large porch across the front, a clothesline extending from one end to a windmill. A young girl who didn't look to be much older than Megan was cutting the small patch of lawn with a push mower. When she saw the car, she stopped and ran up the steps and into the house.

Adam didn't see any place to park. A couple of horses grazed in a fenced pasture to their right. On the other side of the house was a barn and next to it were several outbuildings. He pulled up in front of the house and turned off the engine.

A woman appeared at the door wearing a long dark blue dress with an apron. On her head was a white pleated cap. She looked to be in her late twenties or early thirties. Standing next to her was the girl who'd been pushing the mower. Another small child pushed the door open and tried to run out onto the porch, but the woman pulled her back inside.

"Are you sure this is the right place?" Adam asked.

Faith looked at the buildings scattered about the farm. "This should be it."

"Are you ready to see if it is?"

She nodded and they climbed out of the car.

The woman at the door disappeared and Faith said, "Not exactly a warm welcome, is it?"

The clopping of horses and the clanging of wheels had their heads turning. Approaching the house was an Amish buggy. It came to a halt only a few feet away from the house.

The driver jumped down and came toward them. He wore denim pants that were held up by leather suspenders and he had a long scraggly beard that touched the top buttons on his blue shirt. On his head was a straw hat, covering most, but not all of, his hair. He squinted in the bright sunshine, his stride cautious as he walked toward them.

"Is there something I can help you with?" he called out, the distrust evident in his voice. The suspicion disappeared, however, when he saw Faith. "Es?" he called out in disbelief. "Is that you?"

She nodded and a smile slowly spread across his face and his steps quickened. He reached out, grabbed her and swung her around, lifting her off the ground as he spoke in German.

"Speak English," she ordered him as he set her back on the ground.

"It's so good to see you, Es. When you left without saying goodbye I thought we'd never see you again." Overcome with emotion, he had to dab at his eyes with a handkerchief.

Adam thought it would be a good time to introduce himself. "I'm Adam Novak."

"Levi Miller," he said, taking the hand Adam offered.

"He says he's my brother," Faith added.

"You may leave and cut your hair and wear English clothes, but I will always think of you as my sister, Es," Levi said gravely. He turned back to the buggy. "Boys!" It was then that Adam saw the two kids standing shyly beside the buggy. They looked like miniature versions of their father, minus the beard. "Come say hello to your aunt Es." To Faith he said, "You remember Jacob and Martin."

"No, I'm sorry but I don't," she answered, bending to say hello to each of her nephews.

Seeing the puzzled look on Levi's face, Adam explained, "Your sister has amnesia. There was an accident and she sustained a head injury."

"You have forgotten your own family?" He stared at her in stunned disbelief.

She nodded. "I have no memory of anything that happened before the accident last winter. It's only because John and Mary Miller recognized me that I am here now."

Her brother stood looking at her with his mouth open. "And that is why you've been gone? Because you didn't remember that you belonged here?"

"Yes."

The disbelief changed to relief, followed by a smile. "If that is the case, then everything will be fine."

Adam was as puzzled as Faith was.

"There will be no shunning, not if you are ill and do not know you're Amish."

The screen door opened and the two little girls who'd

been gazing out at them earlier poked their heads outside. Levi looked at them and said, "All right. You can come and say hello, too." Once he waved they came running over to see Faith.

He put a loving arm around his daughters. "Don't tell me you've forgotten these two, as well?"

"*Ja*," she said with an apologetic smile.

"Mary Ellen and Katie." He touched each of their shoulders as he introduced them. "Say hello to your aunt."

Faith conversed in German with them briefly, then turned to Adam, amazement lighting her eyes. "I have nieces and nephews."

"*Ja*, lots of them," Levi added. "Gideon has two boys and Samuel and Ben each have one." Seeing her confused look he said, "You have four brothers. You're our only sister."

"It's a big family," she noted.

"With more on the way," he said with grin. "Sarah's pregnant." Seeing her puzzled look he quickly added, "My wife. She's inside with the little ones. Does Dat know you're home?"

She shook her head. "I thought he'd be here."

"Dat has moved into the grossdawdy house." Seeing her confusion he said, "Don't worry. You'll make sense of things soon. You go inside and visit with Sarah. I'll get Dat." He headed back to the buggy.

Faith's nieces and nephews gathered around her, looking at her expectantly as they waited for her to go inside. She gave Adam a helpless look and he could see that she was overwhelmed by the discoveries she was making.

"You go on in. I'll wait out here," he said out of respect for the Amish.

Faith asked the oldest of the children, "Do you think it would be all right if Mr. Novak came inside?"

Jacob closed one eye and cocked his head. "Mam has English friends who come to tea."

Faith looked at Adam. "I think it's okay."

But Adam remembered the look that had been on her sister-in-law's face when they'd first arrived, and he decided against it. "No. This is your time with your family. I'll sit out here. It's a beautiful day." He took a seat on one of the cane rockers.

It was peaceful on the porch. The house sat on a hill, giving it a vantage point overlooking the fields of alfalfa and corn. As he looked around the homestead, he tried to imagine Faith as a little girl running around barefoot in the grass and sitting on the wooden swing that hung on a rope from an old oak tree next to the house.

Time passed slowly as he waited and wondered what she was learning about herself inside the house. It wasn't long before she came back out.

"Are your questions getting answered?" he asked as she sat down on the rocker next to his.

"Some of them. I know my mother died last winter, right before I disappeared."

He placed his hand over hers. "I'm sorry."

"This used to be her and my father's house. It felt strange to touch the things inside." Her face was pensive as she talked.

"Do you feel comfortable in the house?"

"Yes, and no…. It's hard to explain." Faith went silent and he wished that she'd try to explain.

"Any memory flashes while you were inside?"

She shook her head. "I think I should take a walk around the farm…see if I can't find something that looks familiar."

"Would you like me to go with you?"

Before she could answer, the sound of a horse-drawn buggy approaching again had them glancing toward the road. She stood as it drew near the house. "Levi's back."

Adam watched a gray-bearded man dressed in the same clothing as Faith's brother and wearing a similar straw hat climb out of the buggy. He started toward Faith, then stopped. She didn't wait for him to reach her, but went down the steps to meet him. From the porch Adam watched her shyly approach him and speak to him in German. He expected them to embrace, but either Ebram Miller was a cold man or he was not happy to see his daughter.

After a few minutes, Faith brought him up onto the porch. He extended his hand to Adam. "I thank you for bringing my daughter home. She was lost, but now is found."

Adam understood the tears in his eyes. Although he and this man were worlds apart in their beliefs, he had experienced the same emotion when Megan had come to live with him.

"You will stay and have dinner with us?" Ebram asked.

Adam glanced at Faith who was once more surrounded by her nieces and nephews, enjoying the attention they lavished upon her.

"It's kind of you to offer, but I need to return to the city," he answered. He turned to Faith. "How much longer do you want to stay?"

Ebram turned to Faith. "You're not going to leave?" His voice resonated with authority, making the question sound more like an order. "This is your home. You are Amish, not English."

Faith looked at Adam, a helplessness in her eyes as the circle of Amish children gathered around her begged her to stay.

"Dat's right, Es." Levi shared his father's sentiments. "There shouldn't be any shunning. You were not baptized."

"I'm—I'm not worried about that," she told him.

"If you want to leave and come back, we can do that," Adam suggested.

He saw a fire burn in her father's eyes at the suggestion. "No, she should not leave."

"How are you going to find those lost memories if you're not in the place where those memories were made?" Levi asked. When she remained indecisive he added, "You can have your old room. Mary Ellen's in there now, but she can move in with Katie."

"But I didn't bring a change of clothes," Faith told him.

"Sarah never got rid of your clothes. They're in a trunk in the attic," her brother told her.

Adam could see Faith was torn as to what she should do. "You can always come visit for a few days when you're more prepared," Adam suggested.

He thought it seemed like a good solution. A visit would be good. In the meantime, she could go home with him knowing that there was nothing in her past to keep them from being together.

He thought it was what she would do. That's why he was caught off guard when she said, "I have to stay…at least for a while."

He wanted to tell her she didn't, but he knew he couldn't put any pressure on her to go back with him. For months she'd been waiting for this moment. Now it had come. He was simply going to have to be patient.

"Wouldn't it be better to go back to St. Paul, pack a few things…? Megan doesn't know about any of this."

Faith chewed on her lower lip before saying, "No, I think it's better if I stay. I'll phone Megan and the Carsons and explain."

"There are no phones here," her father's voice boomed.

"I have a cell phone," she announced.

"We only use phones for emergency, Es, and then it's in town, not here," Levi explained.

"But this is an emergency. I need to tell the little girl I care for I won't be there tomorrow."

Father and son exchanged glances, then the father walked away muttering something in German. It was enough for Adam to say, "You're not going to stay, are you?"

"Yes. I'll be all right. I'll keep the cell phone."

He wanted to argue but he could see that she was intrigued by this new world she had yet to uncover. "I hate leaving you," he couldn't resist saying in a low voice as she walked him to the Lexus.

She bit down on her lip, as if to keep from crying. "I know."

"You know you can call me if you need anything?"

She nodded. "You understand why I have to stay."

He didn't, but he nodded anyway.

"I have to find out who I am."

"I know who you are," he told her.

"You know the woman you want me to be," she said quietly. Someone called out to her in German and she looked back over her shoulder and waved. "I have to go. Tell Megan and Lori I will call them." She choked back a sob and turned away from him.

It took all of his willpower not to grab her and put her in the car and take her home. As he drove away from the farm he saw her being taken into the white farmhouse surrounded by people who regarded him as an outsider.

At the moment he felt very much like he was outside of Faith's life. He only hoped that it wouldn't be long before he was back on the inside.

As soon as Adam was gone, Faith had an overwhelming urge to pull out the cell phone and tell him to come right back and get her. But she couldn't. For months she'd been wanting to find the key to unlock her past. Now it was there right in front of her. She needed to do whatever she could to get to know the woman they called Esther Miller. These people were her family—something she'd been longing to have ever since she woke up with no memory. Now she wasn't going to turn away from them simply because their lifestyle was not what she'd expected.

One of the first things her father had said to her was, "Sarah will see that you are dressed properly." While the

men went back to their work outdoors, Sarah took Faith
to the attic where she lifted the lid on a cedar chest and
said, "These are yours."

Faith looked inside at several piles of clothing, all
neatly folded. She reached for a dark blue dress, shaking it out as she pulled it from the trunk. It looked very
similar to the one that Sarah wore. As Faith held it up
to her shoulders she frowned. She examined the dress,
noticing there were no buttons, only hooks and eyes.

"You should wear the black one since it's not been a
year yet since Mam died," Sarah advised her in a serious tone.

Faith noticed the black one was identical to the blue
one. Next she picked up a black pleated cap.

"Your prayer *kappe*," Sarah said. "Married women
wear white, single women and girls wear black." Which
would explain why Faith's nieces also all wore black.

Faith glanced around the attic, looking for something familiar, but all she saw were somebody else's
treasures. "This is an old house, isn't it?" she said, noticing the aging timbers of the roof.

"*Ja.* You were born and raised here. You don't remember any of it?"

She shook her head. "Some of the past is slowly
coming back—like pictures on a postcard. I see things
pop into my head."

"What kind of things?"

"Like the wash frozen stiff on the line."

Sarah smiled in understanding. "Mondays are not
my favorite days, especially in winter."

"But you keep doing the laundry even though it's

freezing cold." Faith had sorted through everything in the trunk. "Do we have to wear dresses all the time?"

Sarah took it as a criticism, her shoulders stiffening as she said, "It is a good life, Es. You shouldn't run away from it."

"Is that what I did?"

She shrugged. "It's not for me to say. Levi says you may have been taken against your will."

"By whom?"

"Someone English."

Faith wondered if that was why she had been assaulted. "I guess we won't know until my memory returns, will we?"

"You want Levi to carry this to your room?"

"If that's where I'm going to be, yes. Which room is it?"

"You don't remember?"

When she shook her head, Sarah said she would give her a tour of the house. Besides the large kitchen, there were five bedrooms, a pantry and a family room.

"Where do I shower?" Faith asked.

"The washhouse is out back."

After a brief tour of the outbuildings, Faith was relieved to return to the house. Mary Ellen's room was very similar to the other bedrooms and familiar to Faith because it was the one she'd seen in a flashback. It was simply furnished with a bed and a chest of drawers with a quilt covering the single-size mattress. At nine years old Mary Ellen was three years older than Megan, yet there were few things to identify this as a room belonging to a young girl. Except for a shelf that held religious books and a few board games stacked neatly to one side, it had nothing in common with the pink princess room Megan enjoyed. There was, however, a doll made out of cloth on the bed. It was dressed in the traditional Amish clothing and had no face. Suddenly the dream she'd had the night she'd met Adam made sense.

Levi had brought the chest containing her clothes down from the attic. Because Sarah had suggested she change into her Amish clothes for dinner out of respect for her father, she had complied, but after only a few hours of wearing the long, heavy dress she longed to be back in her shorts and tank top. If she'd hoped that putting on one of her old dresses and pinning her hair up under her prayer *kappe* would give her a sense of purpose and an awareness of who she was, she was in for a disappointment. All she felt was out of place.

By the time the sun had set on her first day as Esther Miller, she was tired. She sat on the front porch, listening to the silence. The sound of the screen door creaking told her she had company. She looked up to see Levi had taken the chair next to hers.

"Are you all right?" He spoke in German.

She wasn't. She was lonely and missing St. Paul. Seeing how happy her brother was because she was back she didn't have the heart to tell him that. "I'm fine. Thank you for asking. Everything feels strange yet familiar at the same time. I know that doesn't make sense, but it's the way it is."

"I'm glad you're here with us, Es." His voice was strong and sincere.

"Thank you. I appreciate your hospitality."

"It's not hospitality. You belong here, Es, more than Sarah and I do. Mam wanted you to have this house. Sarah and I only moved here because we thought you weren't coming back."

Curious, she asked, "Where were you living?"

"Down near Granger. Sarah's brother moved into the house we had there." He leaned closer to her and whispered, "No one is supposed to know but he's planning to marry Katie Schultheimer this fall."

"It's a secret?"

"That's our way, Es. All weddings are kept secret until two weeks before the ceremony. People usually guess something's going on though when they see the extra celery being planted."

The wedding food. She knew now why she'd mentioned it that night she'd cooked dinner for Adam's grandfather.

"This is like old times, us sitting on the front porch," her brother reminisced.

"Were we close while we were growing up?"

"*Ja.* All of us were. It is our way, Es."

She sighed. "I wish I could remember."

"You never liked the farm chores. You wanted to help Mam in the house, but Dat used to make you clean out the gutter in the barn and pitch manure the same as us boys. There are always plenty of chores on a farm," he said with a good-natured grin.

"What was our mother like?"

"She was good and kind. She never said a mean word about anyone. You look a lot like her and you have her patience."

She had looked for a picture of her in the house, but there had been none. Sarah had told her the Amish don't believe in graven images. Unfortunately for Faith, the only pictures she had of her mother were locked up in her memory.

"You look tired, Es. You should go to bed. Tomorrow is another day and four-thirty comes early."

"We get up that early?"

"We're not like the lazy English," he scoffed.

"All English are not lazy," she shot back, thinking of how hard Adam worked. "You shouldn't make such generalizations."

"Now you even sound like Mam," he said with a grin.

"I'll take that as a compliment."

"You should."

There was another silence between them before he said, "I know what the English are like, Es. I did my running around with the English when I was a teen."

She looked at him in surprise. "And Mam and Dat allowed that?"

"All Amish parents do. They turn their heads and look the other way while teens experiment with the English way. It's called *rumspringa*. Parents don't like it, but they know that once the children see that fancy clothes and fast cars are not what makes them happy, they'll come back."

Curious, she asked, "You didn't like your time with the English?"

"*Ja,* I admit it was fun for a while. I went to the movies, I played the video games, I listened to rock music, but it's not the way for me. I didn't have to be baptized, Es. I could have left and never come back."

"Why didn't you?"

"Because I belong here. So do you."

"I don't feel as if I do," she admitted candidly.

"That's because of the amnesia. In time you'll see you do," her brother stated.

Faith wasn't so sure. She'd seen the look on her father's face when Sarah had set her place at the table. Although Levi had assured her she wouldn't be shunned, Faith knew that church law was strict. The only reason why she didn't suffer the same fate as others who left the Amish community was because she hadn't been baptized. She didn't understand why.

Most Amish were baptized between eighteen and twenty-one, yet she was almost twenty-seven and hadn't officially become a member of the church. The more Faith learned about the rules and regulations of the Amish religion, the better she understood why she hadn't decided to become an official member of the church.

As she crawled into the bed that she'd slept in as a child, she wasn't filled with nostalgia. It didn't feel warm and familiar, but cold and strange. She thought about all the nights she'd gone to sleep at the Carsons, wishing she were in her own bed with her own family. Now she was and she wished she was back in St. Paul.

She pulled out the cell phone Adam had given her and dialed his number. Her heart pounded in her chest in anticipation of hearing his voice. Only he never answered. She got his voice mail.

Feeling extremely lonely, she dialed Lori's number. She answered on the first ring and Faith could have jumped for joy. Knowing that the rest of the house was in silence and that she was breaking one of the most important rules of the community—having a telephone in the house—she kept her conversation short.

When Lori asked if she, Matthew and Megan could visit, Faith suggested she come on Sunday afternoon when Sarah and Levi would be taking the kids to Granger to visit Sarah's brother. When Lori asked if she could bring her anything, Faith asked if she wouldn't mind picking up a few of her things from the Carsons'.

On Sunday, the first thing Megan said to her when they arrived was "You look different."

Faith gave her a hug. "My clothes may be different but inside I'm the same me."

"I brought you a picture," she said, handing her a drawing of stick people. "It's me and my dad on the boat."

Faith's heart contracted when she looked at the drawing. She gave Megan another hug. "Thank you. I'm going to put this in the house and then I'll show you around the farm."

With Matthew in a stroller and Megan clinging to Faith's hand, the four of them headed for the barn, which was empty.

"Where are the cows?" Megan asked.

"Out in the pasture. They'll be back when it's milking time this evening."

Next she showed them the chicken coop where she let Megan hold a baby chick. Faith expected it to be awkward having them at the farm, but it wasn't. She was just happy to see them.

When Lori suggested they drive into Harmony for an

ice cream, Faith knew she should say no, but she didn't want to disappoint Megan.

She should have expected the whispers and stares. An Amish woman was seldom seen climbing out of an Audi, and although Amish did patronize the ice-cream parlor, it didn't happen on a Sunday and with the English in tow.

"Maybe this wasn't such a good idea," Lori said apologetically.

"No, it's fine. I'm glad you came."

Then Megan said, "When are you coming back from your vacation?"

"I don't know," she answered honestly.

"How come you're not wearing your bracelet?" Megan asked when she noticed Faith's leather wrist strap was missing.

"I put it in a special place," Faith told her, reluctant to tell her that Amish women were forbidden to wear any type of jewelry.

Back at the farm, as they prepared to leave Lori asked her, "When are you coming back?" When Faith didn't respond immediately, she added, "You are coming back, aren't you?"

"I want to," she said.

"Then come back," she stated.

"It's not that simple."

"Why not?"

How could she explain what she didn't understand herself? As much as she felt she didn't belong in the Amish community, there was something keeping her there. Maybe it was her past. Whatever the reason, part of her felt as if she belonged with Levi and his family.

The baby began to fuss, putting an end to any further conversation. "Look, I know you want to understand your past, but if you ever need someone to talk to, I'm here for you."

Faith thanked her and gave her a hug. "Everything will work out the way it's supposed to." She leaned into the car to kiss each of the children goodbye.

"I hope you find what you're looking for, Faith," Lori said, then climbed into her car and drove back to the city.

"I do, too," Faith mumbled to herself as the car rolled out of sight. "I do, too."

CHAPTER FOURTEEN

"LOOKS LIKE THE TRIP wore them out," Adam said to Lori as he glanced into the back seat of her car where Megan and Matthew had both fallen asleep.

"It was a long day," his sister-in-law said, stretching as she climbed out of the car. She didn't close her door, but leaned up against the frame to talk to him. "We did a lot of walking. Faith gave us a tour of the farm. It's beautiful country down there—everything's so neat and pristine looking."

"How is she?" He was hungry for information about her—anything that Lori could tell him.

"She says she's fine."

"And you believe her?"

"Have you ever known Faith to lie?"

He hadn't. "She doesn't return my phone calls."

"She's not supposed to use the telephone."

"She phoned you."

Her face softened in understanding. "She's trying to sort through everything that she's discovered."

"Has her memory returned?"

"I wish it had. Maybe then she'd leave."

"She might not want to," he said soberly.

"Are you kidding? That way of life is so not Faith.

They've got rules about everything…what you wear, where you sit, what you can read, what you can't read."

"I guess unless you grow up in that world you don't understand the attraction," he noted.

"It's hard to believe Faith did grow up there. She may lead a simple life and have modest needs, but she has an insatiable thirst for knowledge. I think she's read nearly every book in our library. And she loves the art institute and the science museum. You know that." He nodded in agreement. "It doesn't make sense that she would want to stay in a society that doesn't allow its members to go to school past the eighth grade."

"You're not saying anything I haven't thought myself," he told her.

"Then why haven't you done something about it?"

"Like what? Kidnap her and bring her back here?" He didn't want to admit that that was a plan he'd considered during a brief moment of insanity. "The Amish way may not be what you or I would choose, but you read the same statistics I do. Very few of their members leave, and it's not because anyone is holding them against their will."

"So you're not going to do anything?"

"I am doing something. I'm giving her what she told me she needs—time to make up her own mind."

Lori sighed in frustration, shoving a strand of hair back from her forehead. "Never mind me. I'm just tired, and it was a shock seeing Faith looking like a peasant out of the nineteenth century." She glanced back into the car. "I'd better take Matthew home."

Adam opened the rear door and undid Megan's seat

belt. As he did, she awakened with a start. Confused, she asked, "Where's Faith?"

"She's in Harmony, remember?" Adam answered, lifting her into his arms.

She nestled her head against his shoulder. "I wish she'd come home," she said sleepily.

"Me, too," Adam told her.

"Then do something," Lori mouthed to him.

Later, as he listened to Megan talk nonstop about her visit to Faith's farm, Adam found himself full of envy. His daughter had spent the day with the one woman he wanted so badly that he ached, yet he couldn't even reach her by phone.

After a restless night of debating whether or not he should take Lori's suggestion and do something, he decided to go to Harmony and see for himself that she was all right. He didn't tell Megan or her latest nanny, Delores, where he was going except to say he would be off-site for the day and to call him on his cell phone if he was needed. Then he jumped into the Lexus and headed to the Miller farm.

As he pulled into the driveway, the first thing he saw was the wash hanging from one end of the house to the barn. Men's pants and shirts, all identical except for their sizes, flapped in the gentle breeze. Then he saw a woman in a black dress bent over the garden, her head covered with a black pleated cap. When she heard the car she glanced over her shoulder and he saw it was Faith.

She recognized the Lexus and rose to her feet, dusting off her hands on her apron. She looked nervous as she came toward him and his heart plummeted. She didn't want him there. Then a young girl wearing a similar dress appeared at the door, a baby on her hip. Faith said something to her in German and she went back inside.

"This is a surprise."

"A pleasant one, I hope." He wanted to take her in his arms and kiss her until she ran out of breath, but she was dressed like Esther Miller, Ebram's daughter.

Then she smiled at him and she was his Faith again. "A very pleasant one," she echoed. "I could use a break." She nodded toward the mound of weeds she'd pulled from the flower garden. "And I bet you could use a stretch after that long drive. Want to take a walk?"

"Sure." He glanced down and saw her feet were bare. "Don't you want to get some shoes?"

She shook her head. "Not for where we're going. Come."

She led him across the gravel road and into a thicket of small trees, never flinching as her feet traveled the rough ground. If it hadn't been for the worn footpath he would have thought she was getting them lost. She chatted nervously, much of what she said being the same things Megan had told him last night.

Finally he heard a gurgling sound at about the same time she said, "This is it." When she pushed aside an elderberry branch he saw why her face glowed with delight. Tumbling over a small cascade of rocks was a waterfall that emptied into a small creek. Wildflowers grew on either side of its banks, creating a small haven of peace and quiet. Faith removed her apron and *kappe,* then gave him an impish grin and said, "Help me out of this, will you?"

This was her dress and she didn't need to ask him twice. The hooks and eyes on her dress were something he hadn't ever encountered in undressing a woman. He was up to the challenge, however, and before he knew it she was lifting the dress over her head.

He wasn't sure what he expected she'd be wearing underneath it, but it wasn't a pair of shorts and a tank top. "I've been doing this ever since I was a teenager," she said as she waded into the creek. "It's against the rules but I don't care."

"You have your memory back?" he asked as he watched her splash about in the water.

"Some. I now know I'm a nanny and a midwife."

"That's why you knew what to do for Lori."

"Yes." She raised her face toward the sky, her eyes closed. "Doesn't it smell heavenly here? You ought to take off your shoes and socks and come in. Or don't engineers like to get their feet wet?" She glanced at him with a twinkle of mischief in her eyes.

He removed his casual loafers and socks and rolled up his pant legs, then waded into the water. "It's cold!"

"That's what makes it special. It makes you feel all tingly."

"I don't need water for that. All I have to do is look at you," he told her.

She gazed up at him then, as if she was remembering the times he'd held her in his arms. Her eyes darkened and she looked away, but not before he'd seen the desire there. It was too great of a temptation for him to resist. He pulled her into his arms and kissed her. She tasted warm and sweet and exactly as he remembered.

When the kiss finally ended, he said, "I've been going crazy—" but she stopped him, placing her fingers on his lips.

"Please don't say anything. Just hold me."

So they stood in the middle of the creek with his arms wrapped around her while the water trickled past their ankles. Only the sounds of nature broke the silence. When her body began to tremble he thought it was because she was cold, but then he realized she was crying.

He tried to comfort her, planting kisses on her cheek and murmuring softly, "Don't cry, Faith. It's going to be all right."

She pushed him away and waded back to the bank where she reached for the long dark dress.

"Don't put that on," he told her.

"I have to."

"Why?"

"Because I'm Plain," she said, then pulled it over her head and down over her body until none of her delicious skin showed. "It's what Plain women wear." There was a challenge in her voice, as if daring him to question the decision she'd made to live by Amish standards.

"How many Plain women sneak around with shorts and tank tops under their dresses?"

That had her cracking a smile.

"I like this place," he said as sunshine filtered through the canopy of trees. "I've missed you, Faith." He hadn't realized just how much until he'd seen her splashing about in the creek.

"I've missed you, too," she said quietly, but when he would have taken her in his arms again, she stepped away.

"I've been trying to give you the time you need with your family, but I want you back in my life, Faith. I want to cool off in a creek with you on a hot summer day and not have to worry about anybody seeing us."

"I am Amish, Adam. Most of those memories I've recovered are from my childhood. And they're good memories. Do you know what *rumspringa* is?"

He shook his head.

"It's a time when Amish teens experiment with what it's like to be English. They can do whatever they want and their parents turn a blind eye. The parents figure it's better for them to see the English world and all it has to offer and then to choose to come back and be Amish."

"And you did this?" He held his breath while he waited for her answer.

"Levi said I did."

"But you don't remember?"

"Not yet, but whether I do or do not remember all of my past does not change the fact that this is the foundation upon which my life has been built, the eyes through which I've see the world."

"I would never ask you to turn your back on your family," he told her.

She looked at him then, her eyes filled with pain. "But don't you see? I can't be with my family and be with you. Our worlds are too different."

"Don't you mean that your world will not allow you to be a part of mine? Faith, do you really want to give up everything you've known in my world to live the kind of life you have here?"

She looked away. "This life isn't what you think it

is. If you look around at the people in this community, you will see contentment on their faces. People help each other. Children love and respect their parents. When someone is suffering, everyone drops what they're doing and goes to help. It is a strong community of caring, loving people. There are no homeless Amish," she finished quietly.

"I'm not saying there aren't good people here and that this way of life doesn't fulfill some people's needs. I'm asking you if you honestly believe that you can be happy living in this world after living in my world." Silence stretched between them as he waited for her answer.

"I don't know," she finally said. She wrapped her arms across her middle and turned away from him.

He wanted to embrace her and convince her that she did know the answer, that she belonged in his world, but ever since they'd met there had been an undeniably strong physical attraction between them. At one time that would have been enough for him to justify having a relationship with her. But ever since she'd left him to go back to the Amish he'd come to the realization that he wanted more than passion. He wanted to share every aspect of his life with her.

"I'm in love with you, Faith," he told her because for the first time in his life it was true.

He wasn't sure what he expected her to say, but he didn't think that she'd start to cry. She turned away from him and said, "I can't be the woman you want— at least not yet."

He walked up behind her and pressed his front to her back, wrapping his hands across her stomach. She didn't

resist, but leaned against him, quietly crying. He didn't
try to kiss her, but simply held her close.

"I should go," he finally said.

She nodded and moved away from him. "I'll show
you the way back."

Adam followed her back to the house, neither one of
them uttering a single word. When they'd reached his
car, she faced him, her cheeks blotchy from crying.
When he would have touched her, she backed away, her
eyes darting to the house. She couldn't risk kissing or
even touching him in view of her family.

"Please don't give up on us, Faith," he said, then got
in the car and drove away.

FAITH KNEW SHE WAS in trouble when she saw the look
on her father's face when he walked into the house with
Levi. He sat down on the bench on the opposite side of
the table from where she was shelling peas. Levi stood
several feet behind.

"Do you know what you've done, Esther?"

No doubt her father had heard that Adam had been
to see her that morning and that she'd been in the creek
in her English clothes. Faith glanced at Sarah who stood
with her back to her at the stove. She was disappointed
in her sister-in-law. She thought she was her friend yet
it hadn't taken her long to get word to Levi that she'd
been in the woods with Adam.

Before she could utter a single word of explanation,
her father said, "Doing business on a Sunday, the Lord's
day, is not our way. You should have been with Levi and
Sarah visiting family."

It was then she realized that he wasn't referring to her visit from Adam, but her going into town with Lori and the children. Not only had she gone in an automobile, but she'd gone into the ice-cream parlor, a place of business on a Sunday.

"I'm sorry," she apologized. "I meant no disrespect. It's just that the little girl I used to care for wanted an ice cream and…" She trailed off when her father raised his hand indicating he wanted no more words.

"I will arrange for you to talk to the bishop," he said, and rose to his feet.

"Because I had an ice-cream cone?" She jumped up. "Dat, that's not reasonable."

"Save your words for the bishop," he bellowed at her before stomping away.

Faith looked at her brother, pleading for understanding. "Levi, you must know I wouldn't deliberately hurt the family."

"You shouldn't have gone to town with the English woman, Es," he said, his eyes expressing his own feeling of disappointment. "Don't worry. It's not a major offense. You can make right with the bishop."

"But why should I have to make right?" she demanded, which had Sarah leaving the room, obviously not willing to be a part of the discussion taking place between brother and sister.

"You're starting to sound English yourself," he commented.

"Why, because I ask questions? And why can't I be both English and Amish?"

"Because you can't live in both worlds, Es," he said

with a sigh of frustration. "Stop trying to defend yourself. All you have to do is go to the bishop and tell him
you were wrong. Stop thinking like the English and
take your punishment. "

Frustration rose inside her. He didn't understand. No
one did. She ran out of the house and back to the creek
where only a short while ago Adam had told her he
loved her. Had she been wrong to let him go? Life with
the Amish was a struggle. As much as she wanted to be
a part of a family, she didn't want to live a life of sepa-
ration from the rest of society. She didn't want to be separated from Adam.

After a brief respite at the creek, Faith went back to
the house. She found Sarah outside hanging the wash
on the line. Faith didn't speak to her but went into the
kitchen where she discovered that someone had finished shelling the peas. She suspected it was Sarah and
decided to make them a cup of tea.

She lifted the lid over the firebox to check to make
sure the coals were still hot from when Sarah had
made coffee earlier. After stirring them with an iron
poker, she added several sticks of wood, trying not to
think of how easy it would have been to zap a cup of
water in Adam's microwave. She filled a teapot with
water from the hand pump and set it at the front of
the stove.

She tried not to think about the scene she'd had with
her father, but it bothered her that she'd brought disrespect to him because of something of so little consequence. She looked about the empty kitchen that had
nothing but the basic necessities. It was Sarah's home,

yet there were none of her personal touches other than a cross-stitched Biblical verse and a small wooden sign engraved with a saying her mother had often repeated. Work Hard, Rest Well.

There were no pictures in the house. No works of art, no photographs. She closed her eyes and tried to see her mother's face. She'd known the gentle touch of her heart and hands, yet she had trouble seeing her loving smile. Suddenly the memory of the last time she'd seen her flashed in her head. Her mother was in bed, her long hair flowing loose at her sides. She'd said many things to her, all of them wise and comforting at a time when Faith needed to be comforted. But it was her last words that Faith remembered best. "Follow your heart and let God do the judging."

Let God do the judging. Not her father. Not her brothers. Not the bishop.

Faith pulled the teapot off the stove and raced out the door past Sarah, past the barn, past the chicken house and past the grossdawdy house. She didn't stop until she'd reached the fenced area that was the cemetery. She searched the cement markers until she found the one that read Lydia Miller, Sixty-Seven Years, Eleven Months, Four Days. She lovingly fingered the engraved letters, tears welling in her eyes.

"I have to leave, Mam. I don't belong here." She slumped over on the ground, sobbing.

How long she was there she didn't know. When she felt a man's hand on her shoulder, she looked up and saw her father.

"You remember her?"

She nodded, biting down on her lip. "She was a good mother."

"*Ja.* She worked hard."

Faith nodded. "It's right that a wildflower should grow so close," she said, fingering the tiny pink flower next to the marker. "She used to tell me that every plot of soil, no matter how small, should give life to some useful plant."

"You have her gift for gardening," her father told her.

"It seems to be the only thing I have of hers," she said. "She knew her place."

"And you always seemed to be looking for yours," he said quietly.

"What did you want my place to be, Dat?"

"Here, on the farm, in a good marriage leading a useful life."

"And if I chose not to have that place, would I no longer be your daughter?" Her voice wobbled as she asked the question.

His shoulders sagged and he looked at her with sadness in his eyes. "Are you telling me you are going to leave?"

The pain she saw in his face tugged at Faith's heart. "I can't be Plain anymore."

"You have recovered all of your memory?"

She shook her head. "No. What will I discover when I do? Did I leave on my own? Did I choose not to be Amish? Do you know what happened the night I left?"

He didn't answer any of the questions she fired at him, but got to his feet and started back toward the farm. She started after him, calling out, "Dat, tell me, please."

He didn't stop but kept going. She knew it was useless to follow him. No matter how she pleaded with him, he wouldn't talk to her. In the short time she'd been back she'd learned that.

When he didn't come to lunch Levi asked about his absence. Faith told him that she'd seen him at the cemetery and what they'd talked about.

"So you're going to leave again?"

"Again?" Frustrated, she said, "I wish someone would tell me what happened that night I disappeared." Seeing Sarah and Levi exchanging glances, she pulled on her brother's shirtsleeve. "Levi, you know, don't you?"

She could see he was reluctant to talk in front of the children. He nodded toward the door, then got up and left. She followed him outside onto the porch.

"Tell me. Did I leave of my own free will?" she demanded.

He nodded. "You had a fight with Dat."

"On the night of Mam's funeral?" She found it hard to believe she'd argue on such a day.

"Most of the relatives had gone. We were putting the house back together when Dat said something you didn't agree with."

"What did he say?"

"You couldn't stop crying and he said you should feel worse at a birth than at a death. Being in Heaven is better than the struggles of life."

"And what did I say?"

"You screamed at him that there didn't need to be so many struggles, that if we weren't Plain, Mam would be alive.'

She gasped. "Why did Mam die?"

"I told you. She had the illness that left her with a weak heart, but you told Dat it was all the hard work on the farm that killed her. Then you left."

She left. *She'd* made the decision to leave. "Where would I have been going when I left here?"

He shrugged. "You stormed out of here saying that you had English friends you could stay with. We figured that you went to stay with someone you met through Mrs. Tucker."

"Mrs. Tucker?"

"She was the English woman you worked for as a part-time nanny. She's the one who got you interested in all the books and encouraged you to leave."

Trembling, Faith sat down on the rocker. She willed her mind to remember that night, but as usual, it was a dark void. "Was it the first time I left?"

He shook his head. "You left one other time, but then Mam got sick so you came home to nurse her."

So she had already made the decision she didn't want to be Amish long before that night of the accident. Suddenly the flashbacks of memory made sense—her mother telling her she needed to confess to the bishop, the man's voice that had screamed at her to get out. "I don't belong here," she said quietly.

Levi sat down beside her. "That's not true, Es. This is your home. It's a good place."

She didn't say anything, but stared out at the field of alfalfa gently blowing in the wind. "Why didn't you tell me when I came back? You and Dat and Sarah and everyone else led me to believe that I was happy here. Why didn't you tell me the truth?"

"Because I was hoping that rebellious streak inside you was gone and that you'd come back to us. It's good to be Plain, Es."

"Maybe for you, but not for me," she said sadly. "I can't stay, Levi."

He slowly nodded his head in understanding. "You'll keep in touch?"

She swallowed back the lump in her throat. "Of course. You'll always be my brother."

Later that afternoon, when Jacob brought the mail in from the box next to the road, there was an envelope addressed to her. It was from Megan.

Inside was a letter she'd written herself, printed in large block letters. It said, "Dear Faith. Next week is your birthday. Can me and Lori have a party for you? Love, Megan."

In a week she would have her twenty-seventh birthday. The words of her mother echoed in her ears. "Follow your heart and let God do the judging."

Faith went up to the room she'd had as a child and found her cell phone. She dialed the number she'd known the longest. When a man's voice answered she said, "Dr. Carson, it's Faith. I need to ask you a favor."

WHEN LORI CALLED and invited Adam to a surprise birthday party, his first question had been to ask whose birthday it was. She'd told him that's what the surprise was. Normally it was the guest of honor who was in the dark about the birthday celebration, but she wanted to do something different for a change and surprise the guests.

Adam suspected it was her way of setting him up with one of her eligible single friends. Greg had mentioned something about Lori wanting to set him up with a blind date to take his mind off Faith not coming back.

He would have refused to go to this party had it not been for Megan. Lori had roped her into helping her plan the thing and she was putting pressure on Adam to attend. When he'd asked his sister-in-law how old the guest of honor was and what type of present he should get, Lori had answered, "Oh, no presents. This is just a fun way of getting people together."

She'd been just as evasive about the guest list, although he had heard from his grandfather that he would be there as well as several other Novak employees. As Adam dressed for the party, he tried not to think that he could be enjoying the weekend on the river had not his sister-in-law been playing Cupid.

As he and Megan were about to leave she said, "Wait here," and ran into the kitchen. When she returned, she carried a bouquet of fresh-cut flowers. "I got these for the birthday girl," she said with a grin.

"I thought we weren't supposed to bring anything," he protested.

"They can be from both of us."

When he opened the door she tapped his arm. "You forgot my stuff."

It was then he noticed her overnight bag and pillow.

"I'm staying at Lori's tonight."

"Any particular reason?" he asked as he picked up her things.

"You'll see," she said with a giggle.

He began to get nervous. It was one thing for Lori to set him up on a blind date, but what did she think he would want to do with this unseen person?

When they arrived at his brother's house, everyone was in the backyard on the patio having a great time, judging by the sounds of laughter he heard. Chinese lanterns had been strung across the yard with pink paper streamers dangling everywhere.

"Oh, good, you're here," Lori said when she saw him. "Now we only have our surprise birthday girl."

"I'll get her!" Megan said excitedly.

As she disappeared inside the house, Adam chided Lori. "I really wish you wouldn't involve my daughter in this."

"In what?" she asked innocently.

He lifted one eyebrow. "You think I don't know a blind date when I see one?"

She smiled and spread her hands. "You're right. I plead guilty." She looked down at the flowers still in his hand. "Oh, good, you remembered the flowers."

Megan's head poked out the door. "Are you ready?"

Lori began singing the birthday song, waving her hands for everyone to join in. Then Adam saw two familiar faces—Avery and Marie Carson—and he suddenly understood why Megan had been so excited.

Faith then came through the patio door, clutching his daughter's hand. He knew there could only be one reason why she would have traded her long black dress for a pink sundress that left her shoulders bare. She'd come back to him and Megan. When her eyes met his, she smiled and he knew he wasn't mistaken.

As the birthday song ended, everyone clapped. He watched as she slowly made her way over to him, greeting the guests with a smile and a hug as she accepted their good wishes with Megan at her side. They could have easily been mother and daughter, they looked so much alike. Her skin had a golden tan from hours spent working outdoors and her blond curtain of hair had grown so that it hung down to her shoulders.

When they reached him Megan said, "Fooled you, didn't we, Daddy?"

"If the surprise is this nice, you can fool me anytime you want," he said, gazing into Faith's blue eyes. "Happy birthday," he said, presenting her with the flowers and a hug. As he held her close he whispered in her ear, "I'll give you a proper birthday greeting when there aren't so many people around."

He loved the tint of color that warmed her cheeks at the thought.

"Welcome back," he said as he released her.

"It's good to be back," she answered. "It's where I belong."

"Faith is not going on vacation again for a long, long time," Megan said, still clinging to her side.

"That's good to hear," Adam said, unable to take his eyes off Faith. "Is today really your birthday?"

"Yes. I can't believe Lori or Megan didn't tell you."

"We wanted it to be a secret," Megan announced gleefully. "You know what birthday means?"

"It's the start of a brand-new year for me," Faith answered her, but her smile was for Adam.

"And a great one it's going to be," Lori said as she

passed by carrying a tray of glasses of champagne. As she handed one to Adam she said in a voice for his ears only, "Now aren't you glad I had Megan pack her overnight bag?"

He most certainly was.

FAITH WANTED THE PARTY to be over. She knew Lori and Megan had worked hard to plan such a joyful occasion for her, but what she needed more than cake and ice cream was to be in Adam's arms and to hear that everything was going to be all right. Lori had told her she had nothing to worry about, that Adam was as in love with her as he had been the day she left. Until she heard it for herself, she wasn't going to take anything for granted.

They had been comfortable in their relationship before she'd learned that she was Amish. And they'd had a respect for one another, too.

But so much had happened since then. She'd learned so much about herself—things that he didn't know. Things she needed to tell him. As he drove them to the marina on the St. Croix, they rode in silence, content to be together again. It was enough to simply enjoy each other's company, casting sideways glances as they headed for their destination. It wasn't until they were on the boat with the water beneath them and the stars overhead that he finally asked the question she knew had to be foremost in his mind.

"What made you come back?" he asked as he held her in his arms.

"I no longer fit in that world."

"Because of me?"

She shook her head. "No, because of who I am. Remember when I told you about *rumspringa*?" When he nodded she continued. "It's true that I chose to stay in the Amish community, but it was because my mother was ill."

"Your brother mentioned something about you not being baptized."

She nodded. "That's the sign that you accept the teachings of the church and you make the commitment to the Amish way of life. I couldn't do that because of my mother."

He frowned. "I thought you just said you went back because of her."

"I did. I loved her dearly. She taught me that women should never allow themselves to be doormats, that they deserve to be treated with consideration and genuine love by men, yet she lived her life in a society that appoints men as the head of the household and leaders of the church."

"It's a hard life for both women and men, isn't it?"

She nodded. "And it works for some people, but it's not for me. When I left the Amish world I found a whole new one that included symphony music and art galleries and museums and libraries. I want to always be a part of that world."

"Have you remembered all of your past?"

"There are still some blank spots, but I have a better understanding of my life before the accident. I was not happy being Plain."

"But you said you had a good childhood."

"Yes, I did. Just because I don't fit in that world any-more doesn't mean I regret having been raised Amish. Part of me will always be a country woman who enjoys watching the sun set off the back porch."

"How about off the deck of a boat?"

She smiled and kissed him. "That, too."

He lifted her hand and glanced at her wrist. "You're wearing your bracelet again. Megan said you'd put it away in a special place."

She nodded. "I'm not sure I'll ever know where it came from, but I do know that my life from this day for-ward will be lived as Faith, the survivor."

"You never found out what happened that night you left?"

She shook her head. "Not all of it. From what Levi has told me, and the bits and pieces I do remember, I have an idea as to what happened." As best she could, she filled him in on the details she did know of her past, including her decision to leave home not once, but twice before today. He listened intently as she poured her heart out to him, revealing things she could only have told someone she loved and trusted. She finished by tell-ing him the last memory she'd recalled.

"That night of my mother's funeral I was in such an emotional state that I would have done anything to get out of there. Unfortunately, I went to the highway and hitchhiked. A young guy picked me up and told me he'd give me a ride to the cities."

"Where were you going?"

"I had worked as a nanny for an English woman in Harmony."

"Your parents allowed that?"

"Yes. Many Amish girls work for the English in town either as nannies or housekeepers. They have reputations of being honest, good with children and reliable."

"I thought they wanted as little to do as possible with the outside world."

"They do, but they often need the money such jobs bring in," she explained. "The woman I worked for had friends from the Twin Cities who would come to visit. They had given me their address and told me I would always have a place to stay if I wanted to visit. That night I left they didn't know I was coming to see them," she explained, knowing he was wondering why they wouldn't have reported her missing.

"Why didn't you make it to the cities?"

"The man giving me the ride—the one I thought was a Good Samaritan—turned out he expected payment for his help. I asked him to pull over and let me out, but he refused, making all sorts of threats as to what he planned to do with me. When he wouldn't stop, I jumped out of the moving truck. He'd put my suitcase in the back so all I had were the clothes on my back."

Adam's face darkened with anger. "Do you remember what he looked like? You need to go to the police and report this guy."

She shook her head. "It's over. I don't even want to think about it. All that matters is that I survived. And I met some of the most wonderful people I've ever known." She kissed him. "Maybe it's the path I had to take to find the real me."

"I want you to be a part of this world always," he said,

holding her close to him. "But what about your family? Will you be able to see them?"

"There will be restrictions about visiting them, but at least I'll be able to write and hopefully we'll keep in touch."

He nodded. "They are good people."

"Yes. And you and Megan and Lori and Greg and the Carsons are good people, too."

"I'm so glad you came back to me."

"Well, I had a slight push."

"And what would that have been?"

"I discovered that when an Amish woman is past the age of twenty-four she's considered an old maid and her chances of marrying are slim," she said with a twinkle in her eye.

"Ah, so you think you have a better chance of landing a husband with the English."

"So I've been told."

Her arms went around his neck and she pulled him closer. "Now, are you going to give me that proper birthday greeting you promised me?"

For an answer, he scooped her into his arms and took her into the cabin.

HARLEQUIN *Super*ROMANCE®

Lost & Found

Somebody's Daughter
by Rebecca Winters
Harlequin Superromance #1259

Twenty-six years ago, baby Kathryn was taken from the McFarland family. Now Kit Burke has discovered that she might have been that baby. Will her efforts to track down her real family lead Kit into their loving arms? Or will discovering that she is a McFarland mean disaster for her and the man she loves?

Available February 2005 wherever Harlequin books are sold.

Remember to look for these Rebecca Winters titles, available from Harlequin Romance:

To Catch a Groom (Harlequin Romance #3819)—on sale November 2004
To Win His Heart (Harlequin Romance #3827)—on sale January 2005
To Marry for Duty (Harlequin Romance #3835)—on sale March 2005

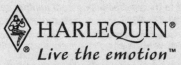

HARLEQUIN®
Live the emotion™

If you enjoyed what you just read,
then we've got an offer you can't resist!

Take 2 bestselling
love stories FREE!
Plus get a FREE surprise gift!

HARLEQUIN *Super*ROMANCE®

A six-book series from Harlequin Superromance

Six female cops battling crime and corruption on the streets of Houston. Together they can fight the blue wall of silence. But divided, will they fall?

Coming in February 2005, *She Walks the Line*
by Roz Denny Fox (Harlequin Superromance #1254)

As a Chinese woman in the Houston Police Department, Mei Lu Ling is a minority twice over. She once worked for her father, a renowned art dealer specializing in Asian artifacts, so her new assignment—tracking art stolen from Chinese museums—is a logical one. But when she's required to work with Cullen Archer, an insurance investigator connected to Interpol, her reaction is more emotional than logical. Because she could easily fall in love with this man...and his adorable twins.

Coming in March 2005, *A Mother's Vow*
by K. N. Casper (Harlequin Superromance #1260)

There is corruption in Police Chief Catherine Tanner's department. So when evidence turns up to indicate that her husband may not have died of natural causes, she has to go outside her own precinct to investigate. Ex-cop Jeff Rowan is the most logical person for her to turn to. Unfortunately, Jeff isn't inclined to help Catherine, considering she was the one who fired him.

Available wherever Harlequin books are sold.

Also in the series:
The Partner by Kay David (#1230, October 2004)
The Children's Cop by Sherry Lewis (#1237, November 2004)
The Witness by Linda Style (#1243, December 2004)
Her Little Secret by Anna Adams (#1248, January 2005)

www.eHarlequin.com

HSRWIB0105

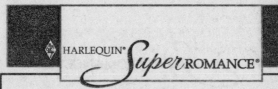

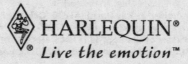